PERFECT IN DEATH

Hailey Arquette Murder Files
Book One

REILY GARRETT

Acknowledgments

To Gunther... This series, as is the case with much of my writing, is inspired in part by my four-footed companions. Dogs have always been a part of the Garrett household. I recently met one who has reminded me so much of my long-coat shepherds that he deserves a mention. Gunther is a 200+ pound ball of love and fur who shares some of the same mannerisms as my fur kids. Yes, I used *who* instead of *that* because in our home, dogs are considered people too. Thank you, Gunther, for keeping all my fur kids alive in my memory.

To Rosie Amber for an in-depth assessment of character and plot, thank you for all your help. You can find her blog and services at rosieamber.wordpress.com/beta-reading-service.

To my editor RE Hargrave, tireless and always patient. Thank you for keeping me on the straight and narrow. You can find her services as www.rehargrave(dot)com.

To my readers, each one of you who selects and reads one of my books, thank you for the opportunity to share my work. If you've enjoyed it, please consider leaving a review. They are the best way to help your author share her work.

Chapter One
Trenton

The red-eye flight from Pennsylvania left Trenton Briner tired and edgy. It'd taken a threat against family to draw him back to the lowlands rife with malice, gators, and insects reported large enough to carry away small children.

When he'd left four years prior, he'd also left his heart.

At least the rental company had an SUV to accommodate his needs as he tossed his go bag on the seat.

Personal demons supplemented his imagination in creating flashbacks of a recent firefight. The psychopathic killer who'd collected beautiful and talented women had threatened his family with her final words, a challenge punctuated in crimson froth bubbling from her mouth. With a sneer of condescension, she'd proclaimed victory, warning one of his sisters would soon disappear.

Both of his siblings were bright and pretty in their own right, but not considered prodigies. Neither bore the stunning looks common to models or television stars. Leigh was a dedicated detective with the Jefferson County Sheriff's Department. Natalie studied abroad in Europe for her final year of college. He'd put his two brothers, Jaxon and Asher, on alert in the event of emergency.

Logic dictated Hailey Arquette—long since labeled a non-blooded twin due to her close friendship with Leigh—was whom the killer referenced. Unique heritage and striking azure-blue eyes that contrasted raven-black hair made her a prime target. Both had been a source of contention and ridicule since childhood.

It wasn't just the older generation who feared talk of witchcraft and Vodou. Schoolchildren had proven themselves as vicious and persistent.

Hailey's ancestors had relocated to Hamchet and used the townsfolk's speculation to hide their unique abilities. A smart move on their part.

The hair on his nape prickled, and his teeth set on edge at the thought of her extraordinary talent. Like many other things, science couldn't explain the strange things Hailey could do, yet she'd always shied away from the term psychic.

His moist palms stemmed from more than the current record highs creating heat gradients transforming distant asphalt into wavy ribbons and promising second-degree burns to anyone foolish enough to tread barefoot.

Like the road he traveled, his life just turned the corner—into a bizarre realm.

Neither Leigh nor Hailey answered their phones when Trenton reached out the prior night. Repeated pinging ended in failure, a frustrating yet common drawback of the area.

A quick check at Hailey's office should grant a location on at least one of them. If he found one, he could find the other.

The noisy hubbub engulfing the airport gave way to quiet briny marsh areas where wildflowers straddled roads, their scents strong in his memory. Small towns blurred by his window, their struggles to survive a difficult economy evidenced in varying degrees of sagging porches, peeling paint, and an overwhelming sense of desperation.

He cranked up the air conditioner.

Wide streets welcomed visitors to Hamchet and boasted its colorful and proud history for a valiant effort during the civil war. Townspeople displayed their heritage in artful depictions covering exterior walls.

The office he sought occupied the first floor of a renovated two-story warehouse lining the town's outskirts. The degree of renovation still needed depended on the eye of the beholder.

Gutsy PI.

Parking on the grass shoulder, he studied the structure with floor-to-ceiling smoked glass windows preventing a peek inside.

Early morning sun reflected off bold white lettering and proclaimed H&C Investigations open for business. He shook his head. To date, Hailey worked alone, claiming she hadn't met her partner—yet. He chalked it up to one of the many mysteries surrounding her.

Warm wind swirled around him as he opened the glass door to a blast of cool air welcoming him in from the morning heat. Large and open, the converted warehouse suited her. The scent wafting from inside was unknown but pleasant, some concoction of herbs grown by her mother.

Stamped concrete flooring beneath a red cheery-patterned sofa along with landscape photos lining the south wall invited him to relax. If only Hailey's sense of self-preservation equaled her talent with a camera.

Chimes over the door hadn't drawn the attention of the blonde receptionist, so Trenton cleared his throat before saying, "Hi."

"What can I do for you?" A quick huff blew a fringe of curly bangs from the twenty-something's forehead while loose strands escaping a bun framed a roundish face. Elizabeth, according to the nameplate on her scarred wooden desk, never looked up.

"I'm Trenton Briner, looking for my friend Hailey. Where is she?"

Another suggestive throat clearing gained him a cursory glance with appreciation lighting the gaze that swept him from head to toe. He understood what cattle felt before slaughter.

Retrieving his wallet, he flashed his credentials.

"She's where she wants to be, I suppose."

"What does that mean? How do I find her?"

"How would I know? You're the FBI. Don't you guys keep tabs on everybody? Hailey's *your* friend. I just work here." Sincere bafflement shone from the young woman's gaze.

Trenton shook his head. If not for the steady but confused stare, he'd think she entertained him with wordplay and wondered what responsibilities came with the job. Maybe she was good with animals and watched Hailey's mammoth wolf dog on occasion.

"Let's start over. I'm Trenton Briner, and I need to speak with Hailey. She's a private investigator here and must be out working since she's never been the lazy type. Do you happen to know what case she's working on at the moment?"

"I have no idea. She's supposed to be done by noon, though. I can tell her you were here."

"What about Leigh? Has she stopped by?"

"Seriously? I'm a receptionist. I get hired by a female PI whose besties with a cop, which makes two people and a small horse in and out of here all day long. Although, I don't mind the dog much. He's a sweetie."

A low buzz turned her attention back to her cell phone in dismissal, his question obviously forgotten.

Beside her keyboard, a manila file bore the stain and weight of her Big Gulp soda.

"I have so much to do with *two* bosses, not just one. How am I s'posed to keep up?" She huffed a frustrated sigh when the office phone rang. "See what I have to deal with? I can't even read one text before I'm accosted by someone off the street and the phone rings off the hook."

Looking around the empty space, Trenton wondered at the alternate dimension into which he'd stumbled. Flashbacks of his earlier years in Texas didn't include such ambiguity.

A low groan escaped Elizabeth's pursed lips as she picked up the receiver. "Good morning. H and C Investigations. What do you need?"

If the girl rolled her eyes any farther, her pupils might never align forward.

"No, she's not here and there is no 'C' investigator. Hailey hasn't taken on a partner yet. And don't ask if she's hiring because the answer is no."

He hadn't flown hundreds of miles for nonsensical antics, so he picked up the file. If the receptionist's work ethic ran commensurate with her ability to interpret and track a conversation, he'd clue into Hailey's whereabouts faster from the folder than having to scour the office for misfiled paperwork.

"Hey! You can't have that. It's confidential." Without excusing herself from the current conversation, Elizabeth punched the phone's hold button and glared her indignation.

Trenton took a step back and ignored the attempted snatch-and-grab in favor of surfing case notes. Hailey's familiar scrawl detailed possible suspects concerning a missing teen. Before he dropped the file back on the desk, he used his phone to snap photos of the two pages.

"Thanks. If you see Hailey or Leigh before I do, tell them I'm in town and looking for them."

Disgruntled grumbling grew louder as he approached the exit.

"How am I supposed to know if you found them or not? I'm not the psychic working here. With all your fancy technology, I assume you'll see them first."

Hailey's not a psychic, at least, not in the way you're thinking.

He wondered if residents still cast wary glances in her direction, whispering about strange and disturbing abilities.

Little do they know...

Moisture plastered the white shirt against his chest when he stepped back into the morning heat, his memories drifting to the girls' antics growing up. Flashbacks made him shake his head as he slid back into his truck. A bittersweet smile creased his lips. Would his world stutter to a halt when seeing her again?

Instead of searching the sticks for the private investigator, he called the sheriff's department and spoke with his sister's supervisor. A short conversation with Lieutenant Colson gave him Leigh's location, also out on surveillance.

Quiet streets hadn't changed much and brought back memories, both fond and painful. If Hailey's boyfriend were still in the picture, there'd be tension during his short visit.

Victor was a narcissistic playboy.

After some consideration, he decided the fast-food joint on the small rise south of the target house would offer the best vantage point if he were setting up surveillance.

Sure enough, he spotted his sister's black pickup at the corner of the lot. She'd found a quiet spot under overhanging maple branches.

The gurgling of his stomach reminded him of his hasty departure hours prior with no meals since. Familiar aromas from the drive-through window made his choice easy—Cajun ham-and-egg muffins. The extras items equaled a peace offering for his sister.

Four years ago, he'd put Texas in his rearview with limited warning, few farewells, and no visits or emailed explanations regarding his abrupt departure. A slow inhale prepared him for the first period of verbal sparring. This could turn physical before his family forgave him.

Unwrapping one sandwich, he devoured it while considering the best approach.

Statistics favored direct methods during interrogation for the fastest results. Wasted minutes could cost lives. He needed to see both women safe and decided on the shortest route.

Experience and training allowed him to stride along the pickup's blind spot. A perverse part of him anticipated the case of shocked shitless that would accompany Leigh's epithets.

Any emotion she experienced would travel at lightning speed to Hailey's pony-sized dog of questionable heritage sitting on the back seat. Sharing the peace offering with the one bearing sharper teeth made sense.

Soft country music drifted through the open window while the occupant's attention remained focused on the neighborhood downhill—until he opened the door.

Shoulder-length blonde hair swung to the side as Leigh swiveled her head to stare with mouth agape. "Down, Gunther. He's not on the menu. Yet."

The animal took up most of the back seat. Startling blue eyes contrasting black fur expressed more than the growl vibrating in his chest.

"Hey, boy. Remember me? If not, I bet you'll remember this." Trenton held out the bacon-and-bagel snack for the animal to sniff, relaxing when the mixed breed snatched it in one bite.

"What the hell? He remembered that from what, four years ago? He hasn't seen you since he was a pup. And let me tell you something, not many are stupid enough to do what you just did, Trent."

"Nonsense. Dogs have a good sense about people, along with a good memory. And for the record, I used to give him one each time I saw him."

"Figures you'd plan ahead."

Trenton grinned. "So, how is it you can bring him on a stakeout? And where's Sparkles?" He thought of Hailey's nickname whenever encountering someone with blue eyes. None had ever compared to what he remembered, either in intensity or perception. Certainly not with the same ability.

"Gunther is part of my cover, and Hailey's working."

Trenton rested his forearm along the doorframe and let his sister finish the sarcastic tirade. He deserved that and more but had wasted all the time he could spare. "Let's start over. Hey, sis."

"Howdy to you, too. Nice to see you. Won't you come in and sit a spell? Or wait, isn't your flight out in an hour?"

"Look, let's drop the sarcasm. I've come a long way, and we need to talk."

"So, it's just drop in and pick up where you left off with no explanations, is it? Sorry, not gonna happen. Where've you been? Don't tell me you came home to initiate a friendly game of firefly wars or a howl-off challenge. Someone on the east coast blow you off?"

His irritation flared with the quirk of her eyebrow. Sliding the pendant on her necklace side-to-side demonstrated intent focus guaranteed to detect bullshit.

"I'm here on business, Leigh."

"Huh. Okay, but before you ask, my supervisor knows Gunther," she hooked a thumb over her shoulder toward the dog, "...comes with me on occasion. At least *he's* proven himself well-mannered and useful."

"Both you and Sparkles are in danger. Have either of you been followed recently?"

That got her attention.

"Hell, what've you stepped in, big brother? We'll talk, but you have to give me more details. I spoke with Hailey last night before setting up here." Leigh gestured to the street below. "We both ignore non-urgent phone calls and only deal with texts. Makes life simpler."

Leigh snagged her phone from the center console and fired off a message. "We've got a girl that went missing a few days ago."

"Where is Hailey now?"

"Um," Leigh swiped the screen on her phone, "she's south in the triangle, closer to the lake."

"Don't you have regular check-ins? You two have always been like twins."

Soft strains of an accordion harmonizing with violin and guitar registered an incoming message.

Trenton snatched the device and read. "Jeez."

On my way back. No luck.

Why in hell have you not answered your phone?

What's the problem?

This is Trenton. Meet me at the loft. ASAP.

Sure, Mom, soon as I get dressed and say goodbye to my dozen lovers.

Blind fury coursed through his veins like the electrical current of a high-voltage wire. He'd traded fifteen hundred air miles for sarcasm.

"We check in every four hours. Scroll back."

"What I see is… bump, grind, sex, and phone pole. What the hell does this crap mean?"

"Short version. We're in sync. If one makes a reference and the response is off, it means the other is in trouble."

"What's a phone pole got to do with sex?"

"Clearly, you're not up-to-date on today's sex toys."

"Oh… no. No more. Please. English is my first language."

"Impatience is a close second."

Odd references were too much to consider. Hiking and rafting proved the only safe topics around these women. Reconciliation came in the form of a nod to the dog.

"Why is he with you and not Hailey?"

"He gets restless on long stakeouts. Easier for me to walk him, considering her location."

"How is it you're both working the same case?"

"The teen's parents hired her to supplement our work. You're still pissed that I helped her get her PI license."

"She has no business doing this work."

"She's good at it, Trenton."

"It's forcing her to use her ability. It'll backfire one day."

"Hey, she wanted to hone it, learn to use it. This is how we're going about it."

Gunther's continued snuffling down Trenton's neck created a shudder. He reached back to rub the dog's chest.

"Don't worry. You're safe, big brother. He avoids food that'll give him indigestion."

Trenton snorted. Without meeting Leigh's gaze, he tossed her phone on the console and slid out of the truck. "Thanks. Sorry for the abruptness. I'll see you back at the loft."

"You're a dick. If she doesn't kick your ass when we get there, I will. Oh, and by the way, nice to see you."

Her assessment was accurate and honest, the parting words hitting the mark more than he could admit. He didn't want to feel comfortable here. By an odd stroke of fate, he'd carved out a good life in Pennsylvania, fitting in with a ragtag group who'd accepted him as family. Better still, he'd partially healed his broken heart. The coming meeting would equate to ripping off a bandage.

The ride back included decisions on how to disseminate information with care when greeting Hailey. To save time, he'd have to accept a mini sparring match.

Since he was here, he'd offer to help while keeping an eye on the two until proving the threat of a dying psychopath devoid of merit.

Hailey's case notes detailed a missing teen who'd attended the school for the gifted elite located in the remote countryside. Perfect hunting grounds for a deranged collector of human souls.

Chapter Two
Hailey

An entire night of surveillance netting zero results topped with Trenton's grumpy texts spurred Hailey's need to vent. Unofficially working in tandem, she and Leigh had split duties to include the missing teen's closest friend and boyfriend.

Wild brush and a long winding driveway denied visual scrutiny of the boyfriend's residence. With no time to set up a remote camera, she'd parked back from the closest intersection. Her first sighting occurred when the teen left for school.

Now, she fumed.

Barely a word from Trenton in four years other than, "Too busy to come home," then he arrives and demands her location?

Screw that. I'll help pick the bones from Gunther's teeth.

Leaning forward, she turned the key of her old pickup. Despite its age, it'd run like a demon since her ex's modifications.

Suspicions of the current situation connecting with a five-year-old cold case nagged at her subconscious as she navigated the remote dirt path overgrown with weeds and narrowed by encroaching saplings.

She couldn't offer enough evidence to connect the cases. However, she would share information with Leigh, a detective with the local sheriff's department.

Five minutes later, she turned onto narrow, cracked, and brittle asphalt leading back to town. Humidity had risen with the sun, doubling her longing for an iced coffee, cold-brewed with roasted chicory and sweetened with organic cane sugar.

Unfortunately, she wouldn't enjoy it until dealing with her stick-in-the-mud friend and whatever issues he'd schlepped from the east coast.

Thoughts of retribution diverted her attention until passing an intersection where an old rusted pickup squealed off from the junction behind her.

Exhaust poured from its tailpipe as it picked up speed. In the rearview, she saw someone wearing a black ski mask.

A small shudder rippled down her spine. Bile shot up her throat in piecing together the driver's obvious intent.

The vehicle surged forward to pass then hung alongside her back wheel well, the position needed to execute a PIT maneuver and spin her off the road. Not many drivers had the skill to pull it off, at least not successfully.

Instinct saw her stomping the accelerator and pulling away to take center position in the road. She palmed the gun at her waist. Practice on still targets ensured she had a decent aim. She'd never shot at anything moving.

She could probably outrun him, but speed plus crappy road conditions and abundant wildlife equaled a recipe for disaster.

The driver tried a different tactic. His vehicle picked up speed, growing in her rearview mirror. She caught a glimpse of stark white against the black mask.

The rear-end collision jolted the weapon from her hand and threw it to the floorboard.

Son of a bitch.

Reflex jammed her foot on the brake, which tossed her field glasses and cell phone atop her weapon. The second collision would at least dent his front bumper if not create more damage.

Her heart thumped hard against her ribs with reverberations spreading throughout her body at a staccato beat. A tighter grip secured the steering wheel under sweat-slicked palms.

Sparring with Leigh combined with solid training ingrained the maneuvers needed to handle herself in a hand-to-hand fight. Challenges between two-ton pickups negated her best assets.

This time, when the driver again tried to pull up beside her, she was ready.

In lieu of her vehicle careening out of control and rolling, she'd flip the tables.

Jamming her foot on the brake and turning her wheel into the attack resulted in a meshing of metal. A long shriek reverberated in her ears as the two vehicles collided. His passenger mirror and her side mirror ripped off.

The grating squeal and grind replaced the low tunes of her radio before his vehicle's greater weight forced her off to the narrow, overgrown shoulder. Uneven ground jarred her body with her teeth sinking into her tongue.

She tasted copper in her mouth.

A glimpse of the driver in passing compiled various points of a denim shirt, broad shoulders, and height that left little clearance in the cab, but no clue as to eye color, weight, or age. A male judging by the shape.

Her vehicle's sudden pull to the right coincided with a low boom and a *whooshing* sound before repeated flapping of a blown tire thudded against the ground. Course correction occurred despite the natural pull to the low marshy borders. Several abrupt taps on the brake brought her to a standstill.

Ahead, the other truck squealed to a stop.

"Oh, no. Think again, asshole." In a split second, she retrieved her backup gun from the glove box and opened her door. She took cover behind its mass and assumed a shooter's stance.

Not ready to concede, the other driver slid out of his truck with a gun in his hand. She noted the unevenness of his teeth when he smiled.

A broken tooth?

His first shot punched a hole in the windshield inches from her face. *Damn.*

Training prepared her to shoot, but not for someone to shoot at her. She stumbled back, losing her balance and her gun when her arms windmilled to compensate. Landing on her ass was something she'd never admit to Leigh or anyone else.

Especially not if dead.

Her vulnerable position equaled an invitation accepted by the shooter, who grinned and proceeded to stalk forward, obviously wanting a close-range shot or to gloat.

Before Hailey could retrieve her weapon, she stared down the barrel of a large bore handgun, recognized despite the twenty-foot distance between them.

Her breath caught.

Time froze.

Nothing existed but the black barrel.

His smile exposed a broken white tooth. He raised his arm to aim. "Time to die, witch, priestess, whatever you claim to be."

Instead of the pistol's bark, she heard him choke. The whites of his eyes contrasted his mask and lent a cartoonish appearance.

Two stumbling steps with one hand scrabbling at his neck compromised his balance. One arm flailed amid choking sounds. He appeared like a marionette to a sadistic puppeteer as his free arm flung wide with fingers remaining clenched on his gun. After several steps, he stumbled back and landed on his butt.

"What are you hexing me with, bitch?"

If rage could create fire, she'd burn to ash in an instant.

Leaning over put her Springfield Hellcat within reach. Her first shot hit his tailgate. The second missed his shoulder when he ducked and scrambled to all fours, now able to control his movements.

Like a terrified animal, he hauled himself back and flung himself into his truck.

The vehicle burned rubber, albeit heavier with the lead pumped into it. She'd missed hitting anything vital.

There was no tag, no bumper stickers, and nothing specific to identify either vehicle or driver except for general shape and a broken tooth. Her insurance company would probably drop her if she claimed the windshield damage.

I need more practice under duress.

Per a national study on police marksmanship, less than twenty-three percent of fired bullets hit their target if more than seven yards away during a gunfight.

"Damn." The incident didn't even confirm she was on the right track. Three years of investigative work accumulated a list of irate cheating husbands along with a few insurance fraud cases.

Tucking her gun in her waistband, she set about changing the tire. In her mind, she reviewed the coming conversation with Leigh and Trenton. *Yes, it was a dark blue, three-quarter-ton pickup, with no bumper stickers or tag. Rust covered most of it. Driver—unknown. Yes,*

Trenton, please put out a BOLO.

She needed coffee.

Wait. Rust covered a large portion of his vehicle.

Her truck acquired some of that paint and rust from their encounter. *Maybe...*

Closing her eyes, she reached out and touched the side panel where traces of blue contrasted the dark maroon of her driver's door. The vision came in a montage of city streets and bustling people.

A man descending steps from his house—clubbed over the head by someone hiding in the bushes. A minute later, the truck sped away. That bastard stole the truck.

It wasn't much to go on, but it was a start.

* * * *

Trenton

Anticipation of the upcoming confrontation energized Trenton to the point he boxed his breathing to remain calm. Coming from a large and boisterous family where they often settled squabbles with a throw down provided entertainment for all.

Today should be no different. Leigh would probably post a video on social media. The fact he'd waited in his SUV parked in the lot behind the building instead of going up to the loft would speak volumes.

A wide grin curved Leigh's lips when she pulled up beside him and slid out.

And so it begins.

"It's bad enough you joined the force, but Hailey has always been a target." His words came out low, barely controlled, and accompanied the firm grip on her upper arms before pulling her in for a hug. "By the way, it's good to see you, too."

"C'mon. Let's go inside, but I'm not helping you deal with her."

"Where is she? Said she'd be here shortly."

Leigh whipped out her phone and fired off a text, frowning when he shoulder-surfed.

Everything ok? Where are you, *klere*?
                              Bumped into a small problem. All's fine.
K. Trent's looking... constipated.
                    Then you'll understand the ugly rug soon. Bringing food.
Please forego necessity of ER visits. I'm tired.

"Come on. Her living space is on the second floor." Leigh opened the back door and waved him through.

A long narrow hallway ran the width of the building and past two doors before exiting to the front. Block walls held a slightly musty odor reminiscent of an old basement.

"Why are there two entrances to the office and her living quarters?" Trenton scowled when the knob turned freely under his hand in passing. "And why is this door to her business not locked? Anyone could come in this hallway from the front and have access to her loft."

"As for two doors, I don't know. One goes upstairs, the other to the first-floor business. This was the configuration when she rented it." Leigh tapped the butt of her gun. "As for the second, we both carry and," she nodded to Gunther padding beside her, "...well, him."

"Having a dog is great, but not enough."

"He's not just a dog." Leigh waited for Gunther to trot up the steps.

"He looks part wolf."

"Think so? Never heard that before, dude. And be careful of who's around when you say that."

"Wolves are illegal to own."

"Not in Texas, Trent, at least not now. Remember where you're standing. 'Sides, there's no written ancestry on him."

Four years hadn't changed his sister's stubborn hide.

Upstairs, he expected the space to be light and airy. White floor tiles contrasted light blue walls while everything else thumbed a nose at color coordination.

A calf-shit-brown rug, thick to the point of being spongy under his shoes, was in desperate need of a purpose.

Leigh looked at him and then the rug. "What? I didn't buy that."

Anything concerning Hailey not immediately understood made him nervous.

A shrug of Leigh's shoulder dropped her field bag on the counter before she moved to the fridge. "Thirsty? I'm gonna start coffee. Hailey's bringing carry out."

Familiarity dropped like a warm blanket around his shoulders, and old habits rekindled with no warning. Still, he looked back at the rug, so out of place and crying out for a reason to exist.

Leigh caught his frown and grinned wide.

Hell.

Trenton snagged a bottle of water from the bottom shelf of the fridge and took a swig. Then, like a pup exploring its new home, he prowled the open space, checking locks and assessing security risks.

"Her security is inadequate. A grade school punk could break in with ease." That was one thing he could help with while here.

"Unfortunate, since that wouldn't make much of a snack for Gunther." Leigh parked a hand on her hip, waiting.

"She depends too much on that dog. You both do. It's not smart."

"He's pack, and he's protective. When you got in my truck, he sensed my assessment. Otherwise, he would've scarfed you down like a tidbit, probably choke on your stubborn ass."

"He hardly growled."

"That's not when you need to worry, Trent. It's when he goes utterly still and quiet. That's what should put your panties in a twist. Whatever he can't handle, Hailey can shoot." She rubbed behind the wolf dog's ears. "Right, boy?"

Outside, the low rumble of a truck tightened Trenton's shoulders. Curiosity drew him to the front window overlooking the road to watch Hailey park.

"Sonofabitch!" He was out the door in the next heartbeat, his shoes thumping down the stairs.

Chapter Three
Hailey

It wouldn't take a cop's mind to determine the scraped, dented side panel and missing side mirror were new. Hailey had always taken care of anything she owned.

Unfortunately, adrenaline washout had prevented preparation for Trenton's greeting. He was the type of man best tolerated in small gulps when riled.

Sure enough, he stalked from the building and circled her truck. Close scrutiny of the damage ended with a growl.

A storm would follow.

"Don't even think about it." Sliding out from the driver's seat, she couldn't avoid his grasp.

She'd missed her best friend for four years, only to have a bearish brute show up in his place.

She wasn't in the mood for verbal war, but a sparring match wasn't out of the question. It would also ease the tension in her shoulders.

Without a word, he pointed to the damage.

Hailey shrugged and leaned against her truck, accepting Gunther's head under her hand with a grin. "Howdy, East Coast, what brings you back to our swamplands?"

Trenton crouched to study the damage.

Despite the truck's age, she knew there were no signs of neglect.

"What happened? I know this is new." He slid one hand over the streaks of rust and blue paint.

That, and a dangling wire from the now missing side mirror marred the otherwise unblemished appearance.

"What makes you think it's new?"

Crossing his arms over his chest, he arched a brow. A heartbeat later, he glanced at her windshield and let loose a string of curses.

Concordial cracks radiated several inches from a hole in the windshield.

"Don't worry. It's part of a matching set with no crimson stain." Hailey pointed to the exit hole in the rear window, knowing her smile would piss him off more.

He closed his eyes on a deep inhale.

A minute later, he circled back to open the passenger door then rummaged through the glove box. His expression embodied the perfect lines to mold a character mask.

"What're you looking for?" Hailey pondered aloud.

"*Hmm*, looking for your backup gun, Hails. If so, he'll want to see if it's been recently fired," offered Leigh as she joined them.

"Well, yeah. That's usually the appropriate response to someone shooting at you. Isn't it?" Hailey acknowledged the tightening around Leigh's mouth with a shrug.

At the passenger door and dangling the Springfield by its trigger guard, he shook his head after sniffing the barrel. "How appropriate you have a Hellcat for your backup. Did you hit your target?"

"No." Hailey kicked at a loose dirt clod in disgust.

"Brother, she's pissed off. I'd tread lightly if I were you," Leigh offered in warning.

Gunther moved to stand between her and Trenton when he strode around the hood. He stopped short when the animal growled.

Retrieving the takeout bags and dangling them at the end of her fingers, Hailey smirked to distract him from the slight shake in her hand. "You have a choice to make. What's it gonna be?"

He took the bags and followed her and Gunther back to the loft. She could feel the animosity radiating from him with each step, most of his grumbled words too low to discern.

Once in the loft, he pivoted to give the carryout to Leigh then took hold of Hailey's arm again. "What happened? We are going to discuss this. Now."

"Hit-and-run. Well, except the guy didn't run until I fired. Funny how that works."

Leigh uncapped her water and leaned back against the countertop separating kitchen from living area. "Dude, you should ease up while you're still vertical. You just got in the door, and this is one argument where I'm not going to interfere."

"Back off, Trent. I'm not in the mood," Hailey warned.

"No. I've flown halfway across the country to find someone's tagged you in a hit-and-run. So, no, I won't back off."

Leigh chuckled. "I've waited a long time for this. Can't say I didn't warn you, bro."

A tick of the clock's hand later, she surprised him with a hip throw. He landed on the ugly rug, back first and arms splayed wide.

"*Oof.*"

The move should've been expected. Her sitting on his chest, not so much. She was careful to avoid prolonged skin-to-skin contact that would instigate a vision. Voyeurism wasn't her thing, and she might lose it if seeing him tangled with a woman among sweaty sheets.

"See? Isn't this rug great, Leigh? Now you understand it." Hailey smiled and didn't interfere when Gunther sniffed and whined in Trenton's face.

Trenton averted his cheek. "Help yourself, boy. You know I belong here, but remember, I don't offer samples."

"Looks like you've put on a few pounds since I saw you last." Hailey patted his chest but didn't stand.

Trenton took a slow deep breath, glancing from her hand to where she sat, then back to her eyes, his message clear.

"Just making my point."

"Fine. Got it out of your system?" He made no move to throw off the weight, instead staring with intent. "Now, tell me what happened."

"It was over pretty much before it started, and I'm not explaining until hearing about what brought you home. Are we expecting a zombie apocalypse? Perhaps an imminent nuclear attack?" Hailey patted his head like a dog then stood, tugging Trenton up. Instead of anger, she pulled him in for a hug.

He didn't object.

Brief skin-to-skin contact revealed Trenton involved in a gunfight inside of what appeared to be a bar. She'd ask him about it later. He obviously fared well since he stood before her, unharmed.

"Why you doin' that after cleaning his clock?" Leigh snickered and took another sip of water.

"So I know how wide to dig the hole out back." Hailey waggled her eyebrows.

"Look, you two, I've been up all night. I'm tired and still hungry." Trenton stepped back and waited.

"Trent, I don't know. Guess I pissed somebody off. Either that or someone doesn't want me looking for the missing kid." Hailey helped distribute the food while Leigh retrieved plates.

"Could you be a little more specific about who you've ticked off? You could've been killed, and I can't interview half of Texas' residents. Did you *see* anything?"

Twisting her lips to one side, she pondered the vision she'd had when touching the paint. "Yeah, but nothing that helps. The truck's stolen from somewhere. A city."

"Could you narrow that down, like which one?"

"Nope."

"Let's eat and discuss this like human beings, shall we? I need to file a report and get back to work. This new lieutenant hired by the sheriff is a real ballbuster."

"Who have you pissed off most recently, Sparkles?" Trenton dusted imaginary dirt from his jeans before taking a seat.

Leigh piped up with, "Anyone with a heartbeat."

Trenton accepted a bag of beignets and took one. "This is a nice place. Bad neighborhood, though."

"There are no neighbors, hence no neighborhood," Hailey countered, lightly touching the coffee pot's carafe on the counter. "Is this fresh?"

"Yep." Leigh sat across from her brother, assessing him as only a sibling could.

"Precisely my point. This place is too open. Exposed." He gestured to the window.

An abundance of space supplied sparring room between the kitchen island and the living area, where the sofa held a pile of clean clothes. Glass walls revealed Spanish oaks and cedar elms lining the woods separating her street from the road beyond.

"You're too isolated here. Who puts up a warehouse in the middle of nowhere?"

"Someone who enjoys their privacy, like me. It's why I opened my office here."

Condemnation in his tone topped her quota and firmed Hailey's decision. With her back to her guests, she pondered her herb selection, her options for a small warning.

An herbal addition to Trenton's coffee would deliver her message better and faster than words could. Best-case scenario, powdered slippery elm would loosen parts of him a bit. Too much and he'd be hugging the toilet for the afternoon.

With her back to her target, she added a small amount to a porcelain mug that read, *I'm multitasking. I can listen, ignore, and forget at the same time.* Her soft chuckle resulted in a raised brow before he accepted the drink.

After several sips, he set it down and pushed his chair back to stand, frowning first at the cup, then at Hailey.

"Neither of you have changed a bit." As if too nervous to stay put, he collected the unfolded laundry from the sofa and strode down the short hall to dump it in one of the rooms.

Leigh stage-whispered, "He's awfully nervous."

Hailey growled low in her throat when he returned. "I see you still need a hug. Around the neck. With a rope. How'd you know which room and whose laundry you carried? Your sister stays over on occasion. Her washer is on the fritz now."

"There was no dog hair on the floor of one room, and my sister doesn't wear a training bra." Trenton lent the direct weight of his stare in tilting his head. "Sorry to hear about you and Victor, Sparkles." A muscle ticking in his jaw declared otherwise.

She made a face at the use of her nickname, bestowed as a child due to her unusual eye color. If only that were her single oddity.

"Care to join us or would you like to try out my new toilet brush?"

"What did you dose my coffee with?" Trenton moved to the sink and dumped the contents down the drain before pouring a fresh cup.

She didn't confirm or deny his accusation, redirecting with, "It wasn't Victor in the truck. I do know that much. 'Sides, he wouldn't come after me like that. It's not his style."

"Okay. Maybe this is all a smokescreen. The psychopath I shot in Pennsylvania indicated she worked with a partner in Texas. Might've been a last-ditch effort to worry me."

"Because a crazy serial killer wouldn't lie," Leigh retorted.

"Tell me about this missing girl. Seems someone is after one or both of you. I need to figure out if it's because of *your* case or if it's stemming from mine in Pennsylvania."

Leigh drummed her fingers on the table in thought. "We have two current cases, well, one's old, but we think it might be connected. A girl didn't make it home from school this past Saturday after their dance. Her parents called Hailey when the police were reluctant to get involved so soon. My lieutenant thinks maybe her boyfriend is hiding her."

"Aren't classes out for the school year?" Trenton looked from Hailey to Leigh.

"Summer session is just winding down," Leigh answered with a waggle of her left hand. "I'm guessing you didn't see anything around the house this morning?" She stared at her friend.

"Not till he left for school." Hailey waved a hand in dismissal, not wanting to relive the nightmare shooting.

She didn't want to detail how the shooter lost control of himself. Strange things like that had happened before, but she'd never discussed them with anyone. Not even her mother. It was bad enough they knew about her visions with touch.

"Not a soul stirred at her bestie's house either," Leigh supplied with a grimace.

"Since Colson also questioned the boyfriend, I sat on the kid's house overnight figuring he'd lead me to her without a lot of hassle." Hailey cast a speculative glance at Trenton. Four years had changed him in ways she couldn't yet define. He appeared leaner, more focused.

"And?" Trenton waited, exhaling a pent-up breath.

"And nothing. The kid never left the house last night, unless he took the swamp express. No visitors, nothing. When I pulled out this morning, someone caught me on Boudreaux Road and sideswiped me. I fixed the flat tire and came home."

Leigh reviewed the notes she'd taken on her cell. "You'll need to file a report for the insurance company."

"I need some sleep first." Hailey finished her food and raised her cup in Trenton's direction. "You get enough coffee?"

"It isn't gonna make me piss red for two days this time, is it? I think your mother was nuts for teaching you all that herbal stuff. If I break out in some kind of weird rash, I'll come looking for you both."

"If that happens, I suggest a visit to your doctor first. You wouldn't want anything to fall off." Hailey chortled and dodged the crumpled napkin thrown at her. "Notice we're drinking it too."

"I wouldn't put it past you to spike the whole pot and have an antidote handy." Trenton strode to the window and scanned the street.

"Well, brother, have you done anything to deserve it? Like being rude or obnoxious?" The accusation hit its mark with his shoulder twitch.

Trenton grumbled, "A little appreciation goes a long way. Since I'm here, I might as well help you both." He retrieved his phone. "You all think there's a connection between the missing girls?"

"I'll send my notes to you, bro, and maybe you could take it a bit easy on my friend? Y chromosome handicap is not a legal defense."

"Explain what you think connects the two cases." This question Trenton directed to both women.

Hailey hemmed and hawed in thinking. "Different ages, but they went to the same school. We might have a crazy with a taste for high school girls."

"I'll talk to Bernadette's friends and teachers after starting the search for Hailey's bumper car buddy." Leigh carried her plate to the sink.

"I'll go with Hailey to the boy's house." Trenton swiped his screen and nodded his thanks.

"Fine, but let Hailey do the talking. She's better at smoothing rough questions over and won't ruffle as many feathers." Leigh pocketed her cell after sending her notes, then hedged, "Wait. I want more details about why you're here. You could've contacted us through Lt. Colson."

"I suggest you spill it before your little sister loses patience." Hailey noticed more things different about her old friend.

Maybe the FBI had seasoned him, or perhaps the combination of work, night flight, and no sleep had added a temporary shell over his emotions. "Otherwise, I'll tell her embarrassing stories about how you tried to seduce a cheerleader under the bleachers in high school." Her smile wasn't full of rainbows and unicorns.

"Fine." Trenton recounted his elimination of a serial killer, finishing with the reiteration that said psycho threatened one of his siblings. "How certain are you no one followed you last night, Hailey?"

"One hundred percent. Which means someone could've put a tracker on my truck."

"Considering you live in isolation; I'd say that's a distinct possibility."

"Keep in mind that would take money, which most folks around here don't have," Leigh made a good point.

"If someone's aware I'm nosing around this case... I don't know a lot about those kids, but I know who might. I bet Laurent is probably already working on this for the paper." Hailey swiped her contact list to find his number.

It wasn't Laurent's job as a journalist that ensured his wide range of acquaintances, but rather his genuine affluent personality. It was a rare occasion he met someone he didn't like.

"Let's think about this. Nearly every kid at the GE school is catered to and pampered. They're groomed for great things. Most are highly motivated, and the competition has to be fierce." Hailey used her hands to gesture when talking until tucking them in her lap after Trenton smiled.

"Money and power breed corruption. Combine that with ambitious manipulators and kids too inexperienced to know when someone's playing them, well, I smell trouble," Leigh agreed.

"Let's backtrack to Trenton's reason for visiting. Did your deranged killer name one of us specifically?" Hailey asked.

"No. Not exactly, and I haven't determined if she lied for effect."

"So, you're here in watchdog capacity," Leigh accused. "We don't need that. Not from you, not from anyone."

"Couldn't let that pass, could you?" Trenton rubbed his eyes as his shoulders drooped.

"Boobs before balls," Hailey chimed in then continued her thoughts in twin speak, "*Katkd liegyd toclpam. degon-hauf donikin du-eh—*"

"Watch him? Who? Trenton?" Leigh translated the obscure but well-developed language as she stared at her brother.

"Stop it, you two. I hate that gibberish." Trenton pointed a finger first at Hailey, then at Leigh. "I'm not an overbearing pervert, or dragon, or whatever you just called me."

Leigh held one hand out, waggling it side to side.

A light giggle escaped Hailey's throat before speaking up. "It's the only way to have a private conversation and get her take on the situation without nosey men butting in. And by the way, you must've talked with Colson to get her location. Tell us about that conversation."

They both knew Trenton would pull out every stop to see them safe, regardless of the frustration it caused.

"I asked him for Leigh's location because your secretary had no clue where you were."

"Oh, that. Yeah. I took Elizabeth on for an internship. Looks good on her resume and all that," Hailey supplied with a shrug. "She's kind of ditzy but loves Gunther to death. Convenient when he can't come with us and we don't want to leave him alone."

More disjointed syllables resulting from years of close-knit communication with her best friend summed up their opinions. Hailey answered the last question, fending off the napkin Trenton tossed.

"I understood that one, and I don't need to get laid while down here." Trenton balled his hands into fists.

His sister snickered.

"Stop." Not easily dismissed, Trenton declared, "I'm here. I'm staying. Deal with it. Both of you. Matter of fact, this is a three-bedroom loft. How about I—"

"No. Absolutely not staying here. You'd try to run our lives and micromanage our work. Nope. No way am I gonna be tripping over your feet." His proximity equaled a distraction she couldn't handle.

"First, I don't micromanage. Second, I'll be either here or in my SUV out front. From there, I can interrogate anyone wanting to enter the building."

"That's blackmail," Hailey growled out, causing her dog to whine and chuff at her side.

"That's life. As I understand it," Trenton turned to his sister, "you and your boyfriend share a house."

Leigh nodded. "Damn Colson and his big mouth."

"Fine. You can bunk here, but if you interfere, I'll let Gunther eat you." Hailey slapped her hand on the table. "Put antacids on the shopping list, Leigh. I don't want my fur kid getting sick."

Trenton's calculating mind always found a way around obstacles. It wouldn't be the end of their clashing.

"I'll go and fill out the report. Then, I need a few hours of sleep." Hailey rinsed and put the dishes in the dishwasher. "The spare bedroom is the third door on the right. Make sure you're dressed before coming out to use the bathroom. I don't want to see your naked butt strutting down the hall."

"And risk you hexing me?" Trenton fired back. "It's a deal as long as you don't come out half-dressed like you girls did during sleepovers."

"First, I don't do hexes. Second, we were children. It's not my fault you jumped the puberty gun."

"Enough. Please." Leigh visibly shuddered then waited at the door. "Hailey, I'll meet you at the station later to go over your report. Meantime, I'll start tracking down this ghost truck of yours. Finding it might lead to our missing girl if, in fact, she *is* missing and hasn't run off. According to the lieutenant, it's not the first time she's disappeared."

Trenton held his hand out when Gunther padded over for another sniff. "Hey, boy. Your eyes are almost the same shade as your mom's."

"You should have a companion, Trenton. It might shave off some grouchiness." Hailey smiled when her furry companion rubbed his head against their guest's thigh. "He's giving you a scent rub. He's accepted you—for now."

"I travel too much to keep one." Trenton stood, regret plainly etched on his face.

She remembered no obvious reason for his commitment phobia. "You need to get a wife, or at least a live-in who could care for a dog while you're gone. I know you do more traveling than is required, but isn't it about time you settled down? Afraid someone's lasso is gonna get you?"

There was a time she took his presence for granted. Now, it hurt to look at him and remember the highs and lows of their friendship.

Trenton ignored the needling and paused at the doorway. "I'm gonna grab my bag and get some sleep. Hailey, I'll be ready to roll in four hours. We'll start fresh."

She nodded. "Hey, Leigh. I need to drop my truck at Dent and Grind. Give me a ride from there?"

"Sure, but you best call 'em first. You know how they are."

"Okay, I'll be down as soon as I finish here."

Hailey admired the view when Trenton left. In the years away, his physique had changed, trading rangy awkwardness for strength and solidity, defining his muscles and sharpening his instincts. He seemed to have more of a runner's build than a weightlifter now.

Might be an interesting match if he decided to spar.

Chapter Four
Trenton

Trenton retrieved his go bag from the back of his SUV, aware his sister stood beside her vehicle. "What? I know you have something to say, Leigh. Spit it out. I didn't embarrass you up there."

While he'd known his return would include granting a certain amount of leeway, he wondered at the extent of the women's collective ire.

"Thanks, but your reluctance to say much stems from self-preservation, and we both know it. She's learned more about alternate uses of local herbs and can make you squirt from both ends while seeing double for hours." Leigh held up her finger to halt his next words. "Let me say this before you carry both sides of the conversation to the wrong conclusion."

A rotating motion of his wrist urged her to get on with it.

"Don't mention Victor again."

What?

He hadn't realized his mouth hung open until Leigh's index finger on his jaw closed it.

"Why? My brother told me they split a while back."

"You barely looked in her direction unless frustration got the better of you. You do your best lying when it's by omission. I know you still care about her." Crinkling at the corners of her eyes accompanied one side of her mouth kicking up in a half grin.

Trenton remained mute. His sister had always been perceptive.

"I also know you avoid looking at someone when you're thinking about them. And… hold on here. She is my best friend. Full disclosure, her ex is having difficulty with the word no. However, you will not stick your nose where it doesn't belong, regardless if it's in the guise of friendship. You've been friends forever, but you've been gone a little over four years. Don't. Muck. This. Up."

Mixed messages from his sister weren't new. "You want to know what Victor has up his sleeve but won't ask," he challenged.

One side of Leigh's cheek puffed out from the thrust of her tongue, a lifelong tell. She remained silent.

"He been hanging around lately?"

"He's stopped by a few times. Knows better than to try and use me to get to her. I don't know why she can't see the parasite under the pretty face. He thinks himself the ultimate bumper crop and feels the need to spread himself around."

His sister wouldn't make a point of the conversation if she didn't have something stuck in her craw. He wouldn't name it without proof, but nothing pissed him off more than a man failing to recognize the end of a relationship.

"Which tells me you're already involved somehow. I'm surprised you haven't hunted him down and fed his balls to Gunther."

"First, I love Gunther and wouldn't do that to him. Second, I gave Hailey my word *I* wouldn't interfere, and you know I always keep my word. On the other hand, she hasn't extracted that same promise from you. And if you don't mention Victor again, she won't think to do so."

"Ah, so you want me to watch over her, deceive her, and beat the crap out of her ex?" The day was shaping up nicely, according to Pandora. If history repeated itself, Murphy would soon join the party. "Anything else while I'm here?"

"Well, when you put it that way, it does sound a little underhanded."

"Ya think?"

"Look. She's nice, smart, and deserves a break. I don't want to see her heart stomped on again. You two were close at one time, then you left and something in her broke. Help her out."

"She can't say no with enough force to get the message across?" Their brief interaction earlier left Trenton with the impression of a decisive, strong-willed, smartass woman who hadn't changed in years.

"Oh, she could, believe me. The problem is, the creep is damn good at covering his motives and tracks when sneaking under her radar. Hell, I didn't catch onto the deceitful bastard until he had his hooks in her deep."

"Covering what tracks, legal or moral? You used to be a good judge of character."

"Still am. Life sideswipes even the best of us at times, bro. It happens. Far as her ex, though, Victor is slick, so it could be either. Look out for him and watch your back when he's around."

Trenton held his hands up, having decided his course at the beginning of the conversation. "I remember him. He must've learned some new tricks."

Hamchet had raised its share of pricks who bristled the hair on his nape, making him thankful Leigh's ex-husband hadn't entered the conversation. Restraint would be an issue.

"Fine. Consider the situation handled." His frown melted when Leigh hugged him tight then lightly slugged him in the stomach.

"Thanks. I'll catch up with you tonight, Trent."

"Stay off the back roads. I think you should—"

"Do not finish that thought. I'm going to do my job, and I'm taking Gunther with me. Just watch out for Hailey. That way I don't have to worry about her. Thanks to your talk with Colson, he'll be breathing down my neck, I'm sure."

"I don't want you doing surveillance alone, even if you have an overprotective hellhound by your side."

Leigh rolled her eyes. "Look. I'll stick to public venues. Just watch over Hailey. She doesn't like guns. I'm the one who insisted she carry, and I also put the backup in her glove box."

"How much practice does she have at the range?"

"Enough, I'd say, but you know as well as I do how stress counters thought and accuracy. At least she keeps that damn bang stick with her when she goes out to Mitts Bayou. *That,* she does have plenty of experience with."

"Bang stick?"

"Damn, you're FBI. You should know about these things. You must've slept through your teenage years. *Tèt di.*"

"I do not have a hard head, and I do know about bang sticks. Just didn't know she got another one. I heard she lost one in the swamp."

"Good to know that you've been keeping tabs. The new one is a forty-four magnum. Great for gators and anything close range."

"Maybe, but it's still only one shot."

Sleep was elusive and fitful despite the air-conditioning vent located over his bed yielding blessed coolness. Not wanting to close himself off from the rest of the loft, he left his door slightly ajar and slept in jeans.

At least he didn't dream of serial killers attacking Leigh or Hailey.

Jostling from a giant fur ball hopping up beside him jarred him awake. The animal took up most of the bed with a mishmash ancestry of wolf, shepherd, and something undefined. Soul-searching blue eyes reminded him of Hailey. They were a good match in temperament and personality.

Before he could hustle the animal off, Hailey stuck her head through the door.

"Oh, sorry. He's a bit of an inquisitive boy. I'll take him out and feed him before we go." Contrary to stated intent, she plopped down on the edge of the mattress beside her four-footed companion. "Gunther, you shouldn't bother our guest."

Trenton held his silence and waited. She had something on her mind as her fingers tunneled through the animal's thick undercoat.

He didn't have to wait long.

"Does your gut tell you my hit-and-run originates from your Pennsylvania psycho?"

Hailey ignored the fact he was half-naked. Considering the summers spent shirtless in the south Texas heat, they were accustomed to casual attire.

"Don't know. Not enough information. You said he stole the truck, so that won't tell us much. You didn't recognize anything else besides a chipped tooth, and you're pretty observant."

"You're worried, though because your sister doesn't work with a partner."

"Yeah. You should both take extra precautions, aside from letting Gunther tag along."

"Why don't you have another talk with Colson? But make sure there's no smothering."

So that's your concern. "Been there, had that discussion. Anything else going on I should know about?"

"No, that should cover it. Leigh's working on a bunch of B&Es, but she can schedule her hours to suit herself."

Trenton nodded. "Okay, but consider this. Leigh's going to be just as worried about you. Since I've been out of touch for a while, how about I accompany you, observant and unobtrusive."

"Fine," she huffed. With that said, she ushered Gunther off the bed and out of the room.

By the time he'd dressed and brushed his teeth, the spicy aroma of Cajun coffee drifted down the short hallway. In the evenings, she'd add rum.

"Hope you don't mind taking a minute to eat. I can't work on an empty stomach."

Trenton watched her prepare a familiar brunch. "What type of herbs are you using? I remember you hated to cook, but loved it when your mom talked about herbs. Are you teaching Leigh?"

"Ha. Yes, we're learning to cook, but we still usually end up with sugary deliciousness more often than wise. Don't worry. You won't be hugging a toilet today. As far as gaining weight, Leigh and I like to spar. That's how we burn off energy."

"Is she still into rafting and shooting at the pistol range?" He'd bought an antique collector's gun recently to smooth his way into his sister's good graces. He had no idea what to do where Hailey was concerned.

Two platefuls of spicy goodness beckoned him to drop into the nearest chair and dig in.

"*Mmm*, eggs and shrimp. I love it. Thanks."

"Breakfast I can cook. I went light with the Creole seasoning and left some for Leigh."

"You're frowning, Sparkles. What's on your mind?"

"I keep getting this itch between my shoulder blades. I think I'm getting paranoid."

"No. Those are your instincts kicking in. Has Gunther been acting unusual?"

"He keeps wanting to bolt into the woods when we go out back. It's not like him."

"Have you checked the area?"

"Yes, didn't find anything. I think I'll set a little trap of my own. Cajun style. If anyone touches it, I'll have them."

Trenton didn't ask anything further but planned a short hike later. "Keep your hellhound close. Animals have better perception than humans. How well do you know this family we're going to interview?"

"Only through research and gossip. Kenny Landry is eighteen. According to local scuttlebutt, he's planning to provide tech services to the area and take over his father's antique store on the edge of town. His dad took off about five years back."

"How about the rest of his family? Does the mother work?" Trenton asked.

"No. His dad was a computer specialist who worked out of his store. They live on an old plantation house southeast of La Belle, moved here from the Louisiana bayous."

"Bet when they heard about a gifted school in Texas, their first thoughts were of Longhorn cattle, horse roping, and dry, dusty land." Trenton pushed his empty plate away, thankful for a good meal that didn't come wrapped in foil or paper.

"You *can* find heaven in the Texas swamps. I think most people don't realize the diversity this area offers. The Landrys might have, before they moved here to be close to their boy genius attending the GE school."

"They live close to the McFadden Wildlife Refuge?" Trenton juggled probabilities and distances in his mind.

"Yep. According to my map, the lands adjoin."

"Nice area to bury a body."

"Are all FBI agents suspicious by nature?" Hailey finished eating and cleared their plates. "I don't remember that in you. Must've been programmed in at Quantico."

Chapter Five
Hailey

Hailey admired the miles of silver, feathery bluestem and Texas cupgrass swaying with the lazy breeze en route to La Belle.

After Trenton finished looking over his notes, he closed the file and laid it on the bench seat with a sigh. "Thanks for driving today."

Hailey shrugged. "No problem. I get that you came to check on your sister. How about telling me what you're holding back?" It was unusual for him to do so, and she didn't like it. At all.

Pinching the bridge of his nose after removing his wire-rimmed sunglasses, he said, "Not much to say. I've had nightmares where you and Leigh were held in underground prisons."

"Damn. That's sick."

"The killer's last words referenced family. None of my siblings would be considered a prodigy or particularly unique. Hell, Natalie's in Europe on an exchange program. I've checked. She's fine."

"So the psycho lied."

"I couldn't take the chance she was blowing smoke, not when you and Leigh are so close. When I found you have a new school here for the gifted elite, figured there could be a connection."

"You think your psycho lady had a partner already down here, and *that* connects to my hit-and-run and the missing girl?"

"Not sure. It's unusual for sociopaths to work as a team, but this one did. Until she killed her local partner. Stands to reason there could be a link to someone down here, maybe some kind of twisted competition. Either way, neither of you should be alone."

"Leigh's not alone. She's got Gunther, who would defend her with his last breath."

"He lacks opposable thumbs. Unless your K9 eats bullets for breakfast, that doesn't reassure me much. Leigh's good, don't get me wrong. I've tracked her record, but—"

"No doubt Colson will reign her in tight. He's been driving her nuts."

"Good. She's still young enough to think she's invulnerable."

"What's really on your mind, Trent?"

"Just wondering if you've had much trouble lately—because of your… ability." It appeared an unseen force dragged the words out against his will.

"It's grown. Actually, that's why Victor and I split." She expected the grimace and the pity, but not the quiet after his apology.

"Grown?"

"Yeah. Weird stuff I'm not ready to discuss." How did she casually enlighten a friend that the would-be killer earlier suddenly seemed to suffer some type of psychomotor seizure?

Trenton respected her decision with a change in subject. "I spoke with the local SAC, Special Agent in Charge. They're extending my stay so I can check this out."

"I know what SAC means. Now you'll have time to visit your family, although I suppose you'll wait until figuring out this puzzle."

He made a low noise of affirmation.

"A school full of geniuses would equal your psychopath's dream shopping spree. I can see why your supervisor extended your stay."

Her friend's gaze slid to the miles of flat land giving way to more of the same. Funny that he didn't bring up missing the Pennsylvania mountains.

"Yeah, there's a lot of gray area. Maybe I'm wrong. Or maybe there's a piece we don't have yet, a bigger picture that ties everything together."

"Which translates into me having my very own FBI stalker and Leigh having Colson on her butt. Hurray."

Before leaving home, she'd headed into the woods behind her house to set up her own style surveillance system with a quart of brown paint. Thin colored stripes wrapped around trees deemed appropriate for cover could catch a voyeur. If the creep who'd run her off the road touched one, she'd have a face.

She caught Trenton's half smile in the reflection of the passenger window.

Paved road transitioned to rutted, craggy dirt long before Hailey turned off onto a narrow, curving asphalt driveway, which led to what could've been the quintessential southern plantation in its day.

Deep overhangs shaded a wraparound porch that offered respite from the midday sun, which would later highlight myriad pinprick shadows from peeling paint.

She parked under a giant oak dripping Spanish moss that inspired more creep factor than awe. Opportunistic weeds popped up through cracks in the brick walkway, more visible hints of disrepair.

The estate had long since passed its prime.

"If they come from money yet don't keep up appearances, must be other factors involved," Hailey surmised in adding to her mental notes.

Reaching to snag her sunglasses, she dropped them when the lenses shattered. "What the hell?"

Trenton looked from Hailey to the broken pieces of plastic. "Um… first time that's happened?"

"Well, not exactly. Guess Fate doesn't want me covering my eyes." Hailey dismissed the incident with a wave of her hand. She didn't want to delve into the mystery's origin before interviewing a suspect.

"Most people would freak out if that happened to them."

"I'm not most people."

"No kidding." Trenton visibly paled but didn't pursue the matter.

On the porch, a young man sat beside an older woman rocking in an ornate iron chair while a young girl, roughly ten, played in the yard with her golden retriever. An idyllic scene contradicted by the woman's vacant stare.

"Kenny's mother looks near catatonic."

Burgeoning heat and humidity created tiny beads of perspiration between Hailey's shoulder blades. In counterpoint, Trenton appeared cool and collected in jeans and a white short-sleeved button-down shirt.

They'd made it halfway to the steps when the young man stood and spoke. His words paused briefly as he stared at Hailey.

"What do you want? If you're reporters, turn around and leave. If you're cops, I talked to them again this morning."

"Neither," Hailey said then noticed Trenton pulling out his credentials.

Guess it paid to have a fed around after all. It didn't hurt that most people found him easy on the eyes. A drop of Super Glue on his lips would make him the perfect friend.

"Kenny, we're trying to locate Bernadette Bordelon. As I understand it, you're the last person to have seen her," Trenton spoke to the young man but appeared to assess the woman who continued to rock and for all appearances was unaware of the strangers in her midst.

Spider lines across Mrs. Landry's nose and cheeks along with sallow skin and vacant expression indicated frequent lodging in the bottom of a bottle. For the children's sakes, she needed to climb out soon. No teen should carry such a heavy load.

"I already told the cops. We were coming home from a dance Saturday night. We left early 'cuz Bernadette picked a fight. Said I was seeing another girl on the side. I'm not."

"But you didn't take her home, did you?" Trenton's words held a note of accusation.

"She kept screaming at me to let her out. Even opened the door before I could stop the car." Kenny's voice escalated, his hands fisting at his sides.

"And then?" Hailey asked.

"And then nothing. I came home."

"You left a young woman in the sticks, in the middle of nowhere, at night, without a light?" Disdain dripped from Trenton's steel-edged tone.

Its effect took the younger man back a step. Lines wrinkled Kenny's brow before his lips twisted into a sneer.

"She's faster than any gator and meaner than any snake. Nothing got to her. We were only half a mile from her lane. She threw a damn rock at my car and cracked the windshield." Angry words echoed frustration as the young man's demeanor morphed into sullen disgust.

"What time was that? That area is pretty remote. Did you see any other vehicles around?" Hailey checked the notes kept on her phone.

"A little after nine. And no, we didn't pass any cars. She lives deeper in the bayou."

"Why didn't you give her a flashlight?"

"Didn't need it. Full moon."

Hailey fixed him with a stare, unable to spot a lie. "Even grade school students know not to walk any distance in this area after dark without protection."

Some locals deemed old enough carried bang sticks capable of firing a hefty charge. Unfortunately, they took too long to reload, making them useless when facing more than one threat.

"Is there anywhere else she might have gone? Anyone living nearby where she would've taken refuge?"

"No. Well, there's the Colby place that sits cattycorner to Shell Road. Also, there's Melford's, and Augustin down from them. I doubt she woulda gone to either of them, though."

"Why not?" Hailey watched the little girl sitting in the grass giggle when a butterfly landed on her extended hand.

"No one goes near Melford's place. After his wife died, he turned into a hermit then had a stroke. The Colbys are nice enough, I guess, but they weren't her type of people. Augustin is a monkey wrench at Dent and Grind auto. Bernadette wouldn't have anything to do with him, certain."

"You two went to school together. Did you share many classes?" Trenton maintained eye contact with the young man who radiated frustration.

"Yeah, so?"

"Seems unusual for two locals in the same county to attend such a prestigious center drawing kids from all over the US and beyond." Hailey observed as Kenny looked out over the nearby marsh.

"My grandmother used to live here. We moved from south of Lafayette years ago. Same swamp, different state. School is where I met Bernadette."

"If she was so mean, why'd you take her out?" Trenton's statement wrapped in suspicion registered his doubt.

Trenton's quick sidestep averted disaster as the young girl barreled past him and up the steps to hug Kenny tight.

The teen wrapped his arm around her. "*Shh,* Jesse. We're fine." One side of his mouth kicked up when he addressed Trenton. "Bernadette's an acquired taste. I learned how to deal with her pretty quick." His voice gained volume but lowered in pitch, the innuendo clear.

"My brother wouldn't hurt that witch." Vehemence in the child's voice betrayed an innocent's honesty.

"Jesse, you shouldn't speak ill of those not present."

There'd be time enough later to delve into the boy's behavior. The goal today centered around getting a picture of Bernadette's personality and viewpoints.

"Why would you call her a witch? Did she claim to be one?" Trenton looked from Kenny to Jesse. He'd never been one to miss nuances.

"She is one. She does Vodou." Fear and awe breathed out Jesse's last word. "But she doesn't have eyes like her!" The young girl pointed to Hailey. "You're a Vodouist. I heard people like you can—"

"Hush now, Jesse. It's not nice to point or talk about others." Kenny's chastisement sent the girl flying into the house.

"It's true. I don't lie." The screen door slammed on the child's continued grumbles, but she remained at the door's edge, peering around the jamb.

"Kenny, I've heard that each student at your school is selected based on their gift. What's yours?" Hailey felt sorry for the child. Unfortunately, misconceptions about religious practices were alive and well.

"Computers."

Simple, flat, no elaboration.

Further conversation led to no new revelations. When the teen crossed his arms over his chest and huffed, she figured they'd done enough damage for one visit.

It had surprised her that Trenton let her take the lead. She'd expected him to monopolize instead of interjecting key questions here and there. Either something shaved a hair off his dominant nature, or he'd learned a new level of patience.

Once back in her truck, she steered down the lane and waited for him to present a theory. Instead of hashing out details, he sat pensive, his gaze taking in the adjacent marsh and the great blue heron wading in shallow waters.

"Mind dropping me off at Claude's if they're still in business? I need to pick up a few things since I didn't pack much." Trenton emerged from his self-imposed reverie to meet her gaze.

"No problem. This place hasn't changed much since you left."

"Is Bouchard's Café still serving the best coffee? I'd like to sit and go over my notes."

"Okay. I have to pop in to see my soon-to-be-ex boss. I'm gonna do one more haunted tour this weekend, and then it's full-time investigator with a side order of photography for me."

"Really? Not gonna continue to burn the candle at both ends?"

"I love giving the tours, but there's not enough hours in the day."

"Good. You need to have a life outside of work, Sparkles."

"Says the robot who does nothing but work. Shame you didn't bring your guitar."

Trenton turned his head to stare but offered no denial. "Why don't you meet me at the café in an hour? It's the least I can do for being gruff this morning."

Chapter Six
Hailey

Increasing investigative work over the prior six months heralded a bittersweet end to Hailey's secondary employment. Switching her major to criminal justice with a minor in photojournalism in college was finally paying off.

She'd miss guiding visitors through Hamchet's old streets steeped in history along with the extra money, but job demands consumed much of her schedule. It was time to concentrate on her private investigation business while expanding her photographic portfolio. Her instincts were good, her pictures better.

Boisterous music blared from Cold Chills Walking Tours and signaled the mood light and energetic with tinkling chimes announcing her entry.

Having grown up amid dinner conversations detailing local history with its gruesome murders and hauntings, she knew the tales of the area as well as anyone. Even her own family history integrated lore with fact.

As a child, her father had encouraged her to learn everything her mother taught, before deciding pastures were greener elsewhere.

She took several deep breaths in deciding how to word her quitting while her boss spoke with a couple who'd signed up for a tour.

As soon as they left, the older woman strode around the counter and opened her arms wide. "Don't look so glum, *mon ami*. This job wasn't supposed to be forever."

"How'd you know?"

A smile creased the corners of her mouth as she touched an index finger to the tip of her nose. "Rumor has it you've finally found a worthy man, eh? One to keep you busy at night?"

"No, the day job is taking more of my time, but I'll miss this place. Most of all, I'll miss the people."

"*Oui*. I've always thought you would meet someone while touring, a rich gentleman to sweep you off your feet, not the likes of that no-account Victor."

Her boss' heart was in the right place despite referencing the ex. Victor wasn't as bad as everyone thought. Immature, yes. Impatient, also yes. Wandering eyes, absolutely. Yet he had a quality, a way of making her relax and understood her in a way few others did, accepting her unique heritage as natural. It was good they'd remained friends after the breakup.

Through the years, her mother had warned her to keep her talent a well-kept secret, shared only with Leigh and Trenton. Words she should've lived by. Like others, Victor suspected her difference, even pried, but never succeeded in confirming the entire truth. His persistence drove them apart.

"Thanks for understanding. I promise to make my last tour memorable." A few minutes of easy chitchat, then a glance at her watch prompted a sad goodbye.

By the time she parked along the curb at Bouchard's Café, Trenton sat at a table under the awning and waved her over. A light breeze sifted its fingers through his dark hair, his sunglasses reflecting a glare. The amount of familiar green plastic bags by his feet revealed his shopping success.

She acknowledged acquaintances in navigating the tables to where he sat. More than a few women watched him with keen interest. Nothing unusual there.

The owner of the establishment approached with a wide grin when Hailey plopped down in a wrought iron chair.

"Where is that blue-eyed baby of yours, Hailey? He should be protecting our up-and-coming photojournalist-detective-whatever else you're into nowadays."

"He's keeping my partner company today."

"And now I see you have a new partner. I approve wholeheartedly. About time you cornered the market on this one. Smart girl." Stout and always wearing an apron with smudges of flour, the owner winked at Trenton, who shook his head.

"No, no. We're just friends, like sibling-type friends." Hailey couldn't get the words out fast enough.

"Good to see you again, Aurelie." Trenton accepted a one-armed hug from the older woman.

Aurelie *tsked*. "Friends make the best lovers. It's been too long since you've visited, young man. You should stay, settle down, and make babies." Her chin tilt in Hailey's direction might as well have included gasoline and a match. At least she didn't mock Hailey's humiliation with a chuckle.

Trenton cleared his throat and studied his menu. "She's a non-blooded sister, Aurelie. We've been through this before." A tightness around his mouth accompanied his slow exhale.

"Ah, but I have the vision, you see. Like your beautiful companion will have one day, yes? I grew up in the bayou, too. I learned the old ways." With a knowing smile and a pat on Trenton's arm, she took their order and bustled away.

Once upon a time, they'd considered making friendship into something more, but the thought faded in lieu of the strong comradery already in place. Hailey wouldn't trade it for the world.

Or would I?

Trenton kept his face toward the menu as he said, "You ever thought about letting the cat out of the bag? Maybe it's time."

"Good lord, no. The townspeople would lynch me." She'd long given up hope of feeling normal and fitting in. Telling others of her ability would create a permanent impenetrable wall.

"People fear what they don't understand and can't control. You could help with the former."

"Wouldn't be enough, Trent. And there'd be no stuffing the cat back in the bag when it backfired."

He shrugged in response.

"Mom's rhetoric doesn't help. She keeps telling me, 'One day soon, it'll stabilize then grow into something more. Bayou talents are different from other psychic gifts.'" That's all she'll say."

"You're extraordinary as you are, Hailey. I wouldn't worry about it. How'd you keep it from Victor?" Trenton grimaced as if not meaning to bring up a painful subject.

"I was a late bloomer, and it wasn't as strong back then. Hell, I'm still learning, and it's so inconsistent. He pried—a lot, which was one peg in the wheel that led to our breakup."

She'd never admit to discovering Victor's infidelity by receiving visions from her own bed. The mattress went to the dump and Victor became persona non grata.

A server returned with their order, and Hailey sipped her favorite chicory-laced coffee in silence.

"I heard rumors about Aurelie's verbal slam into Victor for not picking up a tab. She doesn't pull punches."

"Wow. You have spies everywhere, Trent."

The remark made him flinch. It was rare to see him uncomfortable. He handled situations as a natural course of events and with a calm demeanor. To see his world knocked off-kilter gave her an edge. One she could use to her advantage.

"Speaking of which, why did you leave Hamchet in such a hurry?"

"I didn't leave in a hurry. I was accepted at Quantico."

"Yeah, but no one knew you'd even applied."

"Applied before I left the military."

"I heard you didn't get in through normal channels. Someone pulled strings, and yes, you did leave here with little warning and even less explanation."

"FBI was a natural transition after the service."

"One of these days, you're gonna tell me."

He'd pulled up stakes soon after she'd met Victor. The two men had not seen eye-to-eye despite both attempting a smooth façade.

Trenton cleared his throat and switched gears. Highlights concerning changes in the community yielded to a discussion regarding haunted tour guides and the rich history of Cajun Texas.

It felt like he'd never left by the time they finished coffee. She smiled when he swiped the check from the server's hand. His parents had raised gentlemen in both Trenton and his two brothers.

"When are you gonna drive up to see your folks?" Hailey slid from the chair and stood.

"I called and told them I'd bring steaks for a barbecue next weekend. Why don't you join me? Leigh's coming, and they'd love to see you."

"My last guided tour is this Saturday, but I could do Sunday." A strange prickling between her shoulder blades turned her gaze to the swath of trees backing the property. She felt like a betta fish in a bowl, observant yet ready to strike.

"What?"

"Nothing. Paranoia creeping in again."

Trenton walked her to her truck and opened the door, another trait engrained in his family since childhood.

"Ever the gentleman." She made a face and pivoted to slide in, then growled at what sat in her seat.

In one smooth move, he whisked her behind him and drew his weapon. She now understood why he wore a t-shirt under his button-down. Manufacturers designed it to conceal waist holsters.

On the seat lay a muslin doll fashioned with crude stitches and a face drawn with markers. Bright blue circles for eyes confirmed the target. A long pin protruded from the chest. More specifically, from the X in the center of its painted heart.

"Damn. We've been here less than an hour." Hailey stepped forward and reached for it.

"No. Don't touch it. We might be able to lift prints." Trenton retrieved his handkerchief and wrapped the warning with care.

"Before you ask, I don't know who left it, and yes, I can see I'm the intended target." Her eyes had long been a source of frustration, but she refused to buckle and wear contacts. On specific occasions, she wore sunglasses.

"We're due for an in-depth conversation, Hailey. This is twice in twenty-four hours."

Trenton turned her to face him with a hand on her shoulder before removing his sunglasses. "Sparkles, I won't lose you to nonsense. You hear me?"

And just that fast, their connection hummed through her veins, tightening her chest and restricting her breath.

"Fine. Whatever. For now, I want to do some research before we talk to Bernadette's parents. I also have Leigh's current notes to look over." She broke the connection before doing something stupid, like pulling him in for a hug.

"Okay. Set up the interview for tomorrow AM."

"Before you go off on this, understand something. These crude representations have very little to do with the majority of practitioners." Hailey slipped behind the wheel and waited for Trenton to get in and shut his door.

"Explain."

"Vodou is a religion, plain and simple. Well, maybe not so simple as it blends African religions with Catholic saints. The fundamental principle entails the belief that everything is spirit. Even humans are spirits who inhabit the visible world."

"And the unseen world?" Trenton asked.

"Populated by *IWA, myste, anvizip, zanj*, and the spirits of our ancestors."

"In English, please?"

"That translates to spirits, mysteries, the invisibles, and angels."

Hailey gestured to the wrapped doll he laid on the seat. "*That* is a figment of popular culture and Hollywood's imagination, at least in these parts."

Myriad thoughts rambled through her mind in trying to identify the predator. Anything occult fascinated her ex-boyfriend, a trait earned from parental influence and practices. In his self-absorbed mind, Victor believed she still belonged with him. Destiny. Yet, he wouldn't resort to fear tactics. Gentle coercion was more his style.

In counterpoint, they'd just interviewed the top suspect earlier. Kenny Landry radiated a controlled energy which if unleashed could wipe Texas off the map.

In addition, the threat might link to a cold case from five years prior. They'd never found the young teen who'd not only lived near Kenny, but according to filed reports, went fishing and canoeing with him on a frequent basis.

At the time, he'd just turned thirteen and not deemed a suspect.

Chapter Seven
Trenton

Morning dawned with a colorful array of gold and magenta on the horizon—and Gunther pouncing on Trenton's bed again. For reasons unknown, the animal held a strong affinity for him.

He wondered if this translated to other males who may have visited. The thought shouldn't have bothered him so much. That thought pricked his conscience through Leigh's arrival, their light breakfast, and long after cleanup.

"It's cooler out today. Looks like we'll get a break from the heat." Hailey and Gunther strode back through the door following his morning run. The dog romped around the open loft then sat and tilted his head up. In the next heartbeat, he let out a soul-wrenching howl.

Both Hailey and his sister joined him.

"What are you three doing?" Trenton watched in utter amazement. It seemed some things *had* changed while he was gone.

"Pack meeting. Bonding and all that." Leigh smiled at her brother. "Plus, it always brings him to our side. You could be across town, and as long as he can hear you, he'll come running."

"Jeez, maybe I should have the water checked. There could be a parasite eating your brains."

"Hey, bro. You'll be howling before you know it too."

"Like hell. I may enjoy my own insanity, but I won't add yours to the mix."

"Let's sit and outline the day's tasks." Hailey returned to the table as if she hadn't lost her marbles.

"First, I'd like to say this." Leigh glared at her brother, then Hailey. "If you receive any more dolls, I want to see them for myself *before* you let testosterone bag send it off to the federal lab, got it?"

"Fine, but you know this has gotta be bullshit. I've put up with this kind of crap all my life. People think of me as some kind of dark priestess."

"So, do your thing. Fly on a broom, dance a flame in your palm, or whatever it is you're destined to do. Give 'em what they want." Leigh shrugged with no concern. "Let 'em get it out of their systems."

"That was not bullshit. It was a threat," Trenton countered.

"Guys, you know as well as I do that our religion doesn't use dolls that way. They're used to help people with healing and to communicate with deceased loved ones."

"We're looking for a non-practitioner then," Leigh suggested.

"Any luck with your digging?" Trenton asked his sister, trying to hide his skepticism.

"Not yet, and it's a little harder with my lieutenant breathing down my neck. I did get a tip about a suspicious truck parked out at the old fairgrounds on occasion. I was gonna check that out first."

"I want to interview Bernadette's parents." Trenton ignored his sister's frustration regarding her supervisor.

It's for your own good.

Hailey squirmed in the passenger seat as Trenton drove, her age-old attempt to disguise nervousness by watching the leafy street debris swirl in mini whirlwinds.

"What?" He spared her a glance but tightened his fingers on the wheel. A well-honed sixth sense prepared him for much, although she somehow always managed to throw him for a loop.

"I noticed your direct style with Kenny, but we'll learn more with a softer approach here." She swiped the screen on her cell several times before tucking it into her shirt pocket. "I'm going to record the interview."

"Why?" Trenton noted her fiddling with her necklace, sliding the charm back and forth on its chain. The other half resided with Leigh. "You're plugged into the local culture more than anyone I know. I don't see any motive for them holding back or wanting to threaten you."

"They didn't leave the totem. I'm sure of it. But they travel in similar circles, and I don't want to get sidetracked."

"I want a list of all your recent clients."

"Because of a doll? Listen—"

"No leeway on this. If I have to claim jurisdiction, I'll figure out a way to do it."

"Dammit, Trent. It's just a doll."

"You told me Victor's mother claimed to be a priestess with healing power. Who knows what else they do? I don't give a crap about the symbol itself. I'm concerned about the person who put it there."

"Okay, but Victor wouldn't do this, not this way, even if he went batshit crazy."

"Did you ever observe him doing any rituals?" Trenton knew Hailey's family as well as she knew his brothers and sisters. They were night and day in some areas but had melded during the course of growing up.

"No, not directly. We parted ways a couple years ago, and that's something we never shared. Victor seemed to always want to branch out, and I'm more about tradition."

"And this family we're going to see?"

"Rumor has it Bernadette's mother is steeped in the culture. As deep as you can get. It's not something we discussed on the phone when she hired me."

"Does she share similar beliefs with your mother?"

Hailey offered a noncommittal shrug. "I don't know the family personally. Stories have circulated about their ceremonies, their spirit's names, attributes, and symbols."

"Did they sacrifice—"

"Animals, yes. But hey, don't think of them as dark or evil. We eat meat, right?"

"Yeah, so."

"Think smaller scale and about those who don't go, or can't get to the grocery store every week. They do their own slaughtering and cleaning. They sacrifice the animals, yes, but it's not a morbid fascination with death, it's more of an offering of life-giving energy. It's a preparation of sacred food. Think of it the same way as when you put a package of meat in your grocery cart."

"I never gave much credence to the culture when my folks moved here. Then, when you learned to do what you can do, I... well, I guess I didn't handle it as well as I should have."

"You joined the FBI to get away from us all." A hint of accusation bled into the atmosphere.

"Hailey, I—"

She interrupted with a wave of her hand. "From what I know, this family's ceremonies entail offerings to a specific loa, a spirit who's also the intermediary between Bondyé, or good God, and mankind."

"So, Victor and his family weren't into all that?"

"Why do you bounce between my ex and a missing girl? There's nothing there."

"Just curious is all."

"All right. Vodou 101, something you'll question. Common interpretation of zombies. It's different from the culture's version in that we believe death is merely an extension of life and welcome it as it returns the soul to paradise to watch over living descendants. They, in turn, are revered as guides and are very wise."

Trenton noticed Hailey included herself in this group, even though she didn't *practice*. "So, you must have a dozen ancestors watching over and protecting you. Makes sense with the near misses you've had."

As much as he wanted her take on why the sunglasses shattered earlier, he didn't ask, not even when she'd retrieved another pair from her loft. He'd bide his time.

"Explain about the zombies."

"Okay, the other side—the dark side. Li Grande Zombi is the name of a Vodoun serpent spirit. Think snakes and boogeymen, the latter controlled by a master, not created by a virus, bomb, or whatever. But don't think of snakes as dark or evil, consider them holders of prescient knowledge."

"If I see one, I'm going to shoot it just the same."

"Jeez, you grew up here. You should be used to seeing them."

"I joined the military after graduation. Meaning, I didn't get sucked into the same world as my younger siblings."

"I don't know about Bernadette's family, but some Cajuns and Creoles have encountered enough suspicious and condescending attitudes to keep them aloof. Tread carefully, big guy, is all I'm saying."

"This is bayou country in its purest form." Trenton admired the

French Creole architecture as narrow streets widened and larger homes centered on grounds that were more elegant.

"There's something to be said for living on the fringes, a raw beauty you can't find anywhere else." Hailey breathed deep and exhaled slowly, closing her eyes while the wind rushed in through her open window.

"Never thought anything here could draw me back, but the land is beautiful." If honest, it didn't compare to the raven-haired beauty beside him.

"You like Pennsylvania."

"It, too, has its charms. I've made a life there. Got to admit, my friends' antics are very similar to yours and my sister's." Trenton considered the similarities. "We've grown close. The men have their hands full with headstrong women. One, in particular, builds drones and can't walk away from a mystery. She's much like you. A couple are ex-military guys who view laws as 'mere guidelines.' Group dynamics are guaranteed to give an ulcer to anyone geared toward following rules."

"Sounds familiar. You moved away but found pretty much the same thing you left behind, minus the military part."

He'd long regretted leaving, yet more often than not blamed work for keeping him away. Now that he was back, past misgivings about life here hadn't nipped at the corners of his mind the way he'd expected.

He parked behind a battered, four-wheel-drive pickup at the end of a long, rutted path. Thick oaks, elm, black cherry, and ash offered shade and refuge to the wide variety of wildlife indigenous to the area. The feeling of unknown eyes watching his every move took him back to his days in military intelligence.

An old oak took center stage in the small front yard with two rope swings dangling from an overhead branch. Research had uncovered a family that once totaled four. He imagined Bernadette swinging her younger brother in years past.

A sigh escaped as he regretted his encounter with Hailey on arrival. Worry over her welfare had trumped civility. "I'm not going to bulldoze my way in here. I do know how to conduct an investigation. And I'll stipulate for the record, you have experience in handling difficult people," he conceded.

"Thank you." Hailey removed her sunglasses and left them on the dash, surprising him.

"Um…"

"My eye color freaks people out more times than not. Today, I'm hoping they'll smooth the way. Honestly, sometimes I forget to take my sunglasses off. I did wear them at our initial meeting."

"You shouldn't be self-conscious. They're your nicest feature." *They've haunted my nights since I left.*

"Because you could stare at them all day long?" Hailey's wide grin mocked him with a dramatic flutter of eyelashes.

Trenton snorted. "Because they can't bite, show sarcasm, and don't otherwise normally offend."

"You don't remember me well."

He remembered kids in school whispering behind her back about the striking color, along with various interpretations. Rumor mill long declared Hailey's family steeped in the black arts. She'd used the uncertainty to her advantage and had the frequent flyer miles in the principal's office to prove it.

A blast of hot, humid air hit him while sliding out and circumventing a homemade fire pit.

The home's back steps were wooden and in good repair, as was the rest of what he saw. Like most homeowners in the area, they cut their grass low to avoid large snakes finding refuge among weeds or rocks.

The simple one-story home was elevated to avoid storm waters and allow residents to enjoy stronger breezes. A wide front porch and hipped roof were common to the area. Multiple sets of double windows flooded the home with light while the L-shaped breezeway bifurcated the building's two sections joined at perpendicular angles.

Calm and quiet, one could almost taste the serenity of a cool evening breeze with moonlight filtering through trees and the bayou's natural sonata.

Soft strains of Creole jazz through open windows signaled someone home, and excited chuffing preceded a mixed-breed dog approaching from around the corner of the cabin.

Before Trenton could knock on the screen door, a slim woman dressed in a colorful ankle-length skirt and white gauzy top stepped into view. A soft whistle called the dog to her side after she opened the door.

What he suspected was normally clear mocha skin held blotches of heightened color under puffy eyes.

"'Morning." Trenton grimaced as he reached for his credentials, aware of Hailey's quick strides behind him to catch up.

"Who are you?"

Hailey stepped around Trenton and smiled, negating the need for identification. "Mrs. Bordelon?" Without hesitation, Hailey held out her hand. "Thank you for seeing me again. Trenton is helping me search for your daughter. May we come in and chat?"

"Your eyes... you wore glasses when we spoke last."

"Yes, I'm afraid they startle a lot of folks. I—"

"No. You are a descendant of La Belle Fontaine, yes?"

"I am." Hailey smiled wide. "Only a few people know the specific resemblance."

"Call me Babette. Come in. I'm sorry I didn't recognize this before. My husband and I... please disregard the mess."

There was no need to apologize. They'd all seen the familiar byproducts of grief and recognized the aftereffects.

Trenton accepted the firm handshake and followed the women inside. As suspected, the interior was open space and without hallways.

A large table with bench seating separated the kitchen from the living area where two comfortable looking chairs faced a couch and offered a view of the front yard.

Two plates laden with uneaten food attested to current coping abilities. More were in the sink. A bright red file folder lay open on the counter, a picture of Bernadette with a wide smile holding up a ribbon on display.

"Please, sit. Trenton, this is my husband Enrique." A gesture indicated the male occupying one of two deep, tufted seats.

Babette sat on the arm of her husband's chair.

Trenton nodded, claiming a spot beside Hailey on the couch. Before he could open a conversation, Enrique slammed his fist against the other arm of his chair.

"Have they arrested that *kriminèl,* the Landry offspring?" Anguish mixed with rage suffused the father's tone. "He is the one responsible for the disappearance of our *anj.*"

"Not at this time, no." Trenton moderated his tone to remain even and calm. "We're still gathering facts."

"His is a rich family with much influence, *oui*?" Babette narrowed her eyes, the storm brewing in her gaze not unlike her husband's.

"Affluent, yes. As far as influence—" Trenton began, soon realizing he'd chosen his words incorrectly.

"They go hand in hand in this area," Babette exclaimed with condescension.

"I'd like a little more information about your daughter," Trenton said, making another attempt to steer the conversation away from the parents' growing anger.

"Of course. Anything," the mother conceded, pulling a tissue from her skirt pocket and dabbing her cheeks.

Trenton walked toward the desk in the corner where three pictures took center stage. "You have beautiful children."

"A fever took our son years ago. Bernadette's brother was such a happy boy."

Hailey nodded. "I'm so sorry. No parent should ever bear that kind of loss."

"Is your daughter the same? I mean... happy?" Trenton studied the photo, assembling previous notes and current observations to form a more complete picture.

"You said is and not was, but I no longer *feel* Bernadette's presence, just like I didn't feel my son's aura the night he was taken from us." Babette padded on bare feet to take the picture Trenton indicated.

"Our daughter's beauty cuts through the darkness with the brightest light. Smart and kind, she was very protective of her younger brother. I want to know what has happened to her."

"When did you last see her?" Trenton asked, directing his question to Enrique.

"Saturday, when that *djab* picked her up in his fancy car." Enrique's gaze softened as if he saw through time to a happy memory.

An old sedan parked to the side was the only car Trenton had observed at the Landry house; there'd been no reason to look in the garage since his vehicle was in the shop.

"Were they in an exclusive relationship?" Hailey asked.

"Bernadette was, yes. The boy, I think his hands wandered as much as his eyes. Bernadette said he bedded two other girls after she began seeing him. Ah, but she loved him so much. By the time she discovered his true nature, her heart was stolen by the devil himself." Babette sniffled and held the tissue to her nose. "I know she'd come home if she could."

"How'd she get along with the other students?" Trenton studied the grief-stricken parents, unable to imagine the pain of losing two children.

"As well as any teenager in a school for the gifted, I suppose. There was one recently that she didn't like. I think the new arrival made her uncomfortable in some way."

"Did she give a name?"

"Olivia something." The mother waved her hand in dismissal. "Our daughter had a free spirit within her that could not be contained. When she first went to that school, she didn't like it and wanted to come home." She stroked her dog's ears when he sat at her feet.

"What changed?" Hailey took her seat, her focus on the distraught mother.

"I don't know. Time, I guess. Students come from all over the country, and several from England. The only other Acadian was Kenny. I suppose that's why she got closer to him. I believe they formed a strong co-dependency, and that made the difference."

"The area where Kenny dropped her off, there are several places she might have gone. For instance, the Melford's..." Hailey led with a partial statement.

"Enrique and I spoke with the caretaker. Mr. Melford is in a nursing home after having a stroke. His wife died prior to that. They were adoptive grandparents for lost souls. Bernadette visited the couple on several occasions and seemed to like Mrs. Melford." The mother again dabbed her cheeks before blowing her nose.

Trenton nodded, realizing visits there would add to a bond forming between teens. "How was your daughter gifted?"

Babette's face lit with a sad smile. "Numbers, recall, and language. She could've done anything. She had a special knack for puzzles. She wouldn't speak of her future, except to say it *didn't* include Texas, but Enrique and I figured that out a long time ago."

Further inquiries and a cursory look at Bernadette's room formed the image of a young woman on the cusp of discovering the world.

Large blocks of light from the window highlighted the brightly colored homemade quilt on the twin bed. Crude bookshelves lining two walls were crammed with countless volumes of both fiction and nonfiction books. Trenton saw no conflicting insights or clues as to where the teen would go of her own accord.

"I'm sure you've heard Kenny Landry claims she picked a fight with him. He also said he paced her with his vehicle so she wouldn't be alone—until she threw a rock and cracked his windshield." Trenton expected denial, but not the simultaneous outburst.

"She wouldn't be so stupid as to walk around at night, alone and without protection. There are many dangers, humans being the least of them. No, I do not believe those lies. She would never do such a thing. As far as the windshield, a jealous ex-girlfriend, or maybe not an ex?" Babette shook her head in disgust, effectively closing that aspect of conversation.

Hailey placed her hand on Trenton's upper arm, a light squeeze of warning. "We didn't mean to insinuate anything or slur her reputation, Babette. We merely want to get to the bottom of what's happened and find her."

Trenton moved toward the door with Hailey's urging. Challenging the couple with Kenny's version of the truth had produced the expected result. Both parents believed their daughter to be everything they claimed.

A greater truth existed though. Only a rare couple saw their teen with a high degree of accuracy.

Once back in the truck, he shoved the key in the ignition but paused to lend the weight of his stare after lowering his glasses. "How many know of your ancestry concerning La Belle Fontaine?"

Hailey sighed. "Trent. We're in the Texas bayou, not the badlands or open country where you can feel the thunder of hooves from cattle drives in the distance. I've lived here all my life. People talk. Sometimes it's with revulsion, sometimes reverence. The town is small enough that many think they know everybody else's business."

"Sorry. Didn't mean to step on your toes."

"I know. It's okay."

"How 'bout we meet with Leigh at Bouchard's. I wanna set eyes on my sister."

"Fine. As far as the references to the occult, you know my mom has always viewed the world in a different light. She raised me to stand up for what I believe in."

"She shares the same eye coloring. You never talked much about that aspect of your life growing up. Why?"

"Didn't want to be *that* different. Leigh and I caught enough grief over twin speak. I remember the first time a kid poked fun of me because of my eyes. She decked him flat."

"I remember my mom squaring off with the principal. Said if he wasn't going to protect the kids, they'd protect themselves."

"Everybody hated the twin speak in particular."

Trenton shrugged. "Hell, I have to admit that I'm jealous. To be able to converse in front of a co-worker without them deciphering your words? Priceless."

"I suppose. Anyway, that's not what Babette referenced. Mom subscribes to particular beliefs and has always shared them with me."

"I remember her talk of Bondyé, or Gran Met, and his loa intermediaries." Trenton shrugged. "To each his own."

The more time he spent with Hailey, the more changes he saw in her, and the stronger fate pulled him back to southeast Texas.

"My mom is descended from a great mambo and destined to pass her powers to her children, blah, blah, blah."

"*Hmm*, unless she also practices cannibalism, I don't see the problem. What kind of powers are you supposed to inherit?"

Hailey harrumphed but continued. "Doesn't matter. I don't want to be pigeonholed. I'll choose my own path and my own destiny, thank you very much."

Trenton nodded in understanding. "Do you think that's what drove your father away?" He wondered if the subject was still taboo.

"I–I don't know. Leigh and I were so self-absorbed, and Mom never discussed it. I remember my folks argued a couple times before he left, but I figured all parents did."

"I was just curious, not trying to pry. We're both trained to investigate. In the field, it's essential to know how your partner will react in any particular situation. That means knowing a bit of their significant history."

Spouting that bullshit would've earned a lecture from his parents, especially when Hailey wasn't his partner but someone under his protection. She settled for a serious case of side-eye.

Trenton guided the SUV onto the state highway before activating his Bluetooth to call his sister. She answered on the first ring.

"*What's wrong?*"

Family always expected the worst from him.

"Nothing. Just wondering what you've learned. Were there many summer students present?"

"*A few. There's a student assistant in the office who said a new kid wouldn't take any of Bernadette's nonsense. I have a local address. Apparently, the kid just moved here.*"

"If she's carrying a big chip on her shoulder, I'll talk to her since I don't carry a badge." Hailey rolled her eyes with Trenton's suggestive throat clearing.

"*We're getting nowhere fast. We've no clue who ran you off the road, Hailey. No clue about what's behind Bernadette's disappearance, or who's making Vodou dolls.*" Leigh transmitted her frustration through the line with a sigh. "*I hate to ask this, but is it possible—*"

"No, don't you dare say it. No need to jump to conclusions. I've no idea who left it. I just know it was for me," Hailey interjected.

"It's not like this sleepy town has video cameras," Leigh commiserated. *"Except at the one traffic light, the intersection of Henley and Baker."*

"I don't have anything back on the doll yet," Trenton offered then invited Leigh to join them.

"If you two want to speak with the new girl at school, I'll send you what I have on her."

"We certainly don't have much else to go on. Kenny swore Bernadette picked a fight on purpose. He let her out and followed her until she threw a rock at his car." Trenton sped up to pass a utility truck.

"There's gotta be something to this. Someone didn't like my surveillance and ran me off the road," Hailey added and glanced at Trenton.

Leigh clicked on something in the background. *"I've alerted the local body shops to call with any pickups needing work or a new side view mirror. Colson and I also spoke to the groundskeeper at the fairgrounds. Said kids are using that area for parking, at least until the fair starts up. The manager makes rounds every weekend and runs a few off but doesn't remember seeing Kenny or Bernadette."*

"Someone doesn't like Hailey's participation on this and could've seen you from the river if they'd been out at night." Trenton didn't like the fact she'd continued to work the case, regardless of consequences.

There were too many variables to make sense of the timeline or events. In years past, Leigh and Hailey pissed off everyone from neighbors to teachers and coaches.

"It could be that the two attempts aren't related," he mused.

"Which would leave us with two threats and two disconnected cases," Leigh finished on a sigh.

Chapter Eight
Hailey

The distant laugh of a loon announced its perceived threat along the narrow waterways interlacing lower parts of the county.

Hailey appreciated the unspoiled beauty devoid of oil rigs and processing plants. Few people, hence less pollution, marred the remote area.

Trenton navigated the back roads like he'd never left after stopping to pick up Gunther on the ride back.

Hailey looked over her printout from the previous night's research. "I hope this kid likes to talk. If she had a run-in with Bernadette, maybe we'll see another side of the coin. Let's leave the windows down for Gunther to join us if appropriate. He has a way of loosening tongues of all ages."

"This kid have any personal connections to the area?"

"No. None that we know of anyway. We'll have to play it by ear."

"Only child?"

"Yep. Adopted." Hailey shuffled through the notes for specifics.

"Ability?"

"Didn't find it... Odd. Plus, she's been homeschooled up till now. The adoptive father is an ex-military big wig. Travels a lot. Best let me start off with the questions."

Trenton turned off the single lane route to navigate a labyrinth of smaller roads leading to their destination. "What else did you find?"

"Not much. She just enrolled in summer classes. Getting a feel for the place before the fall semester, I'd guess."

"Who would adopt a teen then spend so much time on the road? Who's the guardian when he's away?" Trenton's tone suggested he didn't like the way things were adding up.

"Dunno. Sound fishy to you?"

"Sounds like there's more going on behind the scenes." Trenton tapped his fingers on the steering wheel and slowed for a passel of opossums crossing the road.

Country living endured its drawbacks.

Two miles farther down, a riot of blooming flowers straddled the entrance of an asphalt driveway under the graceful arc of willow branches.

The home came into view around a sweeping bend, choreographing each visitor's arrival with landscaping designed for maximum impact.

Vertical white siding covered spaces between broad floor-to-ceiling windows of the large southern home bearing a wide veranda and a gray metal roof. Sturdy white pillars, thicker at the bottom, contrasted the slate porch and added to the overall effect of elegance. Three rocking chairs and two small tables offered a serene view of the secluded, well-manicured country acreage.

"Huh, even their parking spaces are marked. Can we say OCD?" Hailey surveyed the extensive landscaping and snorted.

"It's not OCD. It's called everything in its proper place." Trenton cut the engine and put all four windows down for Gunther. "Something tells me your fur kid might not be welcome here."

She smiled at the amount of dog hair Trenton would have to vacuum before returning the SUV to the rental company. She slid her sunglasses in place as a small tuft of black hair floated out with the door's opening.

Trenton raised a brow. "I don't think you should wear them.

"I've told you; they tend to unsettle folks."

He matched her steps along the travertine walkway. "You didn't cover them at Bernadette's home."

"Because of my mother's, um, status, I'm welcome to some. Others, not so much."

The ornate door opened before Trenton raised his hand to knock.

"Good morning." A petite blonde pulled the door back with a smile. Wire-rimmed spectacles perched on a straight slim nose added to the prim effect. A small space between straight white teeth accentuated the symmetry of her features.

"Hi. I'm Hailey Arquette and this is my associate, Trenton Briner. We—"

"Are you reporters?"

"No, ma'am. We're looking into the disappearance of Bernadette Bordelon, who went to the gifted school. I understand Olivia knew her. We'd like to ask her a few questions to get a better idea of our missing student." Hailey looked beyond to an exquisitely curved staircase with wrought iron insets. That one feature probably cost more than her vehicle.

It was difficult to avoid rolling her eyes when Gunther leapt from the truck and bounded up the steps. Mindful of his manners, he sat by her side.

"Is there news?" From behind the door, a teen wearing ripped jeans and a knit tank top stepped into view. Her odd stance indicated one who carried something on the left shoulder or perhaps recovered from an injury.

"Sorry, we can't comment on an ongoing investigation." Trenton held his hand out to shake then retracted it with the teen's smirk.

"I've already talked to Lieutenant Colson. The guy's got a stick wedged up where the sun doesn't shine." A pink bubble erupted from pursed lips and grew until popping with a loud snap.

"Yes, Olivia, we realize he's been here, but we'd like to ask a few follow-up questions." Hailey studied the teen, aware of the discrepancy between casual speech and shrewd eyes that studied them with focused attention.

"I don't answer to that name. Call me Casper if you want to talk." The door opened wider. "It's all right, Sarah. I've got this." A small headshake signaled the older woman not to interfere.

The interplay was interesting with the teen taking the lead. They'd witnessed the same dynamics at the Landry house.

Casper's demeanor transformed from curiosity to excitement when Gunther leaned forward for a sniff. Kneeling to greet the animal, she held her hand out. "What a pretty boy you are. Love your eyes."

The dog approached warily and accepted her hand on his chest. A second later, he hopped straight up in the air then backtracked with a short *yipe*. His head tilted side to side but lowered to the ground.

"Gunther? What's wrong? I'm sorry, Casper. He's always well-mannered." Fine hairs on Hailey's arm prickled with goose bumps.

Something felt *off.*

The teen snickered and glanced at her left shoulder while her fingers held tight to an amulet around her neck. "No problem. Must be my perfume or something." Green eyes reflected amusement before assessing Trenton. "You look like a cop."

"FBI," Hailey murmured, feeling the presence of something she couldn't define. Something significant.

Gunther returned when Casper held out her hand again. "C'mon, boy. I'm not so bad. Take another look and you'll see."

The dog crouched low with his tail tucked and ears down but approached with a whine. Acceptance of Casper's touch coincided with his normal stance returning in slow degrees.

"Come in. I'll grab a pitcher of tea." Casper stood and stepped back.

"I'll get it." Sarah gave them each a once-over before leaving.

The sitting room was airy with an elegant sofa in cream-and-brown toned geometrical patterns. Two wing chairs sat opposite to form a conversational seating area. Bookshelves lined two walls with hundreds of old tomes. A hint of almond and vanilla blended to add to the bright and cozy atmosphere.

"Quite a collection of books you have here." Hailey perused the titles while Trenton surveyed the visible part of the great room beyond. Three long shelves dedicated to the history and geography of the area and another four represented someone's interest in the occult. *Oh, crap.*

"My dad likes to read," Casper tossed out with an air of nonchalance.

Hailey turned and *sensed* a presence on the teen's shoulder. Caught staring, she blushed when Casper cleared her throat. Her mother's talk of spirits all came home to roost, and not in a good way. Keeping the frown off her face in favor of professionalism was difficult.

The gem Casper fiddled with must've held significance, its color defying definition. Maybe she'd remember its reference in one of the many stories heard as a young girl.

"I take it you haven't found Bernadette yet. I thought you guys had, like, electronic surveillance everywhere." Shoulder-length black hair swirled when she sat on the arm of a wing chair.

Like father, like daughter. Taking a position of power?

"No, not hardly. I understand you haven't been here long but are attending summer classes. Can you tell us what you know about her?" Trenton nodded to Sarah when she returned with a tray containing tea and glasses.

Setting her phone out, Hailey asked, "Mind if I record this?"

Casper shrugged but nodded.

"Not much to tell. Stuck-up twat thought she was all that and more. She's smart, but more importantly, she's clever and knows how to manipulate others, even the teachers."

"Casper! That's no way to talk about a classmate." The teen's guardian held her hand up to halt any protests. "You can answer a question nicely, without slurring someone's character."

Hailey wanted to interrupt, to hear what the kid had to say uncensored, but knew better. "Wow. She doesn't sound well-liked." She nodded for the girl to go on.

"I heard you don't go against her unless you want to be viciously torn apart, 'cause she holds onto a lot of secrets."

Casper spoke of the missing girl in the present tense and without hesitation. That fact plus the sincere disdain radiating from every pore lent credence to her sincerity.

Hailey wondered if Bernadette had anything on this new kid, but it seemed unlikely. Instead, she asked, "Do you know if she was seeing any other boys, or was her relationship with Kenny Landry exclusive?"

Casper nipped both lips between her teeth, but the stifled smile reached her eyes before saying, "I don't think she's the type to keep her knees closed. According to her, the entire world is hers for the taking, whomever she wants, whenever, and however. All hers. She probably thanks her lady parts every night for whatever comes her way."

Sarah groaned.

Hailey chuckled.

Trenton's choked cough drew everyone's attention. "You're in several of her classes. Maybe she joined a club that didn't hold her attention, or signed up for an activity you'd think peculiar?"

"Now that you mention it, yes." Casper returned his smile with one of her own.

Keen intelligence and current assessment didn't match the teen's gaze radiating amusement. Whatever she found funny was lost on Hailey. Her attention focused on Trenton.

"She did drop a few hints about older men having more experience in all the right ways. Is that fact or fiction?"

Trenton covered his mouth then scrubbed his hand over his chin. The kid was wise beyond her years but lacked the filter attained with time.

Sarah's sharp rebuke saved him from answering.

"Did she ever mention any specific man or perhaps a clue about a specific subject?" Hailey enjoyed watching Trenton squirm. The kid had moxie—along with a secret if her initial assessment was correct.

"Nah, she likes being all mystical and sh—crap. Once talked about slipping a homemade *zemi* in someone's car at lunch just to see his reaction. She really believed in all that Vodou hogwash."

"But you don't?" Hailey asked.

"Not hardly. I didn't grow up hearing that crap. We just moved to these backwater boonies."

Sarah groaned, but didn't admonish her charge.

Casper reached out when Gunther stepped forward, placing one paw on the sofa to stretch up until face to face with her.

On second thought, the wolf dog appeared more interested in her shoulder than her face.

What's there that I can't see? Hailey *felt* a presence.

"Anything else, Casper? Like, did she ever brag about receiving anything special from someone? New clothes? Jewelry?" Trenton ignored Gunther's behavior in favor of obtaining insight.

If Bernadette was the manipulator everyone thought, it made sense there was a greater design driving her.

"She always had spending money. I know her family's poor, but I figured it came from her boyfriend. Other than that, I wouldn't know."

Hailey made a mental note to dig further into Kenny's family background and finances. It probably wouldn't unearth anything significant, yet many investigations traveled false leads before hitting pay dirt.

Casper tapped her forefinger against her chin in thought. "Wait, I did see her wearing a fancy necklace one day. Shaped like a heart with a diamond in it. When I asked if she was getting serious, she told me to mind my own business. After that, she stopped showing off her lady bits."

"Can you tell us who she hung around with between classes?" Trenton looked up from his phone where he made notes.

Casper spouted off several names. Two studied in the accelerated summer program that extended the school year by six weeks.

"I've answered your questions, now, you mind answering some of mine?"

"Sure." Hailey pocketed her recorder.

"What happened to your sister?"

The bottom dropped out of Hailey's stomach. Of all the times she'd felt a presence, now was the strongest. She narrowed her eyes and zeroed in, not on Casper, but on the amulet she wore.

It *was* significant. She couldn't pin how or why. Yet.

Hailey tilted her head to the side and crossed her arms over her chest. "I don't have any siblings. You must have me mistaken with someone else."

"Huh, I've been doing some reading," she nodded to the bookshelves, "...and heard twins are common in certain families." Casper shrugged before continuing. "Whatever. Why are you wearing sunglasses inside? Did he slug you?"

The teen looked offended when Sarah groaned.

"What? Dad preaches about how women should be able to take care of themselves. I certainly can."

Again, the worldly knowledge radiated piqued Hailey's interest.

Instead of answering, Hailey removed her glasses and smiled. Seeing was believing.

It was Casper's turn to gasp. "Damn. That's intense. Are they natural?"

"Yes."

"You're kin to La Belle Fontaine. I've heard rumors." The corners of Sarah's mouth tilted up in a smile worn by those working at the DMV or IRS. She stood and smoothed a hand over her bottled blonde bob as the air temperature dropped twenty degrees in an instant.

"Yes, I am a descendant, and the rumors are lies."

"I've heard stories about her." Casper's eyes lit with interest.

Before anyone could speak again, Sarah raised her hand for silence. "Well, I think we've talked quite enough. I'll show you both out."

Stiff movements carried the guardian to the foyer where she opened the door wide. "Good day to you both. Do not ask to see Casper again without a warrant."

Chapter Nine
Trenton

"Well, that was interesting. Something spooked both you and Gunther. Spill." Trenton nodded toward the house where Casper's guardian watched them get in the SUV.

Hailey held the talent to dissect someone's motives with quick efficiency; he'd seen it firsthand on more than one occasion. She may not intend to follow in her mother's footsteps, but she had keen observation and accurate assessment skills, and never hesitated to follow a hunch.

"Something was off with that kid, well, other than the fact she's a teenager."

Trenton hadn't spent much time with his nephews or nieces, but prayed they didn't turn out like Casper. "Why would she think you had a sister?"

"Don't know."

The fact a stranger might know more about Hailey than he did set Trenton's teeth on edge. He intended to do a deeper dive into the student's history. "Gunther's reaction was weird."

"He sensed it before I did."

"Sensed what? What did you feel?"

"I don't know. *Something*..."

"If you tell me you're seeing spirits, I'm gonna need a few minutes to adjust." He wouldn't condemn anything she said as hogwash but braced himself for hurricane-intense impact.

"No, I'm not seeing spirits, but that amulet she wore, it meant something." Hailey held one hand up. "I don't know what. I just know it's important."

"Shame you couldn't touch it. What about the furniture, et cetera?"

"Everything was new, like factory new, so any impressions I'd get aren't from locals. I don't think they've used that room much."

As if sensing his companion's mood, Gunther leaned in from the back seat and nudged Hailey's neck. Absentminded tunneling of her fingers through his fur quieted his whine.

"Yeah, there was definitely something off about her," Trenton agreed. "The bored façade didn't fool me for a second. The problem is, we don't know what she's hiding."

"Or if it's even relevant to the case. She is a teenager. Even Gunther didn't understand her." Hailey's gaze turned soft. "It was weird, but not in a threatening kind of way. At least, I don't think so."

"Your fur kid ever have a reaction like that to anyone else?"

"No," Hailey admitted. "At first, I thought it was Casper, but it wasn't. It was like she carried an invisible chip on her shoulder only Gunther could see. And he didn't like it."

Trenton reached the end of the lane and tapped his brakes. "We may not be able to speak to all the students since the spring semester is over, but Bernadette's teachers are local. I'd like to interview them myself."

"Let's touch base with Leigh first. She's already had first run at them. Mind if we make a detour to the hobby store for a sec?"

"Sure. Got an itch to put a model plane together?" Trenton put the windows up and turned on the AC.

"No. The new lens I ordered is in. I need it for some special shots at Mitt's Bayou."

"I looked over your landscape and nature shots on social media. Nice work. What's your preference?" He'd liked them all.

"Wildlife. I got a tip on my blog about a den located in a tree hollow. I've been watching it, and if I can catch the little ones coming out in the right light, one shot would pay for the lens."

"What aren't you telling me? I know there's more to it than that." He gritted his teeth, waiting.

"A lot of chicken-neckers don't like the bayou, but they don't realize the rich potential it offers. There's so much to see and experience. It's a twofer. I get an award-winning photo, and the general public learns that Texas bayou country doesn't equate to hillbillies and illegal stills."

"Sure. Let's go play with crocs, gators, and snakes that'll either eat you or poison you with venom. Can't forget the mosquitos." He hated the latter the most.

"You're such a drama hog. We'd have to go to southern Florida for crocodiles."

"Which is why you put your bang stick in the back of my SUV today."

"Girl's gotta protect herself from the big critters, both two-legged and four."

"Hailey, that bang stick gives you one shot. What if you face two threats? Fun fact, I'm *not* a chicken-necker. My family's lived here for years."

"You're originally a transplant from Arizona. You can't fully appreciate the area. There's so much more to the bayous. Pelicans, hawks, and herons, along with creatures like armadillos, bobcats, and black bears. Regardless, it's not as dangerous as you think."

"I'm betting you have quite a portfolio from what I saw posted online. Why are you working as a private investigator?"

"Good jobs for inexperienced photographers are rare, but it's something I'm getting better at."

"What about the ghost tours?"

"I can get by without the extra income. I started guiding haunted tours in college. The PI business has gradually picked up, though. Enough that I can concentrate on what I want to do. Private investigations and photography."

Trenton remained quiet, a testament to training and willpower.

"My last tour is this weekend. You should come."

"*Hmm*, I might tag along. Sounds interesting." In truth, he had no intention of letting her out of his sight.

The drive back to Hamchet and the small hobby shop was quiet. Trenton wondered how much debt rode his friend's slim shoulders. She wouldn't ask for help until it swamped her, but he could do the research and find out.

A long, block building advertised model planes, trains, and ships in bright bold colors with a big welcome banner.

Hailey collected her camera case from the floor of the back seat and opened her door after he parked.

"No leash?" Trenton asked when her four-footed partner bounded out behind her.

It was such an unusual pairing. He'd read where animals and their companions took on traits of each other. Here, they both had striking eye color, quick tempers, and an abundance of energy.

"No need. Joseph loves Gunther. Hell, he'd spend time with him before a paying customer."

A light jingle over the door announced their entrance before Hailey's aura lost ten years in stepping over the threshold.

On one side, various cameras and accessories lined the enclosed glass shelving. On the opposite, remote-controlled vehicles, model airplanes, trains, and ships lined the walls, all well lit by track lighting overhead. In the back, video games had drawn the interest of several teens.

Everything was clean, neat, and organized, if a bit overstuffed. Two long center aisles carried crafts, computer accessories, and a variety of paints.

A father and young son debated the merits of a military aircraft carrier versus a private airplane model for their next project while three couples with children perused merchandise in the center aisles.

To his left, a low-slung counter held an assortment of glues and a special case bearing a virtual reality headset. The caption on the card read: *Toys for all ages.*

Gunther made a beeline to the left as soon as the owner rounded the curve of the long counter and crouched.

"Gunther. I was hopin' to see you today. How's it going?" Early-thirties with a thick thatch of chestnut hair, the jean-clad proprietor smiled broadly and accepted Gunther's paw in greeting.

"Hi, Joseph. How's business?" Hailey stepped forward and accepted a hug.

"Good, very good." Joseph retrieved a large bone from behind the counter and held it up. "May I?"

"Sure. He loves those, thanks. Well, did it come in? Is it a thing of beauty?" Hailey radiated energy like a small kid at Christmas, shifting weight from one foot to the other.

"I have it right here. Come."

A large box with the shipping label still attached sat on the shelf on the back wall. Joseph retrieved it and opened the top. Foam lifted away revealed a sleek new lens.

Unable to contain herself, Hailey accepted the item with reverence and then swung her case forward by lowering her right shoulder. Within minutes, she'd attached it to her camera and aimed for a distant spot through the half-window behind the owner.

"Wow. Fabulous. No more risky shots getting too close. This is fantastic. Thank you."

"Anything to keep my favorite photographer out of a gator's jaws." Joseph acknowledged Trenton with a cool assessment.

"Aw, there's no critter that could best Gunther and me. You know that."

"I also managed to get a discount for you. I told the vendor you're a rising star and could use a break." Joseph's smile was warm and appreciative as he held Hailey's gaze.

Trenton rolled one shoulder, thankful the proprietor couldn't see his eyes narrowing.

"I'll take all the breaks I can get. Thanks." The long lens detached with a twist then settled back in its foam cradle. "I can't wait to get out on Little Mitt's Bayou."

"Please, be careful. Any predator with a taste for sweet meat will hunt you." The warning said with a smile held the concern of long-term friendship and unfulfilled infatuation.

"Ah, if I run into trouble, I'll just throw out a hex and stop it in its tracks." Tossed out as a joke, the words had more impact than expected.

Joseph hitched a breath as interest widened his gaze.

Regardless of what Hailey thought of her ancestry, few remained neutral. Encounters ranged from abject fascination to fear and revulsion with little gray area between.

"Ha. You know I'm faster than any gator. They wouldn't dare. You also know my mom." Hailey handed over her credit card and waited for Joseph to complete the transaction.

"Yes. Your *belle mere* has lived here all her life, but your papa, he—"

"Was pretty much a stranger to me. I never really knew him."

From behind, a deep throat clearing caught their attention. "I did. Real well, in fact."

Hailey whirled to address the sly rejoinder. "Henri. I'm surprised you're not out hunting gators."

"I'm surprised you're not singing, dancing, and shaking your rattle." Henri worked his scruffy jowls side to side while his gaze traveled from her chest to lower areas with a grin. "Why don't you come visit me at my shop?"

"Why don't you take a midnight walk through the bayou?"

"Aw, you break my heart."

The gator hunter with a bull neck and greasy black hair had always given Trenton the creeps. Considering the way he eyed Hailey like a piece of candy, he deserved a black eye at the very least. Sooner rather than later.

Hailey turned her attention back to Joseph with a smile. "I really appreciate you ordering this and getting me the discount." Accepting her credit card back, Hailey collected her purchase.

Henri continued with, "I can tell you things about your dad you don't know. It would be very... enlightening. Why your dad an' I were bosom buddies back when I started working at the antique shop." He sidled three steps closer and tucked a card from his back pocket on top of the camera lens case. "Feel free to stop by anytime."

Gunther growled.

Henri's retreat included an outstretched hand jerking to the side and swiping boxes of model planes off the shelf. He stumbled two steps, as if not under his own steam before his sudden inhale and dropped jaw signaled shock. "What the hell?"

"Might want to lighten up on the booze, man." Hailey reached for Gunther's collar when he continued to growl low in his chest. Her gaze shifted from Henri to the dropped boxes then back.

"It's not a good idea to mess with me," Henri warned.

Hailey's face went pale and her gaze jerked to the side, her eyes wide as if listening to a response no one else could hear.

Henri growled but bent to pick up the merchandise, stumbled, then landed on his ass. Dusting his jeans off, he stood, his face a mask of rage. His first step forward stopped when eyeing the dog. "You're lucky today."

Gunther lunged with teeth bared, situating his body in front of Hailey. Forward-leaning posture with tail out, ears perked, and whites visible around his eyes detailed his threat. If that didn't convince the dirtball to back off, the growl emanating from his deep chest did.

"Dogs aren't supposed to be in public stores," Henri sneered at the owner.

"This is my place, and I'll dictate who's welcome and who isn't. Trust me, that boy there," he indicated Gunther, "...has a standing invite anytime, under any circumstance. I also see he's quite the good judge of character." Joseph's hand shook slightly when pointing at the animal.

"Take a hint. She's obviously not interested." Trenton had moved beside the dog to intervene if necessary.

Hailey sidestepped then touched Trenton's arm. "I'm ready to go. How about you?" With a wave to Joseph and nudge to Trenton, she guided Gunther toward the exit.

"Send me your photos. I promise not to share," Joseph urged as the door opened.

"I will. Promise."

A wave of moist heat blanketed them as soon as Trenton stepped out. It was preferable to watching Hailey navigate both ends of unsolicited attraction. Such trials and tribulations of her daily life had never occurred to him. He wondered if slim stature, beauty, or mystique proved the biggest draw.

"Was Henri involved with your family back in the day, Sparkles? I don't remember him that well."

"I don't know for sure. I'd have to ask Mom."

Hailey's act of nonchalance didn't mesh with the visible tension of her neck and shoulders. There was more to learn from this interaction, but would require time and tact to unravel.

"Must be a powerful lens to be so expensive." Trenton glanced over his shoulder to see Henri watching them through the window.

"Now you sound like my mom. Yes, it might seem like a foolish expenditure for someone almost drowning in debt, but it's not."

"Not when you're the 'glass half full' kind of person. That's what you've always been."

"Exactly! And once I have a roommate, things will be a lot easier, even though the photography isn't quite holding its own. This addition," Hailey pointed to the boxed lens, "...will not only pay for itself in short order, but further my career. It's a necessary investment."

"Which means you're always working."

"Student loans." Hailey loaded Gunther in the back and hopped into the passenger seat.

"If you needed a little short-term help, why didn't you call me?"

She leveled her old stare at him. The one declaring her capable of putting him down if he continued the same line of thought.

"I'm fine. As I said, when I take on a roommate or partner, things will ease up considerably."

"The mysterious partner you haven't found and aren't searching for?" Trenton made a silent count to ten. He wondered from what universe this supposed partner would drop.

"Don't need to look. You know how you always tease me about my heritage? Maybe it stems from that, but I know I'll have a partner soon. It'll be perfect."

"You've chosen dangerous professions, both of them." Regardless of his intent, his disapproval must've shone through with the dark look she shot him.

"Maybe. I do my best to stay safe. Plus, I have Gunther."

Which doesn't change the fact someone challenged you—on familiar ground—with a homemade totem, he condemned her in his head.

"You mind making a stop on the way back to the office? Normally I like dawn and dusk for scenic shots, but this one, well, I think now's the best time."

Great. She's preparing to jump down a rabbit hole.

Trenton offered a serious case of side-eye as he cranked the engine.

"You're up to something. What?"

"Because I want to try out my new lens? Don't ya think you're being a little paranoid?"

"No. Spit it out."

"Okay, okay. This spot I've found… it'll make the perfect backdrop, especially at this hour. The land's a little low, but it's flat."

"You mean it's underwater."

"Well, it's still flat. As I was saying, afternoon sun filters through the Spanish moss and creates the most dazzling effects on the water."

"Which is surrounded by marsh. Hence, you need a lookout. Someone with a gun who's a reasonably good shot."

"Wow, Trent. You still don't think the best of people, do you?"

"Maybe, maybe not. You've always been a risk-taker." He turned onto the recently paved road and sighed. "Sure you can't use a boat?"

"No. It's a secluded oasis shadowed by overlocking branches. I need it to complete my wildlife portfolio. I've contacted the editor of *Bayou Life* and she loves my blog, said she'd like to see what I've done. Also said she could hook me up with a few advertisers online."

"Wouldn't that be like cutting her own throat?"

"No, she hasn't gone digital. I'm thinking they want to broaden their scope, hence the need to expand into online e-zines."

"Digital magazines?"

"Yep."

"So, you'll eventually stop the PI work?" If he got lucky, maybe he could get his sister into some other line of work also. The idea had merit.

"Nope. Love that, too. Keeps me in shape."

"Running for your life is not the best way to do it."

Trenton took in her earnest expression so full of enthusiasm, and knew he'd say yes before the words slipped out unbidden on a sigh. "As long as you do as I say, when I say to do it, we'll go. Deal?"

If he said no, she'd go alone, putting herself at risk without backup. Any man who could keep up with this woman deserved a medal.

"Sure."

"What happened to no more shots getting too close?"

"This will give me distance but still let me get the brass ring." She indicated the new lens. "That specific portion of the bayou is difficult to navigate. There's no way to get to the spot I need with a boat, which makes it a two-person job."

"I'm not convinced."

Hailey sighed as if explaining the intricacies of sugar highs to a toddler. "I want two different shots at different angles. There's too much stuff in the way to capture the look and *feel* of what I've seen. There's a cluster of mangroves with severely gnarled roots. One is hollowed out and home to a bobcat who's just had kittens. I think there are four. I know they're common enough, but this would be a real money shot, something to give viewers that warm and fuzzy feeling."

Love of nature decorated one wall of her loft with cameo appearances of various four-footed critters, any of which would've eaten her without hesitation. Her passion for photography added another dimension to her personality, and another distraction to sideline her focus from their immediate threat.

Her directions guided them away from civilization to where heat waves cracked asphalt before hard-packed dirt morphed to weedy paths. Cordgrass, marsh elder, and square-stem spike rush among the small yaupon and cedar elm surrounded them.

Heading east led them toward the intertidal zone where mangroves curved and arched overhead, lifting their limbs to the heavens.

"We'll have to park ahead and hoof it the rest of the way. I'll put Gunther on a lead so he doesn't get the notion to chase something. He's pretty good, but I don't like to take chances out here."

Hair on Trenton's nape prickled after sliding from behind the wheel. He took his time studying the vast and fertile yet vacant land while Hailey slipped her camera strap around her neck.

Earlier, she'd mentioned feeling watched. Not asking specifics about the trap set behind her loft, it obviously included something a stalker would touch.

Accepting the dog's leash in one hand, he kept his other one free. Knee-high grasses brushed his pants. He hadn't dressed for a ramble through the swamp. On a positive note, he noticed she'd dropped casual indifference for alert and wary with a side order of wonder.

Bayou life dwelt in her blood even as small gators, snakes, and a host of unsavory inhabitants watched them in anticipation.

Despite being female, younger, and lacking formal training with a gun, she insisted on taking the lead through increasingly dense brush, bald cypress, and a host of plants only she could define. The bang stick held at the ready likened her to a warrior of old before stepping onto a battlefield, ready to overcome any opponent.

She was more at home in the bayou than on a college campus, more in tune with animals like her dog than a party crowd, and more trustworthy than anyone he'd ever met.

He'd missed her more than she'd ever know.

Ahead, he noticed filtered light from the multitude of overreaching branches obscuring their trail. "This path's been well traveled. By you?"

"No, well, I've come a few times. Victor used to come here. Maybe he still does. I don't know. There's an abandoned shack several hundred yards in where I took shelter during a hard rain several months back."

"Wonderful. We should've brought a picnic basket."

Hailey turned to fire off a sarcastic remark then shook her head before moving forward.

The sudden crack of a rifle dropped them both to a crouched position. The near miss chipped bark from an oak tree that left a thin line of crimson across her cheek.

Gunther growled and would've bolted if the leash weren't wrapped around Trenton's fist. Of all the things he suspected they might encounter, this hadn't made it on his list.

Chapter Ten
Hailey

"Damn. Where'd that come from?" Hailey stumbled as Trenton tugged her behind a winged elm. Her fingers steadied her camera then tightened around her bang stick.

"Off that way." Trenton gestured to the left while visually scouring a sixty-degree angle of thickening underbrush and broad-trunked oaks. "Some cowardly monkey brain wants to play hide-and-shoot."

If she'd come alone, she could've educated the asswipe about the many dangers in the lowlands. Leading someone through a beautiful but dangerous section of bayou would see them either stepping within a poisonous snake's striking range or becoming gator chow.

"Metal shine at eleven o'clock." Hailey reached for Gunther's leash. "Here, let me take him. You'll have two hands to shoot.

"Okay." Trenton retrieved his gun, indecision written in every line of his face.

"Don't even think of suggesting we split up. I won't run while you fight." The land was too low and sparsely treed for her to circle around and flank their shooter.

"He's too close for us to make it across the open space to the SUV. He'll pick us off." Gunther wasn't the only male growling.

"Ground's too low to circle him," Hailey saw the frustration lining Trenton's face, mirrored by her own inner turmoil.

"Then we don't have a choice. We'll have to run for the truck. Zigzag, but keep moving. I'll carry your bang stick." A nod to her wolf dog accompanied, "Is he going to go willingly with you or attempt to search out the shooter? I can take him—"

"No. We'll move faster if he stays with me." Hailey caught a glimpse of dark hair and a baseball cap peering out between the branching base of a broad oak.

As the shooter aimed his rifle again, Hailey ducked back, expecting the tree to absorb the impact of the next shot.

Instead, she heard a howl of surprise, followed by a shrill scream.

Thrashing and gargled shrieks dictated a fight ensued, but not the nature of the participants.

When she slid from cover, she saw the shooter entangled in the grasping branches of a honey locust tree. His current position a half-dozen feet from where she'd last seen him posed the question, how did he get there?

Long three-pronged thorns designated locust trees the Freddy Krueger of the botany world, avoided by any creature with a shred of self-preservation.

"Let's go." Hailey reached to unbuckle Gunther's leash but maintained a grip on his collar. She held tight until knowing he'd follow her command, "Load, boy. We're going home."

She let her four-pawed companion pick the path as he'd be more alert to ground level dangers.

Running went against her nature, but she didn't like the odds for Gunther otherwise if he rushed the shooter without fear or hesitation.

Trenton's steps didn't falter as they bolted through the woods at a reckless pace.

A string of broken curses signaled the shooter's continued flailing. Hailey imagined him bloody with torn flesh and clothing after his fight with surrounding flora. Whatever fright had tossed him into the arms of the locust tree might've saved their lives.

Alert to the sounds of footsteps behind her, she took note of Trenton's broken rhythm. He moved quieter than anything she'd ever known.

Gunther cut through the brush ahead as she leapt over a fallen tree. Twice she stumbled but regained her balance without face-planting.

Hunters in the bayou were generally good shots since their survival depended on having good aim. This asshat had missed, but not by much.

Her heart stuttered at the wood's edge when two more shots rang out. No doubt their shooter was on the move, which would affect his aim.

Lack of obstacles in the open would hasten their progress but leave them vulnerable for forty yards. She paused to catch her breath. "We'll be sitting ducks."

"No choice. Run to the far side and dive in low on the back seat. Call Gunther in behind you."

On a silent prayer, she bolted with Gunther by her side. Tall grass with clumping bases made footing treacherous and almost took her to ground. Her camera bounced against her flank despite the attempt to keep it steady.

Twice her dog hesitated but a firm command captured his attention and kept him moving forward. "Almost there, boy."

She'd been in tight situations before but never on the receiving end of such a concentrated effort. When Leigh learned of her circumstances, there'd be days at the shooting range scheduled.

Something solid moved underfoot and forced her to stumble-step sideways. Her ankle twisted as she threw her one arm wide. The ground rose to meet her at a frightening speed.

The bite of a snake never came as she braced one arm for the fall and used the other to protect her lens.

Pain shot up her right arm before she rolled while protecting her camera. She ended in a sitting position facing the tree line—and the black muzzle of a gun hugged up against a tree trunk not thirty yards away.

"*Move it, klutz.*" The order came low and harsh.

Hailey snapped her head around, but Trenton was looking over his shoulder. The voice didn't belong to Trenton.

No one else was present. *Now's not the time to lose my sanity.*

A cap pulled low denied identification of the shooter. Instead of firing a mortal wound, his barrel jerked up into the air as the firing pin struck the primer. The shot went wide by a large margin.

Strong arms jerked her to stand and spun her around in one move. Trenton pushed her toward the SUV's passenger side, urging, "Go. He's gotta reload."

Her lungs pulled in moist air rich with the scent of composted marsh grass and other materials left by scavengers.

She'd just reached the corner of the SUV when another shot forced her to glance through the window to see Trenton opening the other door and tossing in her bang stick. She hadn't noted any dirt kicked up, nor did she hear a painful gasp from Trenton.

With one hand cradling her camera, she snatched the door open and dove onto the back seat, sweat plastering the ends of her long ponytail to her shoulder blades. Gunther hopped up behind her before she slammed her door shut.

A minute later, Trenton stomped the accelerator and rocketed them over the jarring trail. "Damn, I hate this."

"You wanted to hunt. I saw it in your face." She'd never seen such rage in her friend and was glad not to be his intended target.

"I can't risk a civilian. Of course, we retreated. That was a rifle, which means he could take a long shot. Keep your head down till I say otherwise."

She didn't argue. He was right, at least in part, but she knew another truth. Something saved their lives. Something she couldn't see but had heard and felt just the same. She'd felt that same entity in the hobby shop and after some prick ran her off the road.

"Who knew you'd be coming out here today?" Trenton's shoulders relaxed in slow increments as his gaze flicked to the side and rearview mirrors.

"Um, I kinda keep notes on my photography blog…"

"Jeez, seriously? Let me guess, you put your itinerary on it?"

"No. Just where I took some shots and what I might get in the future. I leave the comments section open so I can interact with locals. You'd be surprised what folks will say online when it's anonymous."

"So, the killer could lure you here with a half-ass picture, knowing you'd want a better one?"

"Possibly… but that's not what happened here." She caught his look in the rearview mirror.

"Who? Give me a name."

"Um, well, I've had a back-and-forth discussion about this place with someone online. Just the same, anyone could've read the posts."

"How many knew where or when? We obviously weren't followed out here."

"You're right. He was waiting near my destination."

"Hence the eleven o'clock position."

"Damn this sucks, Trent."

He tapped his fingers on the steering wheel, waiting for her to cough up a name. "Hailey? You're dodging. Who've you been talking back and forth with?"

"Victor, but there's been another person who's interacted frequently, too. And it's open for anyone to view."

"What happened to him settling down in—where was he going?"

"He tried that but didn't like it, didn't want to stay. Said there were ample opportunities here. As far as others who follow my blog, I don't know. Hell, lots of people use handles or false names."

Though he didn't speak for several moments, Trenton's knuckles turned white.

"You can sit up now."

Leigh snickered at seeing her brother's fuming expression at the office door. He'd made a beeline for the small space designated as a break room, leaving them to follow.

"Have that good a time, bro? What's the matter? You step in something?"

"No. Someone took a shot at Hailey." Trenton opened the mini-fridge and pulled out two bottles of water, tossing one to Hailey.

"What?" Loose papers fell from Leigh's file as she turned to scan her friend from head to toe.

"We're fine." Hailey dropped into a chair and uncapped the bottle. Since her fingers were shaking too much to hold the water, she bent to rub her cheek against Gunther's head.

Trenton disclosed details of their encounter in clipped phrases as he yanked out a chair and sat. His gaze flicked between her and his sister. "Leigh, sit. From now on, I want to know where *both* of you are at all times."

"Hey, you know Colson's breathing down my neck at every turn." Leigh sat and reordered her file. "Damn, girl. You find more trouble than I do."

"I don't see Colson here now. Matter of fact, I think—"

"Do *not* finish that sentence. I will not hide, and I can guarantee you she won't either." Leigh smirked when Hailey offered Trenton a one-finger wave.

Trenton ignored the exchange, standing and turning his back to make a call. Short phrases using abbreviated commands detailed specific requests regarding Hailey's website and time frames.

His brother Jaxon was well-known for his skill on the keyboard. Soon to be ex-military, he'd spent part of his youth hacking and coding.

Once finished, Trenton alternated covering his mouth with his hand and scrubbing his fingers through his hair before speaking again. Brows drawn low and eyes briefly closed, he swore intermittently before making another call.

After pocketing his phone, he sat, removed his glasses, and studied them both. "All right. I want you two to stay put. I'm going back with Asher to see if we can find anything on your shooter." Holding his hand up, he gestured them to quiet. "No, neither of you are going. I want to know where you are and that you're safe."

"Asher hasn't been out there in ages, Trent. I know those lowlands as well as anyone," Hailey argued.

His middle brother, known as one of the best trackers around during their younger days, now pursued criminals as a DA.

Trenton leaned over and closed the distance between them, placing his hand on the table beside her. "I'm going to find and eliminate the threat, by whatever means necessary. You and my sister will stay here with your hound from Hell. Is. That. Clear?"

Hailey shrugged her shoulders. She'd rather be dragged behind a skiff through shark-infested waters than sit on her butt. However, Special Agent Cryptic and Overprotective didn't need to hear that.

As soon as he stood and turned to go, he shrugged his shoulders as if knowing what transpired behind his back.

Hailey grinned at her partner and mouthed the word, "Ready?"

At the door, Trenton turned his head to make eye contact with each before leaving. "Seriously. Both of you stay." A lump appeared in his cheek from the thrust of his tongue, a common habit when evaluating a situation.

"Any ideas who pulled the trigger?" Leigh asked once they were alone.

"Nope. But they weren't far enough to miss three times, and I don't believe for a second they intended to miss." The echoes still rung in her mind and she touched the dried crust of crimson on her cheek.

"Maybe he wanted to scare you off, not kill you."

She felt the heat drain from her face when remembering the voice in her ear. This was something she hadn't broached with her best friend, and didn't want to now.

"What?" Leigh leaned forward in her seat. She wouldn't relent until hearing every detail.

"It's happening again. I don't know who or what intervened, but I should be dead. I... saw the gun barrel jerk upward just before he fired."

"Hell. It's like you've got a guardian angel or something."

"Or something."

"Explain."

"Something happened when I stopped to pick up my camera lens. We ran into a sleazeball who had more than pictures on his mind. You remember Henri? We used to see him by the bait shop."

"Yeah. He's got a record for B&E, but I'm sure has gone farther than breaking and entering. Why?"

"He said he knew stuff about my dad, said he could tell me a lot about him. My gut says he wasn't lying. I think... I think he's tied up in this. There was this look in his eye."

"Your instincts are better than mine. You're going to snoop, because you think he was the shooter." It was a statement, not a question.

"Dunno. I remember once when Mom saw him on the street. She made us cross through traffic rather than walk by him."

"If I don't go with you, you'll go alone." Resigned, Leigh stood and offered Gunther a pat. "You'll have to stay in the truck, boy. Don't want you getting into trouble."

"I'll tell Elizabeth we're making a dinner run for some jambalaya and won't be back before she leaves."

A high-five sealed the deal.

"I'll drive since your truck is still at Dent and Grind. Let's not risk damaging the loaner. Gunther can keep me company while you find trouble."

"Leigh—your job…"

"My priority is to protect you. C'mon. Let's go."

"You can park down the street. He gave me his card." Hailey pulled it out of her jeans pocket and flicked it with her fingers. "Technically, he did say I could come by any time."

Once settled on the front passenger seat with her note pad and pen in hand, Hailey flipped through the pages. "Okay. Let's make sense of this." She began detailing her assorted notes aloud while scrawling on the paper:

Sophia disappeared five years ago.
Bernadette missing since Saturday night's dance.
Bernadette picked a fight and walked home, at night, in the bayou.
Bernadette is controlling, vicious, and shallow.
Asswipe runs me off the road after surveillance.
Student assistant indicated possible older guy romantically involved with Bernadette.
Bernadette has fancy necklace. No ID on suitor.
Asswipe leaves handmade totem in my truck.
Someone shot at Trenton and me in the bayou.
What made the shooter miss?
Why did Henri fall at hobby store?
Who told me to move and called me a klutz?

"Okay. Time to pick this apart." Hailey tapped her pen on the pad. "Even a reasonably intelligent teen wouldn't walk alone in these parts at night without protection of some kind, and I can't see her carrying a gun to a party."

"Then it'd make sense she had someone waiting for her." Leigh cranked the engine and pulled away from the grass shoulder. "If she did pick a fight, she had plans to meet someone nearby. What's close to where Kenny let her out?"

"*Hmm*, Melford's place—but it's been abandoned for years. Maybe she planned a bit of one-on-one there? Or maybe Kenny lied, lost his temper, and buried the body where we'll never find it." Hailey added the note with a question mark.

"You said the student assistant indicated a boyfriend who's older, maybe a teacher? I've talked with them and didn't see anything out of the ordinary. They all claim she was brilliant and ambitious."

"Did you interview ancillary staff?" Hailey pointed down a street straddled with red flowering crepe myrtle trees. "Let's grab a bite to eat. I can't snoop on an empty stomach."

"I talked to the staff present. What's sticking in your craw?"

"Trenton and I interviewed a new kid, nickname Casper. Unlikely she was involved as she just moved here a few weeks ago."

"And..." Leigh made a hurry up gesture with her hand.

"She was... I dunno. Something was off. She's hiding something, plus, she's way wiser than her declared age."

"Send me her info. I'll run her through every database available to the sheriff's department."

"Don't get me wrong, I don't think she's our killer, but I want to know more about her."

Leigh pulled up to the curb in front of their favorite café and pocketed her keys. "Looks like we hit the lull before dinner. You want the usual?"

"Yeah."

With only Gunther's quiet breathing, Hailey studied her list while Leigh made the grub run. Each point stood on its own but with little to no connection to the whole. She wondered if this was how Trenton felt during his cases.

By the time Leigh hopped back in the truck, there was no blinding insight to offer and no new thread to pull. Hailey accepted the bag of carryout, contemplating the situation.

"I got the smaller bag for Gunther."

"Thanks, Leigh."

"Been thinking." Leigh cranked the engine. "All this may or may not be connected to the five-year-old cold case. That girl Sophia was a little younger but still a teen who disappeared without a trace."

They followed the narrow street to the park on the outskirts of town and took shade under a branching willow to eat and chat.

"Sophia wasn't gifted the same as Bernadette, and I don't see another connection. Unless we have a pervert with a taste for young flesh."

"Also, the totem could've been left by your ex or connect to a different case, a cheating husband perhaps?" Leigh took a bite of her sandwich and chewed thoughtfully. "It might not be related to this in any way."

"A stretch, but possible. Victor wouldn't take a shot at me. He's not involved." Hailey unwrapped Gunther's burger and palmed it.

He scarfed it down in two bites.

"Maybe it was intended to warn Trenton off? You might not have been the target," Leigh suggested. "We'll need to review old case files, just the same. What about Kenny?"

"His dad owned that antique store."

Leigh popped a heaping spoonful of spicy goodness into her mouth and turned Gunther's head away when he tried to sniff her food. "I asked for seasoning, boy. Sorry."

"Little Treasures was the original name. Years ago, Henri worked there for Kenny's dad."

"I checked Landry's finances while you were strolling through the bayou. Kenny's mom holds the title to the store, but I can't see her dipping her fingers into antiques, not from how you described her at their house."

"No, but maybe Kenny has aspirations for the place, and drops in there from time to time while letting Henri run it as he sees fit, as long as he turns a profit. That kid is ambitious. Looked to me like he runs the household."

"If Kenny wanted to keep something of Bernadette's after an enraged mishap, maybe it'd be at the store, not that we have enough to get a search warrant." Leigh finished eating and tossed her trash in the bag.

"I'll slip in and take a look. Just let me off nearby. Not gonna risk your badge."

The truck purred to life with a throaty rumble. Leigh weaved the vehicle around a kid riding his bike down the street, oblivious to the scant traffic. "The shop's just ahead."

"Park a bit down the street. If Gunther needs to stretch his legs—you mind?"

"No problem."

"Shouldn't be anyone there now. I'll creep, you peek." Hailey gathered their trash and reached for the door handle.

On the curb, a community trash bin sported a sign with bold print: ***Don't feed the animals.***

Hamchet's sleepy population had doubled with the advent of a new refinery transferring to the upper end of the county. The influx of employees from metropolitan areas instigated small shops and the need for more housing.

Instead of revitalizing the old, newcomers branched out on the far side of town with modern construction.

Leigh parked on the curb behind a white utility van with "Furniture Movers" blazoned in bright red letters along its side. Abandoned buildings straddled the narrow street, a testament to flourishing enterprises of yesteryear.

"You sure about this, Hailey? Maybe I should go in."

Hailey harrumphed. "You always get the fun parts. 'Sides, Colson would have your badge if you got caught. It's my turn. What's the worst that could happen?"

"Hey, I know you'll want to touch everything to see what you can pick up, but don't. Please wear these." Leigh handed her a pair of latex gloves from her center console.

"From the girl who's always prepared. Thanks."

Chapter Eleven
Hailey

Early summer twilight extended into evening with a light breeze blowing an empty paper cup down the street. Scant traffic dwindled after the end of the workday with shadows coalescing to blanket the ground.

A dark alley ran the length of either side between concrete block walls where a few seedlings pushed up between cracked concrete.

Next door, a shoe store with a threadbare awning offered little shelter to pedestrians during the heat of the day. Elegant heels worthy of prom night recently passed contrasted sturdy hiking boots. No lights shone from within.

Boarded windows blocked the view of the interior on the other side.

A small convenience store across the street once sold the best shrimp po'boy sliders around and boasted advertisements for bread and milk under a roof with missing shingles.

At present, all was quiet.

"Why'd Kenny's mom keep this place after her husband split anyway?" Leigh leaned back in her seat to ruffle Gunther's fur.

"Maybe Kenny wanted it for nostalgic reasons, and his mom has the money to hold onto it. Can't imagine it supports itself being open four mornings a week. Looks like there's a lot of junk inside from what I can see." Hailey checked her shirt pocket, noting the pick set therein.

"Maybe they sell more than antiques, like something fresh out of the field." Leigh rested her hand on Gunther's collar to keep him from bounding out after Hailey.

"If someone wonders what you're doin' parked here, tell 'em you're waiting to meet your boyfriend for a nostalgic evening stroll. Text me a warning. I'll set my phone on vibrate."

Slipping out and scanning each side of the street again, Hailey hustled through the narrow alley's concealing shadows.

Leigh had taught her to look for alarm systems, but she had little experience in disabling them.

Fractured concrete between buildings heaved with time made passage treacherous. Hailey stepped lightly down the side toward the back corner to survey the rear, slipping twice on loose crumbles.

Beyond the store, chain link fencing divided barren land and a copse of trees, with more of the same running the entire rear of the block.

Glass shards, remnants of a security light, dotted the ground around the back door. The lengths of the buildings were near equal, which meant anyone residing in the second-story apartment on the far side couldn't see her sneak in the back entrance. Considering the circumstances, she doubted the presence of the most meager security system.

She made quick work of the lock after slipping on gloves and scanning her perimeter. The door opened on a low squeak.

Pitch-black interior indicated no windows linked the storage room with the main display area. Musty and only slightly cooler, the concrete block under her fingers bore no coat of a water sealant and snagged her latex gloves.

Although she might learn something through bare touch, she heeded Leigh's warning. Antiques held decades' worth of memories and weren't worth the risk of leaving prints behind. Anything of value wouldn't be kept back here anyway.

Her phone provided light while her eyes adjusted to the cluttered mismatched pieces of furniture. Boxes piled on tables filled the small space while chairs stacked along the perimeter left a narrow path for passage.

She stubbed her foot on a table leg and wondered how a man Henri's size navigated the space. Logic dictated he didn't venture back here often. By the smell of it, no two-legged critters did.

Why wouldn't they take steps to avoid mold on antiques?

Then again, if they intended to sell anything, wouldn't they also repair tattered rattan, broken chair slats, and the like?

In reaching the door to the shop, she tested the knob and found no resistance. Dousing her light before inching it open a crack, she took a slow breath to calm her heart. Whoever had taken a shot at her in the bayou had upped the stakes in their endeavor.

Residual light streamed through the shop windows up front to cast the main floor in a gradient of shadows.

No stealthy slide of material or quiet intake of breath offered proof of another presence.

Intuition and the goose flesh on her arms dictated she wasn't alone.

Henri's eclectic taste ranged from antique perfume bottles to flatware, tables, and old guitars. The last almost paused her step in thinking about Trenton and his sexy baritone voice.

Now wasn't the time for fanciful dreams.

Abandoned treasures and castoffs, items others would label junk, covered each flat surface. Desks took up the middle with a small pathway leading to what appeared to be an office.

Trenton's warning flared in her thoughts. He'd be so pissed to discover what she'd done. The smile sliding into place faltered with the reason for his warning. It was well-founded.

I won't learn anything by sitting on my ass.

If Bernadette had indulged in an affair, her lover could have killed her and now attempted to block their investigation.

It didn't seem unusual for a banker to own the store, as many had struggled to stay afloat in the shriveling economy. Maybe the father chose to abandon his family rather than live off his wife's inheritance.

A skittering noise nearby alerted her to another presence. With her luck, a pack of rats expanded their nest to make room for guests.

Henri claimed he ran the business, handing her a printed card. Would he soon be unemployed if Kenny took over? Framing the boy to take over the shop would be Henri's MO.

The shop's office took up a sizable section of the building. Her small light cut a swath around the room until highlighting a ripped pair of jeans, t-shirt, and shoulder-length black hair. The face was that of the teen interviewed earlier.

Oh crap. She fumbled the phone, sending fragments of light across the desk and floor.

"Casper?" She remembered the kid didn't like her given name.

"Um, yeah. Your stealth mode needs work." Standing stock still except for the hand that slid the pendant necklace back and forth on its chain, her expression equaled one part resignation and two parts belligerence.

"What are you doing here?"

"Breaking and entering. Just like you."

"Why?" There couldn't be much present to interest a high school student.

"Thought I might find some knickknacks for the house on a five-finger discount."

Hailey propped one hand on her hip and waited.

"I'm curious about what's happened to Bernadette. I love solving mysteries."

"What led you to this place? And how'd you get in?"

"You wouldn't believe me if I told you."

"Try me."

"Okay. First, I'm eighteen and working undercover. Second, well, I can't tell you that."

Even in the dim light, the student's façade lacked signs of deceit, as did her tone. Stated age was a little more consistent with her demeanor. If her intent was to play a game, it didn't show. Suddenly, all the occult books seen at her house took on a new meaning.

This was a complicated young woman, so Hailey pressed forward with a test of her own. "Guess you may have heard the rumors. I'm the decedent of a powerful *loa*, a spirit well accomplished in the art of Vodou."

Casper tilted her head to the side and gripped her pendant tighter, as if in concentration. "Huh, maybe we should talk later, I don't think we have much time right now."

The student assumed to be another brainiac turned out to be so much more.

"Agreed. And count on it." Hailey's thoughts strayed between the student and her implied goal. If a federal agency employed her, Trenton would've known. If semi-local, Leigh's department should've been aware. Few agencies would insert an undercover operative without alerting *someone* local.

A wooden desk took up much of the office space, with a black leather executive chair slid back for the girth of a sizable person. Little light filtered through the small window high in the sidewall, but a stray shaft spotlighted two picture frames beside a calendar.

One, in particular, caught her attention.

Henri stood beside Kenny's father, recognized from research. They both smiled, neither appearing strained. Before she could set the photo down, her phone vibrated. The frame crashed to the desk and sent glass shards scattering across the scarred wooden top.

Crap. I need to get us out of here.

"Not a natural-born snoop, I see. Henri's on his way. Let's get out of here." Urgency filled Casper's harsh whispered command.

Checking the phone, Leigh's number glowed on the screen.

Trouble's coming. Get out.

"Casper, how'd you know?" Maybe she received a warning via ear mic.

"You're not the only one with spies." With that, Casper turned toward the office door.

Amid broken glass, Hailey plucked the picture up, using her light app to avoid sharp fragments slicing her glove and leaving a blood trail. There was no date written on the back.

She caught sight of a familiar-looking shape when she turned. The outline of a large frame covered by cloth sat cattycorner against the wall. Aiming her small light, she recognized the dust-covered gray material from long ago, the same type her father had used to protect his works in progress.

"C'mon, Hailey. We gotta go."

Cold dread knotted her chest in stepping around the desk. Lots of people painted as a hobby. Many would cover their work until completed. Those cloths were a common fixture in any painter's life.

Henri didn't seem the type.

Her fingers shook in reaching for the material.

The bottom of the frame rose on one side as the cloth slid away to reveal a unique setup. Stretched on an internal frame, a younger version of herself stared from the canvas prison. In her heart, she'd known its composite before seeing the first hint of rich greens in the bayou background. Leigh sat on the stool beside her.

Distant memories assaulted her mind. She could almost hear her mother's admonishment to hold still for the portrait in progress.

It remained unfinished.

So, why is it here?

She'd spilled chocolate sauce on her new frock dress that day and kept one hand over the stain. Cecile Arquette had been so disappointed in her.

Her phone vibrated again, the soft purr coinciding with commotion from the store's front. Leigh's voice raised in anger didn't concern her as much as Gunther's barking.

What surprised her more was the reappearance of Casper in the doorway.

"Idiot. You're gonna get yourself killed. Grab hold." Casper held her hand out, the expectancy clear.

They'd be seen moving through the store by anyone glancing through the plate glass from the sidewalk. Looking around, she saw no place to hide.

Bile shot to the back of her throat with panic engulfing her mind. Hiding was the sole option, but the only place to go would see her exposed as soon as someone rounded the desk.

Angry voices charged the air. *Leigh?* Specific words didn't clarify intent.

Tinkling chimes indicated the shop door opening.

Casper smiled. Either the teen lacked mental stability or she held onto a bigger secret.

Hailey stumbled in her haste to move. Her graceless fall included sudden pain when her temple struck the desk corner. Nausea boiled up. Her cell phone dropped to the floor.

She was vaguely aware of Casper picking it up.

"Damn. Are you okay?" Casper grabbed her by the shoulders and hauled her to the chair.

"Yeah, just need a minute to see clearly."

"We don't have a minute. I'll get us out of here."

"Go, kid. Leave. Henri's dangerous."

"So am I. But you're gonna have to help. If I guide, can you walk?"

"Yeah." Hailey wasn't sure of anything except her arm around Casper's shoulders. "There's not enough room for us to walk side by side." She tried to pull her arm back, but Casper held tight.

In the background argument occurring, Leigh's anger flared.

"You can't treat people like that, asshat. It's beyond rude, and I demand an apology!"

"You'll get nothing but my fist if you don't leave my store."

A muted thud indicated the front door slamming again. Hailey lost track of who'd entered or left. She should've left when she had the chance.

"C'mon. This way." Casper walked her toward the back wall of the office.

"Are you nuts?" Hailey planted her feet so as to avoid a broken nose.

Instead of halting, Casper wrapped her other arm around Hailey's waist and walked her into the wall.

Except—they never made contact.

Everything existed in varying shades of black, yet she now stood in the back storeroom. The one behind the office.

They hadn't maneuvered to the door. Without her phone's light, Hailey couldn't see the placement of the furniture or narrow path, yet Casper urged her in a straight line.

She'd never had a concussion, and now wondered about her sanity.

The next thing Hailey knew, open air brushed her face. She dropped two feet in the air before her sneakers touched cracked concrete.

Her touch instigated the onslaught of confusing images assaulting her mind. Between them and the instant nausea of dropping to the ground, her legs buckled.

On all fours, dry heaves racked her body.

She was outside. On the ground.

Shadow arms of nearby trees waved a macabre warning while a fresh breeze brushed Hailey's bangs aside.

Everything was fuzzy, but she inhaled deep once able. Her head hurt, and something sticky dripped down her temple and along her cheek. *Blood.*

"What's happening?" She looked around but stood with Casper's help. Her young accomplice led her behind the shoe store and toward the end of the block.

"How'd you do that? Did you, we... walk through a wall?" Her vision blurred, normal sounds muffled by the blood rushing through her ears.

"Keep moving, Hailey. No time for talking now."

They hadn't passed through an open door or even paused to let one open. No swath of light had lit the teen's way.

How did she get to, much less navigate, the storeroom without light and without Henri seeing them? Secret passage? There wasn't a wide enough path.

Opening one eye, she tried to lift her head. All she saw were weeds on the strip running behind the buildings. Casper moved stealthily. The kind that came with experience.

She's more than a prodigy... but what?

Concentration on maintaining balance prevented Hailey from looking around, but the next thing she saw was an alley entrance and street beyond.

Walking helped stabilize her mind, until the slight grind of hinges indicated a vehicle door opening. Leigh's truck.

Jostling onto the seat brought bile back to her throat. She swallowed hard, settling on the seat and closing her eyes.

"Next time, leave the snooping to others." The door closed with a quiet snick, but not before her phone was pressed into her hand with a, "Text your buddy that you're clear."

How'd she know where to guide me when she was already in the store?

Blurry fingers fumbled a text to Leigh before closing her eyes. She had no idea how they'd escaped unseen and unscathed.

The teen couldn't be involved with Henri's scheme when she risked getting caught helping a fellow burglar.

Honor and integrity had been the theme in Hailey's family during her formative years. Yet she couldn't reconcile that concept with her father's association with Henri.

Maybe the gator hunter was more of a hired hand five years prior and had stolen the painting. That didn't solve the puzzle of why he'd keep a portrait of someone else's kids.

Had her father been blackmailed? The one person who could offer insight would also be the one least expected to give it.

Her mother.

On a positive note, Leigh slid into the driver's seat a moment later and growled low. "What happened to you?" Grabbing a towel from the back seat, she held it to Hailey's temple.

"I floated through walls, then gravity kicked in and I fell to the concrete. Oh, and I think I have a guardian angel."

"Damn. I've got to get you to a hospital."

"No. Don't. That'll raise too many questions."

"Damn it, Hailey. You're not lucid."

"I'll get there. Give me a minute. Take me home."

"Fine. But I'll only be able to hold my brother off for so long. He knows you were in there."

"Yeah, he always knows when I find trouble."

At least Leigh would be there to diffuse the coming fireworks, helping explain and defend her actions. It was her last positive thought before closing her eyes to review the strange events.

Chapter Twelve
Trenton

"What were you thinking?" Trenton slammed the loft door closed with a snarl on his lips, then pivoted to face Hailey, lying on the couch holding an ice bag to her temple.

It wasn't the ice bag that sent his thoughts into orbit as much as the dazed look in her eyes. With each approaching step, he saw images from past cases flitting through his thoughts. Dead bodies, brutalized then dismembered.

"What happened?" Snatching the ice away, he examined the wound. "Well?"

"Give her a minute, Trent. She's been mumbling about floating, falling, and angels. Other than that, I got nothing other than she hit her head." Leigh snatched the ice bag and handed it back to Hailey. "It'd stopped bleeding by the time she got to the truck, but..." She looked around as if uncertain what to say.

Risking a reprimand from his superior while technically off-duty was the least of his worries. The possibility of losing his job paled against the very real fear of finding Hailey and Leigh's lifeless bodies in a dumpster.

"Neither one of you have a lick of sense and could have been killed. Has it sunk in yet that Henri might be the one who took a shot at us, Hailey? Or maybe he stole the truck that ran you off the road." He swung a scathing glare between Hailey and his sister. "Your actions are risking Leigh's job. What if Henri calls in a complaint?"

"I didn't cross any legal lines." Leigh arched a brow in Hailey's direction, an unasked question burning in her gaze.

"Okay. I recognize that look, Leigh. What is it you want to say to Hailey but not in my presence?"

"Nothing. You found her by pinging her phone."

"I had an inkling you two might pull a stunt like this, despite telling you guys to stay put."

"I'm not a dog," Hailey retorted then closed her eyes and hunched her shoulders as if in pain.

"No, your dog has more sense," Trenton retorted, eyeing said animal when he growled a warning.

"How'd you hurt your head? Couldn't have been Henri's doing. I don't see pieces of flesh between Gunther's teeth."

"I tripped."

"She was woozy and uncoordinated when I got back in my truck." Leigh moved the hand holding the ice to check the injury. "Did you lose consciousness?"

"No, well, maybe. Everything's fuzzy."

"How'd you get out of there without Henri or us seeing you? He was in the door before I could stop him." Leigh moved with her brother's urging.

Whereas his sister embodied bafflement, Hailey garnered something else close to the vest. A direct approach would do him no good.

Leigh moved to the kitchen and started a pot of coffee. "Anybody else want some?"

Hailey snickered. "Trenton does, but he's not sure how to go about it. Did you order the blow-up dolls?"

Trenton swiveled to glare before slumping to the sofa and closing his eyes. The image of Henri choking the life from either woman wouldn't dissipate despite his pinching the bridge of his nose and concentrating on the case.

"*Sackld meocl paksdhe.*" Hailey's utterance preceded Leigh's giggle.

Trenton shot to his feet and whirled on Hailey. "Don't you dare twin speak about me when I'm yelling at you! I'm not being a dick."

"Well, you're sure inflating like one." Hailey's shoulders shook despite the blush sweeping her cheeks. "Surprised you remember that."

"I should. You've called me one enough over the years."

Ignoring him, Hailey continued her gibberish, answered in kind by Leigh. Their "conversation" escalated into heated territory before Leigh threw up her hands and grumbled.

"Damn it, Hailey. Trenton has a point, this time."

"Thank you." Trenton's glare flicked to the one most likely to keep a secret. "I know you had common sense knocked out of you as a kid, but how'd you let stupidity stick a puck in your head?"

Hailey cast a speculative gaze first at Trenton, then Leigh.

"Oh, no. No, just no. You two don't shut me out that easy. I may not speak the language, but I read the nonverbal just fine." Trenton stalked toward Leigh, intent on reaching through to the one who might hold more reason, if only by a small margin.

Seeing his approach, Gunther took position in front of her and growled, stopping Trenton in his tracks. It wasn't the animal's fault neither woman subscribed to logic.

Loud knocking interrupted Trenton's assertion that he had a chance of instilling rationality within the group.

"I'll get it. My head's clearing with all Trenton's yelling." Hailey stood and strode toward the door, stopping when Leigh yanked it wide first, and then tried to slam it shut without a word.

The visitor's boot inserted in the gap prevented it from snapping shut.

"I love quick visits that skip the niceties of social etiquette," Hailey quipped in casual fashion. "Need I guess who's there?"

"Nobody you need to see right now." Leigh shoved the door against the offending boot as if imagining a small hatchet in hand.

"C'mon, zaffre, I just want to talk." Cajoling on the border of irritating, the male obviously didn't understand Leigh's mood.

"What do you want, Victor? We're busy." Leigh growled with menace.

The boot's owner nudged open the door and cataloged the occupants, his gaze resting on Trenton with narrowed eyes. "Hey. I just wanted to touch base. Hamchet grapevine has it you're running into trouble. You know it's faster than any wire service."

Trenton smiled. Instead of having to track Hailey's ex down, the sad sack of shit arrived when he was in the mood for a special interrogation.

My lucky day.

"You hunt crawfish, now, Victor. You're not a reporter."

Tall and wiry, Victor swept his longish black hair to the side. Green eyes burned with curiosity and something else just under the surface.

"But I went to the same school and attended the same classes as her, remember?" Beseeching eyes locked onto his target.

"How can I forget when you keep popping up?" Hailey stepped between Leigh and Victor, who reached out and lightly gripped her forearm, arrogant beyond measure.

Gunther growled and bolted forward, forcing the intruder to relinquish his hold and sidestep.

"Call off your wolf. I just wanted to see how you're doing. C'mon, Hailey, take a walk with me. You know you can't think straight with all this commotion."

"I don't need you to help me think."

"You never did, but sometimes it's nice to have a neutral sounding board. Remember when we used to bump ideas around after journalism classes?"

"Not a good idea, Hailey. This is how he sucks you in." Leigh's warning echoed Trenton's thoughts.

Victor's unwavering stare remained glued on Hailey.

During his career, Trenton had witnessed varied manipulation tactics and was trained in many. Much about the smooth-talking Casanova didn't sit any better with him than with Hailey's four-footed companion.

"Fine. I need a break, guys. I'm just gonna take a walk. I know what you're thinking. You may not realize it, but I know Victor wouldn't take a potshot at me."

Trenton thought twice about actions that might have an adverse effect but couldn't help himself. "You're not in any condition to go anywhere. You might have a concussion."

"I'm fine, just need some fresh air."

"Take Gunther with you." Leigh's warning elicited Hailey's nod.

A self-satisfied grin stretched across Victor's face as he winked at the occupants in shutting the door on the way out.

"Well, big brother. Congrats. You may have single-handedly shoved Hailey back into the toxic arms of that no-account Cajun swamp dog."

Leigh slapped him on the back in striding for the front windows.

Looking down, she shook her head. "If that coonass wangles a date out of this, you're gonna be stuck with surveillance. I won't spy on my best friend."

A minute later, the low rumble of Leigh's phone answered Trenton's unspoken worry. Her muttered curse after reading the text raised the hair on his nape.

"She's going to catch a late-night snack. Looks like you're up, dude."

"Damn it. That shooter could've killed her in the bayou. I don't know which one of us he targeted, but I haven't been here long. I haven't visited in years and only told a few close friends where I was heading when I left Pennsylvania. Those bullets were meant for Hailey."

"My lieutenant's being an asshat too. Took a uniform and scouted the area. I was wondering how he'd found out. Damn meddlesome, micro-managing, mini-brained control freak is getting plugged into the county fast, and he seems to have ears everywhere." Leigh poked Trenton in the chest with her finger. "I know you've asked Jaxon to snoop around her blog and Asher to tromp around the bayou. I do not like hearing information secondhand. Got it?"

"Jaxon's on administrative leave pending discharge, so I asked him to work remotely. How did your lieutenant find out about her?"

"Apparently, your brother had a conversation with him." Leigh threw her arms up in disgust.

"Asher's the best tracker I've seen."

"He's also a lawyer and likes things neat, by the book. I didn't ask my lieutenant, but I'll bet my next paycheck he also talked with the captain. Go figure, Asher's the one lawyer who'd make lots of friends in the department."

"Leigh, fill me in on what Hailey found at the antique store."

She looked outside, a common tell for stalling. Faked distraction granted time to decide what she'd divulge. "Look, I'm not sure what it means, but there's a painting of us in there. One her father did, well, started. It wasn't finished."

"What? How could a creep like that get it? And why would he want it? Why would he keep it?" Trenton's complexion darkened. "That bastard. I wonder if her mom knows, or if she'd even tell me?"

"I don't know. Really. She also found a photo of Henri with a man she didn't recognize at first. It was Kenny Landry's father."

"It's definitely time I had a chat with Hailey's mother."

"I'd wait if I were you. It's gonna be the first thing Hailey does when she thinks things through," Leigh advised.

Trenton felt sorry for the matriarch well known for kindness and willingness to help others. It wouldn't protect her daughter. "Hailey said she set a trap in the backyard and would know if anyone's watching her from the woods."

"*Hmm*, either paint or cloth around trees, shoulder high." Leigh nodded her approval. "Good thinking."

"I'll check with her in the morning about it."

"So, what did the digital snooping turn up?" Leigh asked while ducking down the hall and into the last room.

"Jaxon's initial research into her blog netted little useful information. If our shooter's using the site to track her, he's not interacting, just visiting from a public venue."

"*And Asher? What's he found*?"

"Nada. He searched the old cabin but found nothing. Considering its age and decrepit status, it's defying both the elements and gravity to remain intact." Further details included a section of smashed marsh grasses where someone could've lain in wait for her."

Leigh returned and gestured toward the door. "You ready to shadow Hailey? She's got Gunther, so they'll have to eat outside. There are only two places she'd go."

Chapter Thirteen
Hailey

Hailey relaxed against the wrought iron seat, appreciating the cool breeze sweeping the cobwebs from her mind. Heavy, varnished wooden tables dotted the patio adjoining the restaurant while delicate tea lights supplemented solar lighting on ornamental trees.

Details of how she and Casper escaped the antique store were fuzzy and confusing. It'd felt like they'd walked through walls then dropped to the broken concrete behind the store.

Time had moved differently with an altered sense of consciousness. She couldn't declare anything definitive, except the ache throbbing behind her right eye.

Across from her, Victor turned his plate before picking up his fork. "Thanks for joining me. I've missed casual dining."

She didn't trust herself to answer with the old hurts welling deep within her chest. Tamping them down with the assurance that his carefree good looks wouldn't sway her judgment required constant self-monitoring.

"I needed to get away from Trenton's rant."

"Things looked pretty tense back there. Please tell me they don't think I was the one who took a shot at you."

"Who knows what they think? I don't care. I know you wouldn't do that anymore than you'd place a totem in my truck." Despite his inability to maintain a commitment, he wasn't perverted or a killer.

"What? Now, *that* I hadn't heard. When? Where? You know me better than that."

"I do. They'll catch on eventually. Still, this doesn't mean we're together." She gestured between the two of them.

"I know." He brushed aside her comment with a sad smile. "Looks like you're carrying the weight of the world. Tell me what's going on." Victor leaned forward across the table and placed a light hand over hers.

It took her a minute to pull back, its familiarity and warmth providing genuine comfort. The problem was, his hands didn't inspire the sense of safety and security as a certain bull-headed federal agent.

After dodging a bullet by inches and Henri trapping her in the antique store, she needed the peace a kind touch engendered. It was just dinner, even if he wanted more.

Whatever freakish strand of fate granted her vivid blue eyes had also zapped her ex with a like shade of green rimmed with gold. It was the first thing she'd noticed about him in college.

He used it to his advantage and always knew what to say to a woman, any woman, as she'd found out two years into their relationship.

"This isn't about rekindling what we had. It's simply sharing time and that which burdens our souls. Tell me what's on your mind, *mon chou*."

As if kismet decided to add its own opinion, the soft strains of Marvin Gaye's "I Heard It Through the Grapevine" poured through the outdoor speakers. She didn't need the reminder to put a lock on her heart.

The arrival of their meal postponed her need to answer.

Spicy crawfish fettuccine issued an aroma promising heaven with each bite. Off-dry Riesling provided the perfect complement to the dish's heat, if not her minor head injury.

A drink, a moment of weakness, and the realization his concern was genuine opened the floodgates.

His attention never strayed during her effusive outpouring regarding her current case. She knew him well enough to spot deception and kept the conversation involving specific details of the missing girl's circumstances in reserve, along with the eerie, unexplained interventions that saved her life. Twice.

He nodded and offered occasional suggestions, his insight proving helpful.

"Remember when we used to talk late over coffee and beignets?"

Her trip down memory lane was cut short with Sheryl Crow's "First Cut is the Deepest." Now that she thought about it, this one, and songs like it, had blared from the external speakers on a continuous reel since they arrived. If Victor noticed, he said nothing.

"Enough about my work. Tell me about your mudbugging."

He'd left the rat race of journalism in favor of the familiar, having grown up working on crawfish farms.

Victor grinned. "You would have loved it out there today. Had a cottonmouth set up in the trap, thought he owned it all."

"You keep a rifle on the boat, yes?"

"A Mossberg two forty-three, yes, ma'am." Victor nodded. "For snakes and the occasional gator who thinks he can tag along for the show. Evil nuisances."

Hailey slid back when Victor's mint julep suddenly tipped over and spilled onto his jeans.

"Damn gusts of wind." He grabbed a napkin and mopped up the cold liquid darkening his jeans.

What wind, she wondered. Neither Hailey's drink nor those of surrounding patrons suffered similar results, not the tiniest shake, nor did the awning over the nearby door flutter. Her mind flicked to her earlier thoughts about walking through walls. Weird occurrences had upped the ante where her life was concerned.

"Do you still take pictures?" She remembered when he carried a camera around his neck the way a woman would carry a purse.

"Some. I finally decided to trade up and bought a new printer so I could go digital."

"Nice. I just got a new lens, six-hundred-millimeter Cannon."

"Did you get the pics of the kittens?"

Hailey froze with her fork halfway to her mouth. "How…?"

"How'd I know? I read your blog, of course. So, did you get the shot?"

"No, that's when someone took a shot at me." Hailey watched him rear back in his chair.

"What? Hell. Oh, no. You can't believe that was me."

During their time together, both their tempers flared on occasion, but never to the point of physical violence.

"Obviously not, since I'm here with you. It could be related to the current missing teen or the cold case we're investigating, though."

"Your work is dangerous. You should leave it to the badges."

"I won't quit." She didn't explain the trap she'd set in the woods behind her loft.

"Your missing girl might be dead, shot by the same person who took a crack at you. Did you think of that? People in this area are... different. You know this," he all but whined.

Southeast Texas residents appeared more geographically and culturally attached to southwest Louisiana than the bulk of citizens located north and west who sported ten-gallon hats and leaned more toward Spanish as a second language.

"I'll take it under advisement. Besides, I don't work alone." Her reference to Gunther resulted in Victor's frown.

"I'm sure he's protective, but have you taught him to dial 911?"

"Working on it. We have regular pack meetings and communicate well."

"You mean your howl fests?" Victor chuckled. "Never fully understood them, but he sure does respond well."

Victor remained a gentleman throughout the meal, even grabbing the check before she could claim it.

When he walked her back to the loft and tried to claim a goodnight kiss, she placed her hand on his chest.

"We're not there, Victor. This was a friendly get-together. Remember?"

"Sure, Hailey. Sure. Sorry. Old habits and all that." Disappointment etched his expression but lacked malice.

If he had a vengeful side, she'd never seen it surface.

* * * *

Trenton

Why Hailey set up shop in the current one-stoplight town bewildered Trenton. She was both smart and talented.

Which brought his current actions into question. Wearing a federal badge didn't erase his knowledge of how to tread right up to the line. He'd cross it without hesitation if it meant protecting those for which he cared.

That viewpoint put him in his current predicament.

Hailey was by no means gullible, yet she'd sat across the table from Victor and smiled, accepting the weight of his hand over hers without flinching.

Men like Victor existed as emotional lamprey, absorbing their prey's fortitude until they were drained and lifeless. It was too painful to stand by and watch it before, hence the choice to join the FBI over a local department.

And now I've become a stalker...

The fact remained. Someone had taken a shot at them today. If he didn't narrow the suspect pool, Hailey might not be lucky a second time.

It was time to pay a visit to the ex's lair.

He found the ramshackle shelter near the backwaters in the lower county. No doubt, the man felt at home with anything that could slither, crawl, or made its den underground.

The old, remote house and encompassing woods reeked of evil.

Criminal types often used broken-down facades in undesirable surroundings to conceal nefarious dealings. Unfortunately, many residents in the area didn't have the funds to maintain their homes.

Circling the one-story bungalow and checking windows, he found no sign of an alarm or easy point of entry. Resorting to picking the back door lock, he inserted a tension pick and applied a small amount of torsion to the cylinder. Using finesse, he made quick work of the almost nonexistent security.

Victor either had nothing to hide or was too arrogant to be bothered.

The back door opened to a kitchen, clean but with a damp, stale odor. Ambient light through the over-sink window emphasized chipped Formica countertops and a half-table abutting the far wall. Farther inside, he noted the shape of a low couch facing a brick fireplace.

Flicking on his flashlight revealed spartan rooms free of clutter. Scarred wooden floors lacked dust bunnies in the corner or rugs to add warmth.

The man lived a utilitarian life. In the fridge, a covered plate and a container of coleslaw occupied space above the shelf of bottled water.

Doorless cupboards beside the sink contained four white dinner plates, bread plates, and salad bowls. An iron rack above the extended bar supported a small variety of pots and pans.

To the left, three doors opened off a narrow hallway and offered a view into the dubious character of Victor Abrams. One opened to a small master bedroom with a worn navy bedspread. A lacy bra on the pillow contrasted the starkness of the room.

Two framed pictures sat on the bedside table. From the glossy confines, Hailey smiled into the eyes of Victor. They clearly shared a moment in time cherished to date by at least one.

Shadow arms from a branching oak outside the window stretched across the floor to encompass a low wooden dresser on the opposite wall.

The presence of candles, herbs, and chalk on top chilled Trenton's blood. He didn't embrace the same beliefs as Hailey's family, but certainly recognized tools of the trade.

In examining the floor, he saw various drawn lines too faint to make out a symbol. It appeared someone used it many times. Wiped, but not cleaned.

His head swiveled back to the bed where the bra rested on the pillow. Was Victor enlisting help from another practitioner, then indulging?

Failure to find a hunting rifle in the closet didn't dampen suspicion. Maybe he carried one in his truck.

A small bathroom accessed via a narrow door provided enough room for a toilet, sink, and small shower. No feminine products lay strewn on the counter or in the small medicine cabinet. A travel-sized bottle of aspirin was the sole occupant behind the cracked mirror.

In the spare bedroom, Victor had set up a small office. Uneven legs on the desk caused it to wobble but not displace the single lamp or small laptop. A straight-backed slatted chair sat cattycorner to face one of the two windows admitting filtered moonlight.

On the desk was a rumpled folder. Trenton opened it to find a stack of old newspaper clippings. On top was the story about Hailey's father, presumed to have taken off.

That was ten years ago. Victor couldn't have been mixed up in that.

He'd just opened the computer's lid when headlights slashed across the front yard, flashing briefly over the far window. The sound of an engine grew louder then cut as he flicked off and pocketed his light.

No garage to delay the homeowner's arrival left little time to stretch across the desk and open the window. His gloved hand slipped on the latch. A light shove failed to open the sash as paint melded rails to the frame.

A car door slammed outside. If caught, not only would it mean his badge, but he wouldn't be able to supplement his sibling's investigation.

Adjusting his position allowed him to apply more force behind the next upward thrust. A gap opened several inches wide.

No screen blocked his escape.

Of all the times he'd berated his sister and friend for questionable ethics, he'd not only crossed legal lines but would earn years of censure for his actions if discovered.

Testing his weight on the desk, he paused briefly to see if it held.

While fumbling through the exit, he heard the back door creak open. Victor's grumbling followed by a slamming door declared he'd returned alone.

Trenton's landing on soft ground came as a surprise. It would be more like the dodgy character to plant thorny bushes.

A small blessing.

Light from the hallway leached through the spare room to highlight a window-sized rectangle of tall grass beside him.

Low grinding coinciding with the window's closing forced him to cringe. As if to drive home the point, resistance gave way and the window thudded shut with a loud thump. At least he'd had sense enough to wear gloves and not leave prints.

He didn't have time to take cover behind the nearest wood line so opted to plaster himself against the exterior wall in hustling along the side of the house.

Twenty steps carried him to the corner just as the window produced the now familiar low screech. Grumbled epithets from within hastened Trenton's bolt for the road out front while Victor was still in the bedroom. He didn't dare use his flashlight, instead hightailing it to the rugged gravel lane… and his vehicle hidden a hundred yards south.

To think he'd called Hailey harebrained…

Still, he'd protect her at any cost.

Chapter Fourteen
Hailey

Dark windows in the loft indicated her temporary and meddlesome houseguest was still out. Tired and with a full stomach, Hailey parked behind her building and just wanted to climb in bed.

She favored avoidance over a chance encounter with Trenton, not wanting to endure him spewing overprotective nonsense. She'd had more fun facing off with a gator.

After letting herself in, she ignored the lights that would spear her eyes like a javelin. Moonlight through the floor-to-ceiling made them unnecessary. Her keys clinked in the bowl on the kitchen counter. Despite exhaustion, her mind continued to churn out thoughts of missing girls, Victor, and the return of Trenton. The latter would keep her up all night.

"Hold on a minute, Gunther," she said pouring herself a White Russian and finishing the last of the Kahlua. "We'll go out together so you can run."

The kitchen door opened to a short hall with steps leading to the building's back exit. With all that had happened, she hadn't thought to check the office. Their flaky receptionist didn't always remember to lock up when leaving.

Two doors in the bottom stairwell offered a choice. To the right, the exterior door was solid with the exception of a small window to brighten the entrance hall. It locked automatically.

Stepping left, Hailey tried the door to the office. It turned under her fingers.

Figures Lizzy would forget to lock up.

Another lecture to their ditzy employee probably wouldn't help. Maybe a sign on the door as a reminder would.

The overhead light behind her cast a long shadow through the interior. Gunther's growl stopped her from opening it wide. Unlike her own, her dog's senses were acute and always on target.

Hailey paced beside him, keeping her hand on his back to prevent him from charging. Together, they slipped through.

The rumble in his chest grew louder.

Moonlight sectioned off the open-span interior but failed to penetrate deeper than the file cabinets on the far wall where glass portioned off the office space.

The door was open, another oddity.

She wasn't armed, her weapon locked in the office with the intruder. The time it'd take to retrieve her bang stick from upstairs equaled enough for an uninvited visitor to escape. She still held an advantage.

Her four-footed partner liked fast food. Taking advantage of her hesitation and with a mind of his own, he bolted into the open space.

"Gunther, no!"

Shifting shadows beyond the glass defined the threat moving. Judging by the size, a male. The intruder would outweigh her by at least seventy-five pounds.

Lack of official K9 training didn't dent Gunther's protective instincts. He cut the distance in a few strides as the prowler stepped out to face him. The standing coat rack held as a weapon in front of him thwarted the advancing canine attack.

A black mask denied identification of the intruder, his shoulders broad, his belly wider.

The first jab shoved her dog backward. Undeterred, Gunther darted forward and dodged the next to latch onto a meaty thigh, eliciting a howl of rage and pain.

Before she could reach them, the asshat swung the rack like a cudgel. Her dog went down with a yelp. When he stood on all fours again, a menacing growl rumbled in his chest.

Rushing forward, Hailey intended to level the playing field in grabbing the makeshift weapon.

Before she could latch onto one of the branching wooden feet, it jerked upward and flew out of the intruder's hands.

A gasp was his only response when it landed on the floor ten feet away.

"Quiet type, huh? How do you like the odds now?" Hailey thanked whatever force of nature intervened on her behalf.

Not only heavier, the intruder was also taller than her five-eight frame. Dark clothes, gloves, and a mask denied visual of any identifying marks. White teeth seen through one of the three holes in the mask gleamed in the moonlight.

She did a double take when he retrieved a gun from his back waist. Apparently, he hadn't set out to kill anyone tonight or that would've been his weapon of choice.

Gunther lunged but failed to gain ground against her hold on his collar.

"What do you want? I don't keep money here."

In lieu of speech, the gunman waved her aside with his gun barrel. It would take less than a millisecond for a hunk of lead to rip through her chest.

She backed up with Gunther, whose paws churned against the concrete floor in his bid to gain traction. If the intruder fired a shot, the one left standing would kill him. He must have realized that.

He sidled by, limping from his encounter with her hybrid with little more than a grunt. Side-stepping motions allowed him to track both her and his exit. When he shut the front door and stood on the other side of the glass wall, he leveled his barrel in her direction.

Just before the muzzle flash heralded her death, the barrel surged upward, the shot tearing through the ceiling over her head.

She ducked as the sound of the next round ricocheted off the block wall behind her. The asshat meant to kill, after all, but not at close range.

When she looked up, he was gone.

Gunther dragged her forward, her tennis shoes squeaking against the floor until they reached the door.

An engine gunned to life before tires squealed.

The intruder had hobbled to his vehicle then peeled off down the street.

She was unable to discern make or model through the shadows. Without security or streetlamps along the road, she had no way of tracking him, nor would she try without a weapon.

By the time she'd backtracked to her office for her gun, there was no trail to follow.

"Damn. Somebody's looking for something. Files on a current or past investigation maybe?"

Another loose end she couldn't tie off.

Gunther barked at the open office door. The only space big enough to hold a threat was the kneehole of the partners desk, larger than the one in Henri's office.

With a snug hold of his collar, she flipped on the light.

Files lay scattered over every surface with papers strewn across the stamped cement. A gasp escaped her when she rounded the desk corner. The message left was clear.

In the seat of her chair, coiled and ready to strike, waited a blacktail rattlesnake.

Oh, joy. The prick left his partner.

* * * *

Trenton

Trenton's relief at turning onto the remote street died with flashing red-and-blue lights strobing across the loft and woods opposite.

He sighed.

She doesn't have to find trouble. It lives with her.

A visual check of Hailey and Leigh talking to a uniformed officer by the front door confirmed no major catastrophe had befallen them. Yet.

Figured it would happen when he'd left her alone. He should've known better.

His door closing snapped Hailey's gaze up to find him, a scowl marring her delicate features. She grumbled something unintelligible with his approach.

Visual cataloging of personnel moving about and snippets of conversation signaled the processing of a crime scene, the specific crime yet to be determined.

Hailey turned away from the taller man intent on voicing his disapproval of her chosen profession. He'd be lucky if she didn't flip him onto the grass shoulder.

"Glad you could drop by, dude. Where were you when someone used Hailey for target practice?" Leigh's version of worry generally included sarcasm.

"Jesus. I can't turn my back for a second." He shook his head.

Lights from the first-floor interior accentuated the small hole marring the front window. Hairline fractures radiating from a small hole could've represented a wound in Leigh or Hailey's skull.

"Welcome to my world." Badge and gun clipped to the belt on his jeans, the blond-haired lieutenant held out his hand. "I could use a hand with these two. How about it?"

"What happened?" Trenton accepted Lt. Colson's handshake with gratitude.

"Seems Hailey and Gunther interrupted an intruder in the office. The guy—we assume it was a guy due to his build—fired a couple shots at her. Missed."

"Did he take anything?" Trenton noted Colson's frustration leaking into the conversation.

"Won't know till they can make some semblance of the mess. He did leave a calling card of sorts."

Trenton briefly closed his eyes. "What?"

"Rattlesnake. Guess it's another Vodou warning." Colson held his hands up when Leigh stood toe to toe with him.

"Hey, this has nothing to do with our religion. The snake Hailey removed from her office was a rattlesnake. It was left by a botono."

"A what?" Colson looked to Trenton for clarification.

Leigh continued. "Someone who believes in dark magic, or Bo. Vodou has nothing to do with this. It's not dark. It's not designed to hurt or kill. It deals with healing, life, et cetera."

"I'll call my brother Jaxon," Trenton interrupted to spare his counterpart a cultural lesson, "He can figure out what, if anything, they got into digitally."

"Leigh already called him. Where've you been? Besides not answering your phone." Hailey eyed the mud on Trenton's shoes then cast him a questioning glance.

She trust him with her life, but would also know he'd withhold information.

"Ah, sorry, sometimes I just don't want to hear it ring. Forensics inside?" Trenton's change of subject earned a questioning glance from her lieutenant.

Not wanting to delay information exchange, they headed toward the building's front door.

An officer checked Trenton's FBI credentials and handed him the sign-in log before giving him a pair of disposable booties.

"Going above and beyond. Good," Trenton said as Colson trailed him through the front door.

"Always do when it's one of our own. The guy came out this way then turned and fired." Colson gestured to the side where a forensic tech photographed a muddy boot print. "Looks like he was limping on the way out."

Good for you, Gunther.

Four hours later, Trenton sat on the sofa in the loft going over his notes while Hailey perched on the bench seat overlooking the street with Gunther at her feet.

Leigh moved around the kitchen preparing a light snack. Simple movements would keep her hands busy while her mind sorted facts, which they needed to discuss before small details slipped from Hailey's mental grasp.

"Coffee's ready," Leigh said as she deposited trays on the low table fronting the couch.

Hailey gracefully dropped Indian-style beside Gunther on the floor and picked up her favorite mug. "I've been over this a thousand times already, guys. The bastard was six-foot tall, linebacker build, dark clothes, and gloves. He never uttered a word. He did groan when Gunther bit him, though. Very satisfying, that."

"Good thing for Gunther the bastard won't report a dog bite. Less complications." Trenton plucked a cup from the tray and took a sip.

Mental wheels spun in replaying Hailey's description yet yielded no additional clues. "Great," Trenton said. "We've narrowed down the suspect pool to a six-foot male who may or may not still walk with a limp."

Despite the late hour, Trenton felt wired. He'd added a few more notes to the case, and by the time Leigh stood to leave, he was ready for his own bed.

"I'm going home. I'll be back tomorrow." Leigh patted Trenton on the shoulder and smiled on her way to the door. "Be nice or the wolf dog will give you a very rude and wet awakening."

"I'm too tired to continue tonight, and too wired to sleep." Hailey patted her lap to invite Gunther to rest his head. As usual, the two moved in sync.

"Understandable. That's twice someone's taken a shot at you."

"Wanna watch a movie?"

"*Hmm*, depends on what you have in mind." He'd learned long ago to be specific.

"Something with action, adventure, high seas, revenge, and betrayal."

"Great. I'll get us more to drink."

She settled back with the remote and flipped through channels.

By the time he returned, she hit play on the remote.

"What? No. Not *The Little Mermaid*. Please?"

Hailey smiled and rubbed the soft fur behind Gunther's ears. "C'mon. It's a classic."

"And watching this for the millionth time sounds like fun?" Despite the cinema choice, it felt good to slip into old times and habits. It might even outrank the peace achieved with a makeshift family in Pennsylvania.

Curiosity over her non-date with Victor drove him to the brink of asking direct questions. Instead, he settled for, "How was your dinner?"

"Fine. Says he's changed and all that... I thought about having a philosophical talk with Father Ryan."

"You used to go there to sort out complicated situations." Offering the leader earned him a snort.

"Nice try." Hailey pointed to his stocking feet. "Didn't peg you for a man to tromp through the woods at night. Wanna talk about it?"

"What?"

"The mud on your boots earlier. Unusual for a neatnik. Plus, you have a few pine needles clinging to the back of your clothes." Hailey plucked a thin cluster of said needles from his hair then pointed to his jacket on the back of the couch.

"If someone restrained your hands during conversation, would you still be able to talk?" he teased while avoiding the topic.

"Sure, but it wouldn't matter. Corpses don't hear anything."

Her acknowledgment of his change in subject ended with a wide grin, one made for the devil.

"Share whenever you're ready, dude. I'm a good listener."

"Back at ya." Trenton grabbed the remote and turned up the sound. It all felt so familiar.

"Have you missed *us*, Sparkles?" She'd always felt like a younger sister, until she hadn't. Still, he'd sensed the void of friendship while in Pennsylvania.

"'Bout as much as a toothache." Her smile softened the admonishment. "Yeah, I guess I have."

"Why haven't you married?" From a male perspective, she was beautiful, smart, funny, sarcastic, and loyal. He didn't understand why someone hadn't enthralled her heart and soul.

"No one can keep up with me. What about you? Any near misses?"

"One, but it didn't feel right."

"Why? Didn't she have enough spunk?"

"For the most part, yes, but she wanted to change me. My lifestyle, my work, even my hobbies."

"*Hmm*, couldn't stand your guitar?"

"Didn't like my boxing."

"You left your guitar in Pennsylvania. Not used to seeing you without it."

"Left in a hurry. Didn't plan on beaning a killer over the head with it."

Hailey seemed to mull it over then nodded. "And they say Acadians are slow. Maybe I'll rethink your chicken-necker status."

"How's the noggin?"

"Slight headache, but I'm fine." Brows drawing a straight line declared the lie.

"Sparkles?"

"Okay. I know this is weird, but… something's happening. Something strange. It's like I have an invisible friend with me, watching over me at times. Do you think I'm crazy?"

"No more than usual. Want to talk about it?" As much as he wanted to delve into what she'd just admitted, he wouldn't do so until she was less vulnerable. Taking advantage of her wasn't part of his nature.

"Not now. Maybe tomorrow." She rested her head against his shoulder and sighed.

His world just righted itself.

Chapter Fifteen
Hailey

Dawn's eerie silence equaled nature's warning to brace for the coming day. Dishrag clouds hung low over the horizon with the threat of rain and strong wind.

Dread coated Hailey's throat with the task ahead. She strode up the familiar walkway with a firm goal in mind. The thought of her father's association with Henri rivaled the bleak forecast while fate prepared to paint her worldview in dark, somber colors.

Soft Cajun swing, dominated by fiddle and piano, filtered through lacy curtains fronting open windows. Her mom loved music.

Her need to solve the current case overshadowed the desire to confess the strange occurrences during the prior three days. As much as she wanted to discuss recent, strange events, her personal issues would have to wait.

It wasn't unusual for the front door to be open, but her mother could at least lock the screen. It didn't stretch Hailey's imagination to think her stalker would extend his reach and strike a family member.

"Mom, you shouldn't leave your door unlocked," she called out as she entered.

Gunther bounded ahead for his due of homemade treats.

The aroma of fresh-baked bread quickened her steps through the living room to the kitchen where she found her mother perched on a stool at the counter.

"Try these sweet potato biscuits, Hailey." On cue, Cecile retrieved a plate from an upper cabinet and set a basket of bread on the counter. A mason jar of jelly from the fridge soon followed. "I finished canning blueberry jelly yesterday, and the combination is fantastic."

Cecile had never met a fruit or vegetable she couldn't preserve.

Hailey dug in and nodded when Cecile poured a cup of iced coffee.

"Did you go back out to Mitts Bayou again? By yourself?" A worried frown creased her brow. "Leigh said her lieutenant forbid her to go out there alone to poke around."

She shook her head around a mouthful of bread. Her mother's reliable grapevine flourished. "Huh. Seems the lieutenant doesn't know her very well."

"He's young. He'll learn." Cecile grinned.

"To answer your question, no. I'm gonna give it a little time before I try to get that pic."

"Any idea on your shooter?"

"No, we've got too many irons in the fire to pick one." Hailey provided details of the near miss the prior night.

"A good thing Trenton is visiting. I wonder how long he'll stay."

"Mom, he might have been the first target."

"Not from what I hear. He arrived what, three days ago? Has he been flashing his ID?"

"A little. So, okay. He probably wasn't. But it could've been a poacher or something."

"Hon. The fact you're my daughter does not make you bulletproof. And a poacher wouldn't be ransacking your office."

"Okay, but don't ask me to back off this case. I won't. We have two girls missing, and I intend to find them."

"Could the girl from five years ago have run away? I've seen it often enough."

"Not likely. They found her glasses and shoes on the road at the time, which suggests otherwise."

"I feel you're treading a dangerous path, Hailey. Be careful."

"Always am. By the way, I ran into a rather unpleasant fellow who claimed to know all about Dad."

"Who?" Nipping at her bottom lip declared she already knew. Hamchet's scuttlebutt would've warned her.

"Henri."

"Where did you cross paths with that odious toad?"

"Hobby store."

"Do not believe any filth that beast spits out. It'll be lies."

"If Trenton hadn't been with me, I would've given him five minutes, not that Gunther wanted to. He was ready to taste test on the spot."

"Your protector has such good sense." Cecile crouched down to offer Gunther another treat from the bag kept on the kitchen table. "Who's the best judge of character around here, huh?"

"Mom, the time has long passed for me to understand what happened to Dad."

She'd spent years searching for the man who'd taken her to the Acadian Cultural Museum and canoeing on the lake. They'd become her favorite spots to explore, instilling a love for both nature and history. Each time they took the ranger-guided boat tour, she'd become more fascinated with bayou life.

"*Chère*, please, listen to me. That one is evil, and no good can come from enduring his presence. Trust me on this."

"I'm going to find Dad when this is over."

"Hailey, your father was a good man, regardless of what Henri would say. Let it lie. Answers can only bring heartache."

"There's frequently a grain of truth buried in every lie. It's up to the listener to dig and find it."

A heavy sigh brushed a stray lock from her mother's modified French twist before she set aside her apron. Strength of will visibly vanished in her plopping down on a stool. "I'll tell you what I know. You'll not like it, but at least it will be the truth."

"What are you talking about? You said he took off, and you had no idea where he went."

"That part is true. However, there is more. I've not told you before because I wanted to protect you."

Suddenly, the sweet bread and jam on her tongue tasted like ash. Memory served up only one time in the past when her mother adopted an expression this serious—the morning after her father left.

"Your dad was a good man, with a good heart. He loved you very much."

"But? I hear something else coming."

"No buts. No human is without faults. Your father, he had a weakness for gambling. It started out with small, friendly games. Eventually, he graduated to high-stakes games, poker and ponies, anything and everything. We didn't lose the house because it was handed down to me from my parents."

"No. He was an artist who taught school. He sold his paintings everywhere."

"That is also true, but like every living creature gracing this planet, he had a dark side."

Although the small rip in her heart widened, Hailey narrowed in on her mother's averted gaze. "There's more. Something you're not telling me. What?"

"Let it go, Hailey. It's a road I don't want you to travel."

"Too late." Hailey knew the woman feared some unknown truth. The question remained, would it rip them apart?

"The night he left, it was rumored he got in a car with a young woman and headed out of town."

"With who?" She couldn't believe the man she'd idolized through childhood would be unfaithful. "I don't believe it."

"I wouldn't have either, but the source was a man from our church. The high school custodian."

Skepticism didn't come close to what Hailey felt. "How would he know?"

Pieces of the puzzle fell together. Instead of one complete picture, there existed a montage of unrelated images.

"The janitor worked evenings after intermural sports. I ran into him one night after your basketball game. He's an honest, hard-working fellow."

"Tell me."

"While cleaning up after a game, he saw your father talking to what he thought was a student—down the hallway."

"So what? You know how Dad was. He'd help anyone who needed it. What you're insinuating, it can't be true."

There'd been occasions, social gatherings, where more than once Hailey had heard the soft murmurs of conjecture and insincere greetings, seen gazes that wouldn't connect.

"He didn't see the girl's face, but did see them both get into the car. Your dad wasn't seen again after that night."

"No. He wasn't like that."

"I don't believe he'd have an affair with a student, either. Regardless of the many times he'd counsel a lost soul over lunch through one crisis or another. I got a call from a parent once, thanking me on his behalf."

"Damn."

"As far as talking with Henri... well, I might as well tell you. That lowlife snake encouraged your dad, enabled him to get in deeper with those who held markers in gambling."

"But we've never had a lot of money, nothing for anyone to covet. What was the point?"

"I don't know."

The man Hailey had idolized for over ten years now appeared tarnished, unrecognizable. "All these years. Why didn't you tell me?"

"Hailey. I know you feel betrayed, but I was trying to protect you from gossip, lies, and innuendo."

Betrayal tasted bitter in her mouth. Hailey shoved to her feet and backed away, unable to meet her mother's gaze. "You did lie. All these years."

"No, *chére*. I didn't." Tears stained her mother's cheeks.

"A lie by omission is still a lie."

"Hailey, please don't go after Henri. He's dangerous."

"Is he a botono?"

Of all the practitioners in the area, her mother would have a handle on most of them.

"He keeps to himself from what I understand, so I'm not sure. It wouldn't surprise me."

"I'll do what I need to do. Right now, I need time."

Gunther whined but followed her out the door and across the lawn to her truck.

Her phone rang before she cranked the engine.

"Leigh, what's up?"

"I may have found the truck that ran you off the road. Come on out to the lake at Melford's farm."

Trenton had taught her and Leigh to fish at that lake. "Be there in twenty. I gotta swing by the loft for my camera."

Abandoned for years, the farm made a good dumping site, which meant the killer was probably local. The bayou was better known for holding corpses.

The older couple who'd once lived there, known for their generosity throughout Hailey's school years, had welcomed many a teen in their midst. Their door was always open to visitors. With no children of their own, fostering must have filled a void.

Gunther sensed her change in mood and licked her cheek before turning his attention to the passing countryside.

"I'm okay, boy. Just a lot to take in." She let him follow her up to get her camera. Her thoughts touched on each puzzle piece during her drive to Melford's farm.

One hand secured her equipment bag to the seat as the truck bounced over deep ruts scoring the dirt driveway. The property hadn't seen so much traffic in years.

Three rainy nights earlier in the week would help forensic specialists to create a timeline, and with Trenton's involvement, they'd have access to the FBI's labs.

The old farmhouse had seen better days. Sagging rooflines, broken windows on the first floor, and scrub grass in place of a well-kept lawn made her heart ache. Grief had destroyed the elder homeowner long before his heart gave out.

Behind the barn stood an old shed where they'd stored a lawnmower, gardening tools, and slabs of wood for drying and painting prior to the insertion of clock parts. Anyone lucky enough to have a Melford-homemade painted clock in their home treasured it.

Hailey parked behind a black Camaro and cautioned Gunther, "Be nice, boy. Remember, you're an ambassador here."

A soft *woof* conveyed his feelings before he nudged her arm for attention. Her four-footed partner could express more in a look than any creature on earth.

With her camera bag slung over one shoulder, she set out across the field to where yellow tape cordoned off onlookers. She wasn't the only spectator. A familiar form also watched the proceedings.

Casper.

On the opposite shoreline, the Briner siblings studied dual tracks in knee-high grass leading to the water, interrupted by a small boulder.

Colson directed forensic techs to a spot of overgrown weeds, kneeling for a closer look.

Hailey approached the familiar figure watching the proceedings, curious over Casper's morbid interest.

"Hi, you're a ways from home." She didn't miss how the teen held tight to her pendant.

"Well, this place is miles from any decent entertainment. Girl's gotta find her own. What draws you here?" Like before, shrewd eyes held knowledge locked behind an impenetrable mask.

"I'm a private investigator, remember?"

The youth stared at something to her right, not at the scene, her monotone words evidence of distraction.

It's the best time to get an uncensored answer.

"How'd you know to come here?"

That snapped the teen's attention back. "Um, connections and curiosity," she mumbled before her attention was drawn away again. This time, back toward the house, as if she listened to another conversation.

The kid knew something—or, a lot of somethings. To give Casper a minute for composure, Hailey retrieved her camera to assess the work in progress.

Seeing nothing but black reminded her to remove the lens cap. Before she could grab it, it flew off the end of the lens. Due to the current wind direction and their protected location, nothing stirred.

"Like I said. Connections," Casper whispered with a giggle. "That kind." She nodded to the lens cap on the ground.

"O-kaay." Hailey retrieved the cap, then hoisted her camera and adjusted the focus for a closer look at the distant crime scene.

A winch from the wrecker voiced its struggle with a grinding noise. She saw Leigh's shudder in the distance before a back bumper broke the waterline. A minute later, the cab of a truck came into view. "Don't see a tag on the back."

"No surprise when there's a dead man inside." Casper's gaze remained on the house, in the opposite direction of the lake.

"How would you know *that*, Casper?"

"Huh? Um, how's your head? You took quite a hit the other night." The teen shrugged then gripped the amulet tighter, taking better note of her surroundings.

Not willing to let it go, Hailey persisted. "How do you know there's a dead man in that truck? Did you see his spirit?"

Casper blanched and took a step back. "Are you nuts?"

"Then who were you looking at when I first got here? 'Cuz it wasn't at the lake." She paused for a breath, then tried again. "I know you're not like me exactly, but you're also different in a way that feels... familiar."

At that moment, two news vans with local call letters pulled up in Melford's driveway, briefly drawing their attention.

"Looks like we have an audience," Casper advised. "Not a good time for this discussion."

Hailey acquiesced and proceeded to take pictures.

Water flowed through the open windows and from the truck's bed as the winch jerked it higher on the waterline. "Damn it. It *is* the truck that ran me off the road."

"Really? When did that happen?" Casper spared her a side-glance.

"Not sharing until you illuminate some details for me. Like, why you were in the antiques store and how you got us out?"

"You wouldn't believe me. And it's not like you can tell Trenton without drawing more of his ire," Casper gloated.

"How is it you're so plugged into this whole situation?"

Another glance accompanied a small grin. "As I said, connections."

Hailey turned back to her camera. Through the din growing in her ears, she whispered two words confirming Casper's statement, "Dead body."

The cab lurched sideways after hitting some unseen object under water, enough to send an arm floating out of the cab's window.

"Hell. I see an arm." She couldn't identify the man who'd run her off the road, but the clothes looked the same.

"Told ya."

"Oh, God. The arm's not attached, like, to anything. Just floating away." Current created by the truck's movement pushed the limb in a back-and-forth macabre *Hello* wave.

"Gross." Casper shuddered.

Hailey switched the camera's setting to burst mode for continuous shooting. "No way…"

"What?"

"Shoulders and torso, but no head." Hailey spun to the side as her stomach ejected her mother's biscuits. Several heartbeats later, she repositioned herself for more photos.

"Damn." Her lens captured the shredded remains of a baseball cap, floating out the cab's window to create more ripples in the rainbow oil skim. "Aw, crap. Is that chunks of brain matter?" For the first time, she questioned the wisdom of her purchase.

"Yeah."

The teen's unphased demeanor inspired a closer look. "What do you know about this?"

"I've got an airtight alibi. In fact, I'm on my way to becoming an investigator."

Hailey studied the kid for a minute. "No notes, no camera. Not even your phone out."

"Doesn't mean I'm not learning. What else do you see through the lens?"

"The hat floating away."

One of the crime techs waded in to grab it along with the arm.

Hailey switched her camera's focus to Leigh then Colson, waiting as workers finished pulling the truck ashore.

"No wonder they cordoned off the entire area. Gross way to kick the bucket." Casper turned from the scene and released the grip on her amulet.

Adjusting her direction of focus, Hailey caught the arrival of the ME and state forensics van. "Local law enforcement is too small and undertrained for this situation. Looks like they called in state help."

"Gonna need more before it's over," Casper agreed.

"We need to sit down and have a talk." Hailey couldn't force the conversation, not knowing the background of her companion or Casper's adoptive father, but she pressed, "I have information. Local and pertinent."

"I have sources, too, but I'm open to a short conversation to see how it goes."

"Why'd they ditch the truck, and why here? Someone would discover it sooner or later with the place up for sale. Lots of better places in the bayou someone could've hidden it." Capping her lens, she rolled her shoulders to ease the kinks forming in her back.

"He doesn't know. Dead before arrival." Again, Casper looked off to her right, as if observing a conversation. After a moment, she edged closer to view pictures taken. "Lemme see."

Hailey flicked through the digital photos with only slight doubts about her sanity. "If the guy thought this a good dumping ground, how many other bodies are here, and where? In the house, barn?"

"None inside, I don't think. But there's another place we should check."

"*We*?" Instead of asking for clarification, Hailey asked, "Where?" For the umpteenth time, she wondered over the discrepancy between Casper's age and insight. Arcane knowledge certainly made her a fit for the elite school.

"You'll have to ditch both Leigh and Trenton, but I've got a plan. Meet me here, say, around ten?"

"Make it nine. I'll tell Trenton I'm watching a chick flick with a friend." Hailey snickered. "Have to make it animated and G-rated so he won't want to come."

Casper chuckled then sobered when Leigh glared from across the lake. "You telepathic or something? Even from here, I can tell she's pissed off."

"Or something," Hailey confirmed.

"Damn. You two really are connected, aren't you? How're you gonna get around her?"

"Don't worry. I'll call her boyfriend and tell him she's feeling neglected. Not a thing in the world he wouldn't do for her."

The pitch on the winch's motor changed when the truck's tires caught traction on dry ground. A most gruesome scene with Hailey's imagination supplying finer details, until a large water moccasin slithered out with the water draining from the window.

"Tell me cottonmouths aren't carnivorous," Casper whispered.

Whoa. There's no way she can see that snake clearly from this distance; not the jowls holding venom, or the triangular shaped head.

"I wish I could. No one deserves that. You have a northern accent but seem to know a lot about the area." Hailey tested the waters again, trying to crack the enigma that was Casper.

"Research. Like any good investigator would do."

"It'll be days before we get answers from this." Hailey indicated the crime scene with a sweep of her hand. "Unless we can get something out of Trenton. He's the easier target." Extracting information from the federal agent would require offering like in kind.

"What kind of nickname is Casper, anyway?"

"The kind that fits." A Cheshire-cat grin accompanied a chuckle. "See ya at nine." With that, she checked her watch and walked away.

The questions remained in Hailey's mind, what was Casper's connection to this scene, and what was she hiding?

Chapter Sixteen
Hailey

A corn-yellow crescent moon hung low on the horizon to offer moderate light as Hailey paced Casper toward Melford's side yard.

It'd been years since a dairy herd grazed the pastures and horses romped across the fields. Remnants of fencing lay broken on the ground, with the occasional remaining post tipping over with a touch, rotten and breaking off at or below ground level.

Casper gestured to circumvent the house and led them toward the long-overgrown herb garden. Despite the darkness, she navigated the uneven ground that caused Hailey to stumble more often than not. Walking in the younger woman's steps didn't help.

Gunther moved in sync beside her as she mentally reviewed specific questions and how to approach the subject forefront in her mind. She'd given much thought to how they'd escaped the antique store unseen and arrived at no answers.

"Trenton and the new lieutenant shouldn't have missed this," Casper muttered.

"Missed what? And how'd you know the lieutenant is new to the area?"

"Homework and students go hand in hand."

Hailey's senses were on high alert, like the feeling she got after leaving her apartment and wondering if she'd left the stove on. Nothing moved or hissed, everything remained calm and quiet.

Then why is my skin crawling?

An earlier phone call to Schiffer's Realty confirmed the farm under contract by a local landscaping service to bush hog the grounds once a month. An offshore corporation held the title, for purposes unknown.

The air was humid and oppressive. A perfect night for mayhem, and yet, she didn't feel threatened, just creeped out.

Years prior, Hailey and Leigh visited the farm often, sharing what they'd learned about herbs and gardening with the missus. A ready supply of pie or fresh bread always sat on the counter and included encouragement along with a sympathetic ear.

For years, the Melfords offered their time and resources to help others. Two horses used during rehab classes for disabled children were how they learned to ride.

Casper stood behind the house and stared at the empty field. Her hand tightened on the amulet.

"Hey, you all right?" Hailey asked.

"Yeah... There's an old root cellar around here. They used to store canned goods like the old timers." A slice of moonlight highlighted the teen's confusion morphing into something darker.

An unseen force drove Hailey a step back. The prickles climbing her arms weren't from the breeze. She stared at the teen's back, waiting for... something.

Casper held her hand out, a motion for quiet. Tilting her head to the side, she murmured, "Why didn't you tell me that before now for God's sake? She doesn't need to see that."

In a moment of silence, a shudder running the length of Hailey's spine awakened an icy foreboding deep in her bones.

Death lurked nearby. She felt its presence.

Casper shook her head and dropped her hand to her side briefly. A dip of her left side was the same movement Hailey made when sliding a strap off her arm.

"Fine." Casper's harsh whisper broke the silence. "But you're still a tramp. A stupid one at that. If you're not going to help, then leave."

"Doesn't need to see what? Who are you talking to?"

"Not one of your spirits, that's for sure. I need to get into the root cellar. Alone."

Hailey couldn't think of any way a stranger would gain knowledge of the cellar. She couldn't clarify the reason for keeping her voice to a whisper, but never ignored her instincts, so acknowledged, "They had one."

This is getting stranger by the minute.

"It's just off the kitchen," Casper clarified.

"Yeah. Mrs. M used to brag about how her husband used concrete blocks to build a more permanent structure on a small knoll." Hailey gestured ahead.

Gunther whined at her side. His rumble increased when approaching the home.

The house was dark and silent, a wooden colossus of old, determined to survive both the elements and neglect.

Near the kitchen door, Hailey stopped. "Casper, someone must've filled it in. I don't see the hatch. Maybe someone thought it a hazard?"

"No, there's an underground… something, here. I know it. Help me move this planter. It's got to be underneath."

The homeowners thrived during an era where hardworking people threw little away. If it could be repurposed, it was salvageable, even farm equipment.

For his wife's birthday, Melford had modified a derelict wheat drill with missing discs to use as a raised gardening bed. She'd grown and tended numerous herbs with loving care.

"They had cows and crops?" Casper asked.

"Just a few crops. The mister was more of a hobby farmer and loved his toys. Hence, the small planter."

Hailey hooked a thumb over her shoulder. "This old wheat drill used to be near the end of the house where plants got more afternoon light. Help me move it." It no longer held flowers, but the soil it held increased its weight.

Each leaned against one of the wheels and shoved. The behemoth moved several inches. Successive efforts saw it shifting a few inches each time.

Swiping away the collected leaf litter allowed Hailey to study the ground underneath. "Ah, here it is. About a foot more and it'll clear the hatch."

Gunther pawed the ground. His whine had morphed into a low growl.

"Thanks, boy, but not exactly what we need right now. Save your frustration for something that deserves it."

When the entire hatch came into view, Hailey knelt to find the ring pull. Despite years of nonuse, the hinged door swung up on a low grind, releasing a swarm of flies and stench that knocked her on her ass.

That's odd.

Casper gripped Hailey's shoulder. "Not sure how long canned vegetables stay good. But let me go down first."

"Something's sure spoiled down there. Maybe a jar broke or... I don't know what smells so bad."

Casper edged Hailey aside and slammed the hatch down. "We don't need to go down there after all. Let's call your buddy Trenton."

Hailey reared back in confusion. "Not a chance. I have to know what's there."

"No. You don't. It's rotten, yes, but it's not food." She punctuated her words with a pointed glare at Hailey.

"How do you know?"

"My, um, dad was military. Talked once about dead bodies."

"*Bodies*? Jesus, what was I thinking, bringing an eighteen-year-old on a sneak-n-peek? I'm going, with or without you."

Not only did she have a kid in tow, but one who knew exactly where to look and what dead bodies smelled like? Her mother's words from long ago rang in her ears. *"One day you'll meet someone and just know you've found your partner."*

Hailey had always thought the reference was to a male counterpart. Now, she wasn't so sure. She'd always known she'd call her business H&C Investigations. Maybe she'd found her C counterpart.

"Don't worry about me. If you're set on doing this, let's get it done." Casper knelt by the opening and helped lift the solid hatch. Her flashlight cut the black space into segments. "No telling what's slithered down there. I can't even see the bottom. Let me go first."

"No, you stay here and keep watch. I'm going." Before Casper could take the lead, Hailey flicked on her flashlight and took the first step, not setting her full weight until knowing she wouldn't crash through. The wooden brace creaked under her weight but held.

"Not a good idea, Hailey—"

"Better than you going."

A rail on the right side held the same forty-five-degree angle as the steps and didn't wobble with a hard shake.

Her first steps into the darkness came with an internal warning and urge to flee. Something invisible brushed by her, sweeping her ponytail off her shoulder. A sudden sense of nausea prompted her to pause for a slow breath through her mouth.

The stench became stronger, more intimidating.

Needing a distraction, she asked, "By the way, how is it you've just turned eighteen but are entering your senior year at a school for the gifted?"

"Late start in life, and everyone else thinks I'm seventeen. Hey, look." From above, Casper's flashlight beam swept the lower steps, showcasing several boot prints.

Hailey finished descending, taking care not to disturb potential evidence. "Whoever's been down here came after the storm. Guess that's why there was more leafy debris than dirt on the hatch."

"How do you know that?"

"Because the prints are muddy, but the edges are sharp and well-defined. So, it's been at least a few days." It seemed she could teach the young curiosity a thing or two.

Gunther padded to the top step and peered down at her.

"No, boy. You stay with Casper. I'll be fine."

The dog whined but sat, accepting Casper's hand on his head as she knelt. Not for the first time, he sniffed her shoulder and whined.

"What is it about your shoulder that draws him every time he's near you?"

"Company. We can discuss it another time." Casper's words left no room for discussion. "If someone was down there and replaced the planter afterward... maybe you should leave this for others to poke around during daylight."

"No. I'm here, and I'm gonna check it out. By the way, I only see one broken jar of beets. Looks like someone hated vegetables."

"Careful of broken glass."

"Noted."

"Is Trenton attached?"

The question from out of the blue made her snort. "We're out in the creepiest section of the county, at night, and you're asking about my friend?"

"He's hot. And no, I'm not interested. I'm not on the prowl. But at the lake today, he kept glancing your way."

Hailey shook off the insinuation.

Perspiration slid down her temple and between her shoulder blades. Not showing fear was the first step in conquering it, according to Trenton years prior. Trying it on multiple occasions had yet to yield success.

Most of the ten-by-fifteen space was dry judging by the way her tennis shoes skidded dirt along the cement floor. Along three block walls, deep shelves holding all manner of canned goods collected dust.

"Nothing's down here but canned fruits and vegetables."

So, what stinks so bad?

"C'mon, Hailey. Let's check out the house. I don't think you should be down there."

"Soon as I'm done here." Five strides took her to the far wall where more jars sat. It wasn't far enough to miss Casper's strange murmuring above. Moving back slowly, she picked up the one-sided conversation.

"Well, why didn't you tell me this before? And why don't you know?" Casper's recriminations carried in the otherwise quiet night. *"Busy? Busy doing what? You no longer exist."* Her disembodied words ended with a groan.

"Who are you talking to?" Under normal circumstances, which now existed in another realm, Hailey would touch the person's arm or hand long enough to get a read. Her instincts declared this would be a violation in the severest form where the teen was concerned.

"Ah, no one."

Again, Gunther growled, this time followed by several short barks.

"Shh, Fido. We're going for stealthy here," Casper admonished.

"Casper, pull him back before he takes it into his head to hop down and join me." Relief at not finding anything more sinister than rotten vegetables would've inspired a deep breath if not for the cloying scent filling her nostrils.

Hailey turned back to climb the stairs and halted. It wasn't until she'd pivoted that she put a name to one of the scents assaulting her.

Vomit?

"Wait. There's something else down here."

"Hailey, come up here, now. Leave her for Trenton."

An urgency existed in the teen's voice that hadn't existed before.

"Leave her? Who's her?"

"Just come up here and leave whatever's down there, alone."

An upward glance caught the teen standing beside the access, her medallion gripped tight in her fist. Backlighting from moonlight prevented defining her expression.

Right now, if the girl had been closer, Hailey would've latched onto her hand to see what was going on. Damn the consequences. It might cut through subterfuge and answer many questions.

The distance was too great, and if she retraced her steps to ground level now, she'd lose her nerve to finish what she'd started.

A narrow space between the steps and wall allowed access to more storage shelves behind the stairs. Those stocked more goods, but something lay on the floor, a large, many angled something covered with a tarp.

Her light sharpened the edges of the dirty steps and the relatively clean tarp beyond. The discrepancy was disturbing in a spine-tingling kind of way.

"What is it?" Casper leaned over the opening above and contorted her body to provide more light.

"Not sure. There's a tarp, covering something."

After a pause, Casper continued, "Damn it. All right. I'll lay on the ground and lean in to give you more light. You're more stubborn than me."

Guess she subscribes to the, if you can't beat 'em, join 'em, club.

Closing around her, an ominous foreboding seethed in the dark interior, cloying, expanding. It felt… malevolent. Instead of sending her backward, some indefinable impulse forced her feet forward and her hand to tug the corner of the white canvas. It didn't give, so she reset her grip and yanked harder.

With contact of the cloth came a collage of images thrust into her mind like an ax—a man seen from the back, with a woman draped over his shoulder, descending the stairway. Black jeans, t-shirt, and boots.

Hailey shook her head to bring herself back to the present. Ignoring the vision, she yanked again on the covering.

Strands of black string caught in the grommets flew up as the cloth fluttered to the floor.

Only, they weren't strings.

There was a head with long black hair. It took a split second to register that the head wasn't attached to a body.

Bernadette's face, glimpsed as her skull rolled forward over… something else, etched in Hailey's mind. Gray skin, soulless gaze, and jaw movement dictated by gravity painted a macabre scene of death.

The head thudded against the wall at the bottom, wedging between the stairs and concrete block.

Hailey's scream shattered the calm. Turning away, she took shallow breaths and wiped away the sight of the teen's cloudy, accusing eyes.

The expression had mimicked shock, her mouth hung open and jaw shifted to the side to match the angle of the head.

Hailey's stomach revolted, sending a sour wad of bile into her mouth.

"Oh, God." Horror didn't begin to describe the sight. "Why?" Small swaths of light unveiled the scene in sections, each piece forming part of the whole.

Recognized by her school picture, Bernadette stared sightlessly into oblivion. Hair once glossy with the promise of youth tangled around her face.

The stench of vomit now filled Hailey's mind. She'd expected the probability of finding a dead animal, but not a human.

Casper's flashlight slipped from her fingers to careen off the nearest shelf and thud on the floor. Its beam exposed a pasty white leg covered in part by a ripped piece of fabric from a colorful party dress.

"Bernadette." Hailey had no other words when snatching up the dropped light.

The steps seemed to multiply as she bolted up toward fresh air. She made it in time to crouch on all fours and vomit.

Beside her, Casper fumbled her phone then scrounged to pick it up. "Shit. Shit. Shit. Why…? I couldn't see it all."

"Don't know. Right now, I don't wanna know."

Gunther brushed against Hailey and nuzzled her side, offering the comfort of his presence. She buried her forehead against his shoulder and held on tight.

Slow, deep breaths helped calm another rush of acid. In the back of her mind, she'd feared someone might find the girl dead.

She just didn't figure to be the one.

Once she collected her thoughts, she pressed Casper back. "Listen. You can't be here when I call this in. Authorities can't know you were with me. Got it?" Hailey snatched the kid's phone and shoved it in her shirt pocket. "Go. We'll talk tomorrow."

But she knew there was a body down there.

According to Hailey's research, Casper had only been in the county for a handful of weeks, hence shouldn't know about a root cellar beneath the ornate planter on an abandoned, desolate farm.

She marked Casper's progress crossing the field and disappearing into the dark. Animated gestures and head movements suggested half of an agitated interaction.

She's either mentally unstable or more likely, talking to spirits.

Chapter Seventeen
Hailey

Stark flashing lights strobed the fields and reflected off the house and barn. One phone call turned the farm into a sea of semi-organized chaos.

In the aftermath of discovery, Lieutenant Colson cast frequent glances between Hailey and Leigh, always with a frown. Maybe because he was new, or maybe he always had a stick up his ass, but the tightness of his jaw promised future upbraiding for at least one of them.

Trenton sat Hailey in his car after ascertaining she wasn't injured. Waiting would've felt demeaning if exhaustion hadn't shut her down. Leaning her head against the window, she couldn't close her eyes without experiencing flashbacks of Bernadette's slack mouth, flies, and the need to vomit. Either memory or imagination served up details of insects feasting on flesh.

Gunther sat on the back seat and watched the commotion from his open window. Frequent nudges against her neck detailed his concern.

A tap on the glass snapped her eyes open and sent her heart racing. Swiveling in place, she noted Trenton's half-grin before regret overtook his expression.

"Hey, we good to go?" Hailey stepped out when he opened the door, followed by Gunther who hopped over the seat.

A bottle of water thrust in her hand accompanied his nod down the road. "Take a walk with me."

This doesn't bode well.

"Is Lieutenant asswipe—"

"We're fine. C'mon."

He'd pulled this maneuver once before when imparting bad news to save her from the humiliation of breaking down in front of others. As a kid, she'd fallen off her bike. He'd helped her up, taken her to the house, and cleaned her cuts.

His jaw remained tight, as if he couldn't loosen it or find the right words.

"Hailey…" He handed her a small chocolate bar and waited until she took a bite. "It'll help combat low sugar."

"Spit it out. I'm not a child with a boo-boo."

Slight irritation flashed across his face, caught by a strobe of blue light. Just as quickly, guilt, pain, or some other misplaced emotion took its place.

"The body you found—"

"Was Bernadette. Right? I'm not going crazy."

"You're right, but that's not all. There was another body underneath."

"What? Who? I didn't look." Hailey dropped her candy bar. No surprise she'd missed anything else present.

Trenton retrieved the snack and stuffed the remains in her backpack. "Since it's been there a while, we'll need forensic confirmation."

Acid roared up her throat for the second time that night. Lightheadedness threatened her ability to stand until Trenton slid his arm around her shoulders and urged her closer. She shoved him away and continued walking.

"It's my dad. Isn't it?" She couldn't bear to look in her friend's eyes and see pity. Bending over to give Gunther a hug, she tunneled her fingers in his long hair and rubbed her cheek against his head.

"We think so. His driver's license, credit cards, and insurance card were in the wallet."

"All this time. He never ran away. He was murdered and stuffed in a root cellar."

Gunther chuffed and nudged her leg when she straightened.

"Was he… dismembered too?"

"Appears so." Trenton turned her to face him just as her legs started to buckle.

She absorbed his strength through arms circling her waist and hugging tight. Holding on for dear life, she took slow, deep breaths, willing her heart and stomach to calm. Her mind whirled with chaotic thoughts, but she drew sustenance from their years of friendship.

"They weren't killed there. No blood." Against her wishes, her mind continued to process the scene.

"Yeah. I'm so sorry, Sparkles. Really."

It was a name of long ago, born of comradery and a childhood bond. A time of security when nothing could bruise her heart.

"How long?" An angry swipe removed the tears from her cheeks as she breathed in the comfort of his presence.

"The coroner can tell us more, but it looks like he may have been there the whole time. Jesus. I know you've always wanted an answer. Just not this one."

"It's why I went into investigative work."

"Sometimes the answers we seek and want aren't the ones we need, and rarely the ones we get."

"I want to be the one to tell Mom. Before the local grapevine does."

"All right. We'll go tonight."

"I wanted to confront him someday."

"To get rid of the anger you've always carried. He didn't leave you, not in the way you've thought."

"Guess I'll have to rethink my abandonment issues." Her chuckle held no humor.

"Guess so. Listen, I've already talked with Leigh. Let's go."

"You don't have to stay and referee this circus?"

"No. This is county jurisdiction so far. I offered to help, which they reluctantly accepted."

"Because of the resources you bring to the table."

"Yes. I think Colson's anxious about a possible serial killer in his midst, but it gives me the *in* to hang around and keep an eye on you and my sister."

"If she heard you say that, she'd kick your ass."

"Yeah, she'd try."

"You always hold back with us, why?"

Trenton uttered one word that said it all. "Family."

"Which has always meant something different for you than for me." She envied the fact he had brothers and sisters.

"Yes, but at least you see more than one side to a situation. You've kept an open mind despite your aversion to commitment."

Hailey rerouted the conversation to safer territory with, "Lots of people knew about that root cellar. The Melfords never made a secret of it. Mr. Melford went into a nursing home right before Dad disappeared."

"I'm hoping forensics will give us some DNA other than yours."

"That wasn't just murder, Trent. That was sadism." Hailey thought about Casper's involvement to date. A few pieces aligned loosely but didn't form a picture. It would help to know what her counterpart was investigating.

"Vodou?" Trenton queried softly.

"I don't know. If so, it stemmed from what you'd call black magic, something I'm not well-versed in."

"Okay. Sorry I had to ask."

Hailey shrugged. "I wouldn't have come out here if not for the truck pulled from the lake."

"True. Still can't connect Bernadette with this place, though. She's too young to have known the Melfords." Trenton tightened his arm over her shoulder as they continued walking.

"Do you think the killer wanted us to find the bodies? Yet that doesn't make sense to me. If he were going to flaunt his intelligence, he would've done it years ago." Again, she thought about Casper's prescience but couldn't reconcile the tidbits of information and how they fit.

"Bernadette's boyfriend wouldn't have a motive to kill your father. Sides, he was only eight when Dad—left."

"*Hmm,*" Trenton agreed.

"I wouldn't think his family would be involved, but you're the one with fed training."

"Regardless, I am going to sit down again with Kenny tomorrow."

"I want to go too. I just don't see any link or common denominator between them." Hailey's thoughts tangled in a knot she couldn't unwind.

"I don't either, now. How about we get your statement. I'll help you, then we'll go to your mom's house."

"All right. C'mon, fur ball. Let's get this done. I'm sure Mom's got a snack for you."

The minute her mother opened the door, her shoulders slumped, and her eyes misted. "Leigh?"

"Is fine, Mom." Hailey bit the inside of her cheek to keep the tears at bay.

So many years passed before her mother's grief had lessened to let another man in her life, albeit kept at arm's length. Hailey wasn't the only one with issues stemming from her father's disappearance.

"Dad." One word said it all.

Her mother was well-known in the community through efforts to reach out to those in need, branding her either Vodou priestess or angel of mercy. Half would support her, the other half would condemn.

"Come in and sit. There's coffee in the fridge."

Gunther led the way to the kitchen, where he sat by the freezer, his routine and signal that snacks would make everything better.

When offered a cooked, frozen, bite-size treat kept for canine visitors, he took it with gentle care.

Cecile knelt and accepted his scent rub. His greeting of sliding his forehead down her back and across her shoulders, licking at her neck, and chuffing his low greeting lent obvious comfort.

Once they'd sat on the sofa, the night's events unfolded with her mother's fingers tight around her cup, alternately gripping and relaxing.

Few details were available, which wasn't what Cecile needed or wanted. Instead, an outpouring of memories, both good and bittersweet, added specifics to Hailey's knowledge in rounding out an adult's perspective of her father.

"He confided in me the night he disappeared. I think he knew there was a chance he wouldn't make it back." Cecile took the handkerchief Trenton offered. "Said he had a gambling debt too big to pay off with money. A man offered him a way to clear it all using his art skills—but wouldn't say how."

"He was an up-and-coming artist, as I remember," Trenton said.

"He was quite good and hoped to trade teaching for painting to earn a living. He could've done it. I'd assumed he'd gotten such an offer, except, he wasn't happy about it."

"Was he asked to forge a painting's likeness?" Trenton set his cup down and leaned forward, elbows resting on his knees.

"I—I don't know. He was so tight-lipped about it."

"Who was the man, Mom? Do you remember him, or anything that might help us find him?" Hailey's thoughts turned to Henri and the unfinished portrait in the antique store.

"Your father wouldn't tell me, said it was for our protection." She blew her nose then tendered a sad smile. "I remember he went into your room and just sat while you slept. He loved you so very much."

"Do you know where he gambled, Mrs. A?"

"No. Originally, it was just a group of friends, hosted at various participant's houses, until he traded up. To what and where, he never said."

"Maybe some of the original group would know, Mom. Who were they?"

As her mother rattled off several names, Hailey made notes on her phone.

"How did my husband die?"

"We don't know yet. It might be a week before our lab can confirm the cause," Trenton advised.

When they'd finished talking, Hailey took their cups to the kitchen, then rinsed and put them in the dishwasher. Having something to do with her hands kept her from wringing them.

"Sweetheart, why don't you stay over? I know you're not going to sleep, but if you go home, you'll spend the night doing research. I could use some company."

Hailey started to refuse, but couldn't after seeing her mom's expression. "Okay. If Trenton can pick me and Gunther up in the morning."

"No problem. I'll be here at nine."

"Make it eight and join us for breakfast." Cecile's watery smile didn't reach her eyes. "I made *poutine à trou* today for the Pinther family, plus extra. You remember them, don't you, Hailey?"

"Yes. Mr. Pinther was the firefighter who rescued a family dog during a house fire on Cantner Street." Hailey wiped her hands and propped her hip against the kitchen bar.

"Thanks, Mrs. A. Baked apple dumplings at eight it is." Trenton hugged them both then headed for the door. Before closing it, he warned, "Hailey, don't stay up all night on your mom's laptop. Ya hear?"

Chapter Eighteen
Hailey

Hailey sat on her childhood bed with her mother's laptop in place and Gunther crowding her thigh. Not a thing had changed in her old room. Hand-crocheted white doilies covered both dressers without a speck of dust in sight.

Two pictures taken of a lakeside alligator hung on the far wall. It was the day her father proudly proclaimed her an accomplished photographer. Those were the early years, before tension filled the days and muffled arguments filled the evenings.

Now, news of her father's death on the heels of gambling revelations turned her world upside down.

Her journal detailing case notes to date was at the loft, which meant starting from scratch in summing up what puzzle pieces she'd collected. On the good side, the exercise could uncover different threads that could lead to new sources.

A headache formed behind her right eye. There existed a major piece of the puzzle missing, like the middle of a pinwheel to which all other parts connected and made sense of the whole.

And how is Casper involved?

Mentally listing the facts and adding her father into the timeline formed a bigger picture with no new connections. From her ruminations, a to-do list followed:

Talk to Kenny and his mom.

Follow up with Bernadette's family. Maybe the teen's room contained a clue to her older beau. A second look never hurt.

Talk to my father's gambling friends, find out how and with whom he branched out.

The last item on her list remained questionable. Time had a way of making memories fuzzy.

In addition, Casper's involvement equaled more than a too-curious teen. Hailey doubted it was coincidence she'd shown up both at the antique store and Melford's farm. What was she investigating and how did it tie in?

She referenced an interest concerning investigations. Even so, it didn't explain the strange whispers and uncanny foreknowledge. *Who'd she talked to at Melford's farm?*

If not for finding the vehicle in the lake, Bernadette and her father could've remained hidden for years. According to Trenton, a potential buyer had questioned dual ruts leading to the water's edge.

After pondering the situation, she opened a new window and pulled up the *Hamchet Times* archives. Her friend Laurent could help fill in particulars if she found something of interest.

Could the first teen's disappearance have been a catalyst of some sort? Few secrets stayed buried. Many eventually worked their way to the surface, like a splinter under the skin. First, it would fester and embroil those around the epicenter until one day erupting through a web of lies.

Five years ago, a fourteen-year-old girl was last seen before an afternoon walk a short distance from home. Reports cited finding her glasses and sneakers. The search hadn't started until dusk, with heavy rains washing away evidence police could've examined earlier.

It wasn't until Hailey rubbed her eyes another thought occurred. The missing girl had lived not far from Kenny Landry. Though, at that time, they each would've just entered their teens.

Coincidence?

Those, in real life, were few. There had to be something she was missing.

Police discounted rumors of Sophia running away, supported by family and church friends who knew them. Another possibility existed, though.

A serial killer.

Thousands of forested acres in the vicinity known as the Big Thicket included various parks and National Forests, and provided a killer with ample opportunities to hide a body. Buried or not.

Carrion creatures would've disposed of accessible remains.

When words blurred and her mind failed to focus, she emailed a copy of her notes to herself and shut down her mother's laptop.

Rich scents of coffee and baked pastry snapped her eyes open to find Trenton sitting on the side of her bed with a steaming cup in hand.

He looked weary.

"Morning, sleepyhead. Damn. You don't wake up easy, do you?"

If not for the enticing brew under her nose, she would've smacked him. "No, I don't."

"Your mom said you were on the computer till late."

"How'd she know?"

"Seriously? She has, like, eyes everywhere. You know this."

"Then why are you comfortable walking into a sleeping woman's bedroom and taking a seat on the mattress? What if I'd been naked?"

"Your pjs are always cotton with puppies or dogs on them. It's what you've worn since your sleepovers with my sisters."

"*Hmm*, where's Gunther?"

"I took him out and fed him. While I've been waiting, I also solved world hunger and cured cancer."

"Busy boy. Do you mind letting me get dressed now?"

Trenton studied her expression. If he'd found what he searched for, it didn't show. "And..."

"I did some research last night. Wanna see my notes?" Bouncing ideas off her oldest friend would help her wake up and think things through.

Trenton offered the cup then retrieved the laptop and opened the lid. "Password?"

"Acadianjazz, one word." Her mom's penchant for music normally pervaded every room of the house. She smiled at the soft strains drifting through the open door even now.

Unlike some men who employed the hunt and peck method at a keyboard, Trenton could probably out-type both genders. She gave him a minute to review her lists.

"The missing teen from years prior. You think it's related?"

"Don't know. Leigh and I have been working both cases, and someone—or *someones*— decided to target me. Either the killer doesn't know who's working on what, or they're connected and he's warning us. Until last night, I thought you might be a target, but I don't know now."

"Neither do I, Sparkles. Neither do I."

"I need to meet Laurent at Bouchard's for lunch. He was covering the lake scene yesterday for the *Hamchet Times*. It'd be nice to compare notes."

"Nice you two help each other. I didn't think that was a thing."

"We do, and sometimes it makes a difference. He knows everybody and their brother-in-law, along with their complete social, medical, and financial history. He and Mom are the town's walking encyclopedias. As far as competition, well, I generally work for a client. Clients don't like notoriety. Hence, less conflict of interest."

* * * *

Trenton

"Your mom said Victor called her this morning." Trenton slowed the truck to pull out of the driveway and onto the paved road leading out of town.

He wanted information, but more, he wanted to protect the friend who'd always held his heart.

"Yeah, my ex is pretty insistent. Why is it men wait until they think you're in crisis mode to swoop in and swear they've changed?" Hailey sipped her coffee and hummed her appreciation.

"You really want an answer? You know how I feel about him."

"But I've never understood why. I don't slam your girlfriends."

Trenton ignored her jibe and bit his tongue. Exposing Victor for a two-bit dirtbag would have to wait for better timing. After all, he hadn't determined if the mudbugger was the one who left the totem in Hailey's truck and/or took a pot shot at them on the bayou. Yet.

If he knew more about the religion devoted to deities and ancestors, he'd open a conversation with Hailey. As it stood, he had a better resource, although inaccessible at the moment.

Hailey's mother would do anything to protect her daughter and would probably confront her about Victor after Trenton's snooping. Until he had substantial proof of the ex-boyfriend's wrongdoing, he couldn't involve either woman.

Instead, he took the high road. "I think circumstances change, but not people. Say—someone has a spot of luck and elects a new course for their life. I don't think it means they've changed, just that their direction altered course because of the circumstances."

"Meaning they could revert back to where they started with another change in status or prospects." Hailey nodded, seeming to think it over.

"Exactly."

"Which doesn't necessarily mean that *would* happen, just that it's possible." She was talking in circles, a sign of nervousness.

"That's the way I see it. As far as Victor is concerned, I've always had trouble seeing him as loyal."

"He's charming and knows how to manipulate, but he's sincere in the moment, too," Hailey qualified it with a shrug.

"Yeah, an equal opportunity lover. Leigh might shoot him if you consider getting back together."

"I can't think about that now. There's so much going on."

"Snap decisions and high emotions don't go well together. If you need to talk things out, my phone is always on, Sparkles."

They'd been friends too long to argue about an ex, especially when she needed a sounding board. His family had all but adopted her as a child, which made him the older brother she never had.

"Thanks. My research last night began with the missing girl five years ago. Since my dad's been gone for twice that time, I don't think there's a direct connection."

"The girls might be linked together other than through school. We just don't see it yet." Trenton took his foot off the accelerator, slowing to make a turn.

As he sped up, the radio snapped on of its own accord. Soft strains of an old song, "Love Story," filled the cabin.

Hailey spewed coffee as Trenton punched the radio button. "Your truck's haunted by a seventies hippy."

"Faulty wiring." Heat singed Trenton's cheeks. He couldn't look Hailey in the eye and was glad when he could take an unfettered breath. Though strange, some things were best ignored.

"Last night I couldn't find anything that would even be considered a loose bond. I searched until I fell asleep on the keyboard. Oh, but there is one other thing, a kid from the school I'd like you to check out. Your background checks are more thorough." Hailey shared a few details about Casper, omitting the student's involvement at the antique store or Melford's farm.

"How's she involved?"

"Probably not. Just curious."

"Bernadette went to the school for gifted kids, but your dad taught at Beaumont High," Trenton said, searching his mind for possible connections. "Maybe they had a mutual friend?"

"I want to figure out what that boy's hiding. I did talk to Laurent. He filled in a little detail about the family. The mom's always been a heavy drinker. The parents got divorced before he moved back east. Neither Kenny nor his mom have contact with him. There was no settlement since she was the one with money. The father just walked away and washed his hands of both."

"Charming." His thoughts circled back to Victor, the same type of man.

Each road of good intention led to hell, just as sure as Trenton's intent to protect a friend stemmed from the heart.

Hailey had stood strong through her father's disappearance, his first heartbreak, her triumph of being the first in the family to graduate from college, and his acceptance into the FBI. Would it stand against his discovery in Victor's house?

Passion for another was fine—unless it bordered on obsession. Victor's objectives weren't yet clear.

One thing was certain. The ex-gator hunter turned crawfish farmer was bad news all the way around. Always looking for the easy way out, the younger man needed a loan to start his farm, according to an off-record conversation with a local banker.

"You're quiet. You're the kind my mom said to watch out for."

"Your mom adores me." Trenton felt as comfortable with Hailey's mom as his own family.

"Yeah, more than me. What's up?"

"Just trying to make sense of this web of facts. Maybe this is more about location than the people involved."

"Explain."

"Look at where we are." Trenton gestured to the thick woods on either side of the road. "Two miles from Landry's house. Five times that distance from town."

Hailey shrugged. "So?"

"And the cold case missing teen lived one mile from here."

"Your point? You couldn't possibly suspect Landry. He was too young, unless you're thinking about the father."

"Doubtful from what I've learned, but the girl sure didn't run away. She couldn't see much without her glasses, and she didn't have a second pair."

"Could Bernadette be somehow connected to your psychopathic killer from Pennsylvania?"

"Thought about that. My gut says no. Not only are the MOs vastly different, but the killer didn't hold Bernadette prisoner, he simply killed her in a way befitting a dark ritual."

Trenton turned into Landry's driveway. He still hadn't figured out how to broach the topic uppermost on his mind, protecting Hailey from her own good-natured need to help others.

Victor was a user, a collector, a connoisseur of unique and exceptional finds. He'd have no compunction about asking Hailey to go into debt on his behalf. Like the crocodile's eye mounted in the ring he wore, the man lacked depth perception, or depth of soul. He'd never seen Hailey's value other than as a unique conquest or means to an end.

Trenton parked beside a late model pickup and sighed. "We need to have a talk later."

"Look. If it's about my dad, I'm okay. I appreciate you hanging around yesterday evening, but I'm good."

"You're still mad at your mom."

"She lied, by omission."

"She was trying to protect you."

"I don't need protecting." Hailey hopped out and waited for Gunther to do the same. In the shade of a spreading oak, she put him in a down stay where he could enjoy the morning breeze.

This time when Trenton mounted the steps, Kenny Landry came out on the porch to greet them.

"What do you want now? We answered your questions."

"Just a few follow-ups. Mind if we come in?" Trenton nodded toward the screen door.

"Fine, but you can't stay long. I have to go into town soon. I'm gonna start cleaning up the antique store."

Defensiveness appeared to be the young man's virtual armor. Condemned by the town's residents without a trial, he'd been ostracized, according to Hailey's friend at the local paper.

Kenny led them to the kitchen where his mother sat at the table with a large mug of coffee warming her hands. On the counter behind her, a bottle of coconut rum sat half-empty, its cap nearby.

"Good morning, Mrs. Landry." Hailey offered her hand again like she'd done with Kenny, both refused.

Kenny gestured to the seat.

"If you say so." The blank stare from bloodshot, watery eyes took in her surroundings. Her brow furrowed as if trying to recall some long-forgotten detail.

"Ask your questions." Kenny capped the bottle of liquor and set it in the cabinet.

It appeared the boy took care of his mother and sister as he scraped two plates of uneaten food and put a third in the dishwasher. Trenton assumed the youngest had eaten. After wiping down the counter with a sponge, he tossed it in the sink and turned to lean back against it, insolence his new armor.

"You heard about Melford's farm?" Trenton began, wanting to see if the mother would rise to his defense.

"Yeah, I heard." The teen swiped a hand over his eyes. "I swear I didn't have anything to do with her death. You found Hailey's father too. That should tell you whoever killed Bernadette also killed her dad." Kenny gestured toward Hailey. "Half the town could've known about that root cellar."

"Seems everyone has the details," Hailey muttered. "Bernadette wasn't the first girl to disappear without a trace."

A hiccup followed the sudden gasp from Mrs. Landry.

In response, Kenny pushed off from the counter and stood behind his mother to rest a hand on her shoulder.

"So, now you not only think I killed Bernadette, but another girl too? I was a kid when that other one vanished. She probably took off. Her dad used to wail on her when he got drunk."

"Like your father did to you?" Trenton's prior search through records turned up two incidences where police arrived at the house to find a battered boy.

"Yeah, well, he gave that up when I got hold of his shotgun and told him if he ever did it again, I'd either shoot him or cut his throat while he slept."

"That's one way to solve a problem." Hailey turned her attention back to Kenny's mother. "You know something about the other disappearance."

It was a statement Trenton couldn't confirm but intended to explore since Hailey opened the conversation. "They lived a mile down the way," he hedged.

Mrs. Landry squirmed in her seat. Trenton hadn't missed the tightening of her mouth and eyes.

"So what?" Kenny's attempt to draw attention to himself and away from his mother didn't wash in Hailey's mind either, judging by her intense focus.

"Police questioned you both at the time, didn't they? I read that your son knew the girl. They used to go fishing together." Hailey directed her inquiry toward the woman barely holding it together, refusing to meet anyone's gaze.

"Guilt is a terrible weight. Over time, it can crush the strongest spirit," Trenton added.

"Leave her alone. You have no idea of her strength, or what she's endured to keep us together."

Mrs. Landry hiccupped again, placing her hand over the one on her shoulder. "Kenny. It's time. I can't live with this any longer, and you've come of age. I'm so sorry."

"No, Mom. Not another word. We'll get a lawyer." Again, the son took the lead, a model adopted years prior, physically at least.

"It was an accident. I was supposed to pick her up. I was," she hiccupped, "...late."

Mother and son's gazes met, one asking for forgiveness, the other shaking his head in pleading for silence.

"Your father and I had just had an argument."

"You mean you'd just finished applying makeup to cover new bruises." Hailey held her hand out to offer support.

This time, it was accepted with a watery smile.

Hailey closed her eyes and bent her head, as if suffering a sudden great weight. A small mewl escaped her lips.

Trenton steeled his nerves, unable to help either woman.

The scene unfolding in her vision must be hell.

"I never saw her. I knew I'd hit something, but figured it was a deer or fox, whatever."

Hailey squeezed her hand for encouragement. When no words came, she gently prodded, "Sophia's parents?"

"Said she was heading toward our house. I didn't get out of the car. Her mom was weeding the garden in the side yard when I arrived."

"And when you got home?" Trenton grimaced, his thoughts completing the scene of horror.

"She wasn't here, so Kenny and I backtracked. I saw her beside the road, a hundred yards back. She was so still, already dead."

"Where'd you bury her body?" Trenton directed his question to Kenny, the boy who'd had to grow up fast and strong to protect his mother. Yet, he couldn't shield her from guilt or its consequences.

"McFadden Wildlife Refuge. A place she and I used to go to find peace and quiet. She liked that spot." Kenny fisted one hand at his side, the other clutching his mother's shoulder. "Mom." Tears brimmed his eyes, but he refused to let them fall.

The mother wiped her cheeks and inhaled deep, letting it out slowly. She met Trenton's gaze with a lucid stare. "Thank you. Her parents deserve closure."

Due to the event's local nature, Jefferson County Sheriff's Department would handle the investigation. Both mother and son waited quietly until Leigh's arrival.

Chapter Nineteen
Trenton

Trenton reached across the scarred wooden table in Bouchard's Café to briefly squeeze Hailey's hand. She'd obviously *seen* something horrid at the Landry house, worse than what his experiences could provide.

"Wanna talk about it? I know you're very selective with what you touch and what touches you."

"No." She didn't withdraw her hand and didn't cringe at whatever she experienced from contact with him.

"You need another dream catcher to hang from your bedroom ceiling?" He wouldn't pry into her visions, regardless of the circumstances, but he could offer support.

"With my luck, it would backfire. No, I just need some coffee and a break to clear my head. Too much, too fast, know what I mean?"

"It's a lot to take in. You've solved the case of Sophia's disappearance, though. Good work."

The lull between morning and lunch crowds at the café meant empty tables where servers restocked condiments and meal fixings. It provided a sense of normalcy.

"Not sure how Leigh's boss is gonna take that. Either I'm a meddling PI or I'll receive begrudging respect from Lieutenant I-hate-private-snoops. What d'ya think will happen to Kenny and his mom?"

"Mrs. Landry will face charges of at least vehicular manslaughter and tampering with evidence. It'll be up to the DA how far he wants to take it. As far as Kenny's involvement, that'll be up to the judge. He was thirteen, but juvenile delinquency will be a part of his record."

"Leigh's on her way out to talk to Sophia's parents. That's one part of her job I'd really hate. Oh, and thanks for dropping Gunther off at the office. Elizabeth might be a ditzy receptionist, but she loves my boy."

"No problem."

"I feel sorry for Kenny and his mom. They each got dealt a crap hand by fate and never saw their way through."

"This may be the only way she can rebuild her life. The guilt will always be there, but at least now she can deal with it and maybe, someday, try to make amends."

"Sophia's parents get closure, unexpected after all this time, but at least they'll know what happened." Hailey turned her mug round and round, her gaze viewing something far beyond the earthly plane.

"Kenny's mom will finally get the counseling she needs. It'll take time for the family to heal." Trenton wondered how long it would take for Hailey and her mother's pain to ease.

"So, Bernadette's killer dumped her body in a root cellar. Sophia died by accident. Looks like the girls' deaths weren't connected in the way I'd thought. Where does that leave us?"

Both leaned back to ponder the situation.

Antoinette Blanchert, the server who'd crushed on Trenton throughout high school, arrived to offer refills. Now divorced, she flipped her sleek ponytail over one shoulder and batted thick-fringed natural lashes. Five bright-red manicured fingers rested on Trenton's forearm to gain his attention.

"Anything else I can get you, Trenton? It's been so long since you've visited. Are you here to stay?" Hope radiated from the smile showing perfect pearly whites.

"I think we're good. Thanks, and I'm just visiting."

The brilliant smile faltered as her gaze dropped to Hailey's hand in his. "You should stick around a while. I could show you how things have changed."

As if to prove her superiority, she gestured toward Hailey. "Take, for instance, Victor. He was in here earlier this week with a pretty little blonde from upstate. You know how he's never been able to turn down generous assets." A careless shrug belied the malevolence radiating from her gaze.

With a shrug and condescending smile directed at Hailey, she turned to leave.

Hailey chuckled. She'd never revealed any romantic interest in Trenton but remained as protective as a momma bear. "That's one woman whose claws you don't want to experience on your back. Trust me."

"Thanks, I think I can handle myself just fine."

Tinkling of chimes over the door announced a new arrival. Laurent's energy bounced through the room to the beat of his smooth stride. He slid into the booth beside Hailey as the waitress circled back.

"Hey, cutie. Looking good today. That silver necklace really brings out your beautiful eyes," Laurent said.

Any mother of a gay male would latch onto Laurent for all she was worth. He'd never met a day or a person he couldn't improve.

After placing his order, the journalist turned his brilliant white smile on Trenton, evaluating. A slight nod and hint of disappointment revealed the workings of the younger man's mind. His face turned somber as he wrapped Hailey in a hug.

Their easy comradery raised Laurent's worth tenfold in Trenton's eyes.

"Trenton, thank you taking care of *ma fille*. My boys' night out yesterday was ill-timed. I'm so sorry, Hailey."

"Laurent. We've talked about this. Trouble and chaos never keep schedules." Hailey accepted Laurent's light kiss on the crown of her head.

"I know. I know. Have fun when you can. Someone needs to check your back for trackers, *chère*. One would say guaranteed heart attack," he up-righted one palm, "...the other would say stroke," Laurent finished, tipping up his other hand.

She chuckled. "Thanks for coming. You gonna write this up for the paper?"

"*Oui*, certainly not one of my more upbeat stories, but yes, I will try and do a good send off for Sophia. After here, I'll go talk to her parents. I've known them for years. As far as your papa—"

"How'd you know Sophia?" Hailey changed the subject and gripped her mug tighter.

"Her folks took an extended education class I was in. Remember the refinishing furniture phase?"

"Yeah, I do. Jeez, Laurent, you know everybody," Hailey grumbled.

Laurent lifted one shoulder in nonchalance. "Not to be short, but there's a lot on my plate today. I followed up with the sheriff's department while you were at your mom's. The truck at Melford's was stolen but registered to a man from Houston. The thief destroyed the VIN number on the dash, but not the one on the engine block."

"Good work, you. Well done. And the man's body?" Hailey asked.

"No ID back yet. But it seems the thief kept the vehicle for an entire week. I don't know why or for what purpose." Laurent's expression fell, his short-lived enthusiasm deflated.

"Okay. Well, we'll wait on his ID, but they still might find trace evidence on the truck. It wasn't submerged that long." Hailey fidgeted until Laurent patted her shoulder and withdrew his hand.

"It's possible. I've read they can find latent prints for about five days. Though less on smooth planes like glass, metal, and paint-covered surfaces," Laurent suggested.

"What about sebaceous prints?" Hailey's question earned a dropped jaw from her friends. "What? I read, too."

"Okay, assuming the thief had recently come in contact with an oily surface—" Trenton began.

"Like maybe he's a mechanic?" Laurent asked, accepting his drink from the server.

"Or a painter." Hailey grimaced, no doubt thinking of her father. "When I was in the antique store, I found a painting leaning against the wall, a special project my dad painted for Mom. It was of Leigh and me in front of the bayou."

"And you're just now telling me?" Trenton leaned forward and placed both hands flat on the table.

"Sorry. I-I... there's been too much happening."

"Dear God. No wonder Colson looks like he has a constant headache," Laurent mused.

"We can't get a warrant without evidence. You know, the type a judge would accept." Trenton's explanation held as much frustration as determination. "And you are not breaking in there again. Hear me?"

"Yeah, I got it," Hailey mumbled. "But Henri did say I could stop by *any time*. Doesn't that count?"

"I wouldn't test any judge on that note if I were you. For instance, was the door unlocked? If not, did you have a key, as in, *given* to you by the owner or manager?" The time had long passed when Trenton could keep his badge out of the picture. Hamchet's Agent in Charge had approved his temporary reassignment to investigate the current situation.

"But they're obviously linked," Hailey griped.

Laurent nudged her shoulder. "We will figure this out, *ti kras.*"

"Yeah... I'm not so little anymore."

Trenton retrieved his cell and swiped the screen as it buzzed. "Hold on a sec." Reading the detailed toxicology report brought a surge of old memories to the surface.

He didn't recognize the specific names but knew both Hailey and Leigh would. The pair had grown up with a fascination for indigenous plants, learning much from Hailey's mother, a native expert.

"Well, are you gonna talk or do we have to wrestle your phone away from you?" Hailey tapped the table for emphasis.

"The toxicology report is back."

"That quick? How? I thought it'd take weeks." Laurent wrapped his arm around Hailey's shoulder again, for support.

"Frequently, it does, but the ME started with a specific search. Both Bernadette and your dad were killed with the same agent..." His words drifted off as he realized Hailey's likely interpretation.

"Don't you dare say you suspect my mother. She did not, *would* not, use her knowledge to kill. She wouldn't."

"You know I wouldn't think that, and neither would my sister."

"But the spouse is always the top suspect, and as a descendant of La Belle Fontaine, the police will go to her first," Laurent spoke the words on each of their minds.

"Leigh wouldn't contemplate that. Neither would the other detectives," Hailey defended her family. "But the new lieutenant might go after Mom for quick closure," she finished.

"Lateral transfers are not the norm down here. Word has it Colson goes by the rules, but he's a ballbuster and wants to prove his worth. He's young." Laurent cast an apologetic glance toward Hailey.

"The good news, at least, is he also has a thing for Leigh." Hailey exhaled a deep breath.

"What?" Trenton reared back to study his straight-faced friend. "That's ridiculous. He's always riding her."

Laurent waggled one hand back and forth. "Exactly the thoughts on his mind. I'm never wrong when it comes to these things. He is fighting it, but the attraction is there, nonetheless. Unfortunately, it won't protect your *mere*. This isn't good. We should warn Cecile before she's taken in for questioning, *chére*."

Trenton added, "We'll support her through this. She'll be fine. However, she should have a lawyer present. I'll call Donnelly."

"I agree. But let me stay with her." Small lines crinkled the corners of Laurent's eyes and mouth. "I can smooth the way between you and the lieutenant. You shouldn't make an enemy of him so soon. Plus, your mom likes me better. Remember?"

Trenton reinforced the idea with a nod. The attorney he'd call belonged to a top-notch firm out of Beaumont. "The last thing we need is for you to get arrested for slugging a cop. C'mon, Hailey. You ride with me out to the Bordelon's home after a quick stop by your mom's. I need your help to talk with Bernadette's mother without her husband hovering. We'll divide and conquer."

He remained quiet as they drove toward the bayou. Bernadette's family wouldn't have vented the worst of their grief yet, but timing of interviews couldn't wait when dealing with murder.

When he cut the engine and turned to face Hailey, he still couldn't find the right words for comfort. Her world had gone from chaotic to hell, with more strife on the horizon.

He settled for addressing the most immediate concern. "Cecile will be okay. Your mom is strong."

"I should be there for her. She's always been there for me."

"Your presence wouldn't help, nor would she appreciate it under the circumstances. She needs a little solitude now, Sparkles, though Laurent will be there soon."

"He deals with difficult situations well, and she loves him, too."

"We'll make more progress out here, finding answers. When we go back over tonight, we'll take Gunther, a bag of popcorn, and a movie." He hoped it wasn't a newer version of the last one he'd watched with her.

Hailey nodded. "Okay. Let's find the link between my dad and Bernadette."

Mrs. Bordelon sat on the porch in a rocker and watched them expectantly. Sorrow written in her furrowed brow accompanied her invitation for a cool drink.

Hailey climbed the steps and offered a hug of condolence. "I'm so sorry we couldn't bring her home to you."

"You have suffered your own loss, *bebe*. We will heal in time. Nature provides all."

Hailey sniffed and pulled away. "Thank you. It doesn't help to know, though, does it?"

"Yet we won't stop searching for answers until we have every last detail. Eh?" Babette gestured them each to a rocking chair, set up in a circle.

"You knew we'd come." Hailey lowered herself into the seat and nodded toward the empty glasses by the pitcher.

"Yes. We share some things in common, if different aspects. Sit, I will tell you more about my Bernadette and her gift."

"First, you have to know my dad didn't have anything to do with either Sophia or Bernadette's death." Hailey rubbed her forehead, as if unable to find further words to clear her family.

"I know that. I've always known. I met your father several times. He loved you and Cecile so very much. He didn't have a killer's heart or mind."

Trenton, quiet until now, wanted to grant the women time alone, without his presence. "Mrs. Bordelon, would you mind if I took another look at Bernadette's room? Sometimes, small things you wouldn't think about offer clues to unraveling a mystery."

"You may. Enrique won't be back for hours, so take your time while I commiserate with Hailey."

Trenton nodded and made his way inside listening to a mother's pride in detailing her child's accomplishments.

"Bernadette's gift ensured a heightened sensory experience. She described numbers in unique shapes with different colors and textures. If asked to compute twenty-six to the ninth power, she'd spew correct results out within seconds by various associations..."

Trenton had read a report on the teen's gift, amazed at how fast her brain must've worked. Synesthetes, as they were called, were reported to "see" music as colors when they heard it. Some could "taste" fine textures in various shapes of round or sharp when eating foods. It occurred when information designated to stimulate one of a person's senses, stimulated several instead.

The effects held far-reaching ramifications sought by scientists and corporate headhunters alike. The teen had a lucrative future until a killer altered her path. Was cutting off her head part of a dark magic ritual or a reference to her gift?

He had to find some obscure tie, if not to a local psychopath, then to someone else, someone part of a bigger picture.

Open bedroom windows invited the slight breeze along with tidbits of the women's conversation. He wondered if Babette's intent to sweep away the aura of death helped. Everyone grieved in their own way, at their own pace.

"Wow. You must be so proud of her." Hailey's tone softened with wonder.

"Always. Tell me, can you feel her presence?"

After a long pause, Hailey answered, *"Yes, but I also feel a certain... restlessness."*

"Do not worry. You'll come into your talent soon. Sometimes tragedy creates delay in emerging abilities, and you have suffered more than your share of them."

Tuning out the conversation opposed his instinct to learn more about Hailey's ability but allowed Trenton to concentrate on his task. The daughter's room paralleled the rest of the home—spotless, neat, and organized.

He'd never met a savant before and couldn't imagine the trials of raising one.

A three-dimensional chess set with jade pieces took pride of place in the middle of a wall-to-wall handmade bookshelf. Among the tomes found, math predominated.

Several pictures of her with other teens demonstrated a thread of disinterest with peers. Since her laptop remained with the county's forensics team, he checked the drawers of the old wooden desk. None were locked, either because she didn't hide anything in them or didn't think her parents would invade her privacy. He'd bet on the latter.

A colorful quilted bedspread with matching pillow shams took center stage in the room, beneath which several pairs of shoes peeked from under the bed ruffle.

A small closet held a number of dresses and skirts. Nothing appeared out of order, nor led him to believe she was anything other than a victim.

Spending her weekdays at a school with other gifted youngsters made it likely she'd keep anything of importance at home, away from those with higher intelligence and advanced skills.

Going back to the bookshelf, he studied the picture of Bernadette and the brother she'd lost. In it, neither appeared more than ten years old, standing arm in arm in front of a fishing boat. Their mother stood behind them with a hand around each shoulder, smiling at the photographer.

The frame sat in front of the chess set, indicating its importance. Turning it over, he released the top and side clasps to slide the back out.

As suspected, more photos lay underneath. In the first, Bernadette stood beside Kenny, both smiling wide. The second was of a man standing in front of a small cottage.

Perhaps a family friend?

The last photo set off warning bells.

This teen was definitely *not* what her parents described.

Trenton used his phone to take pictures of the photographs. When he lifted the last one for a closer look, several bills adhering to the back fell to the floor.

Why would she hide money? Three twenty-dollar bills didn't warrant hiding.

In picking up the currency, he held it up to the light streaming through the window. Tilting it back and forth, he failed to see color-shifting ink, from copper to green.

It didn't take ultraviolet light to prove the money counterfeit.

Where would she get this?

With the levels of intelligence and access to the newest technologies, it wasn't an unreasonable stretch to suspect one or more of the students involved in such endeavors. They'd need connections to launder it. A staff member seemed probable, though each underwent thorough scrutiny through background and reference checks.

Could the fake bills have caused a fight between Bernadette and Kenny? He was, after all, a computer genius and could have the skill to pull it off. However, he wouldn't have the raw paper or experience to make a higher-end product.

Trenton wasn't in the habit of carrying evidence bags. Making do, he wrapped the bills in his handkerchief before pocketing them to continue his search.

The chess set was exquisite, each intricate piece hand-carved. Beside it sat a wooden box with an inlaid design around the rim and an elaborate sculpted queen on top.

Not a king. Interesting.

Light in weight, it appeared empty, the clasp without any type of lock. Expectation of finding some other clue inside left him disappointed until noticing the difference in depth compared to the box's outside dimensions.

In setting it down, a soft rattle issued from inside.

Studying the structure, he expected to find a false bottom. What he couldn't see was how to get into it. He'd considered himself decent at solving puzzles. How could he not with four younger siblings, all with a penchant for finding trouble?

Minutes passed where he pushed, pulled, and prodded each corner and along the inlay. Toward the front, a small piece gave way before a slight click sounded.

Inside, a hinged bottom popped up to expose a hidden compartment. A baggie containing dozens of white pills sat nestled on a thin layer of cotton. Lack of numbers or identifying symbols defied their identification. It would take lab analysis.

Grabbing a tissue from the desktop, he wrapped the small baggie and pocketed it too.

Further exploration of the room yielded nothing out of the ordinary.

When he returned to the porch, the women were still reliving fond memories of years past.

"Hey, Trenton. What's that?" Hailey nodded toward the photo in his hand.

"I found this in her room, behind a family picture." Holding it up for Babette to see, he inquired, "Do you know this man?"

"Yes. That is Armond. He teaches art history at her school, but I've never seen that photo before."

"To your knowledge, what was their association?"

"My daughter mentioned him on several occasions. Several students went to him as an unofficial counselor. You'd be surprised how many gifted children are also troubled."

"And Bernadette?" Trenton asked.

"She looked to him for advice. My girl had plans to take the world by storm but didn't have the experience or foresight to make it happen. I think he was one of those people who knew how to communicate with students at their level using their terms. Many listened to him."

"Then it was good she had someone to talk to when not at home." Trenton didn't detail his other finds.

Since Bernadette had hidden the bills, they'd have little or nothing to do with her parents. Another picture was of a local, a well-known dirtbag he intended to keep away from Hailey at all costs.

That and the pills weren't appropriate directions for Hailey's curiosity. Keeping her out of the coming investigation would require help and a bit of luck.

"Is it all right if I hold onto the photo for now? I'll return it in good shape."

"Certainly. If it helps you find her killer. Keep it. Lieutenant Colson said Bernadette was killed with a poison."

"Yes. We don't know much more at this point. I promise I'll fill you in when I can." Trenton nodded to Hailey. "Ready to go, or would you like to stay a little longer? I can circle back. I—"

"I'm ready."

He saw curiosity blazing in her eyes and knew she'd want to drill him as soon as possible.

Chapter Twenty
Trenton

Time spent reminiscing with a kindred soul had softened the visible tension in Hailey's shoulders despite lack of offering clarity to the investigation. Regardless of what her father had or hadn't done, the man had loved his family.

"Thoughts?" Trenton asked, turning on the air conditioning. It was a matter of time before curiosity made her pry, but he hoped to hold back at least one aspect of his morning's finds.

"You look more hopped up than when we snuck into the school cafeteria and replaced sweet peppers with my mom's super hots." Her arched brow equaled a demand of its own.

Redirecting her focus, he said, "I called my folks. They're insistent we all visit; said it's been too long." He hadn't realized how much he missed them until stepping into the Texas heat.

His brothers Jaxon and Asher understood delving into work and not coming up for air. Leigh was the same. His youngest sister was absorbing European culture, delegating family to another realm.

"Nuh, uh. Not happening. What'd you find in Bernadette's room?" Hailey twisted in the passenger seat to face him. "You're hiding something when you go off on a tangent."

Damn.

"I'm just glad you found a like soul to share your burden."

"Pretend you're talking to someone who has sex with other humans. What'd you find?"

That reference brought his thoughts to a stuttering halt. He released a pent-up sigh. She'd always been perceptive. "Only if you *swear* not to go off on your own."

"Sure. Now, spill."

He'd known this was coming, even planned on it. With any luck, divulging two-thirds of his discoveries would distract her from the last. He turned onto the paved road and pulled over to the shoulder.

"Do me a favor and grab a couple of evidence bags from my briefcase on the back seat." From his pocket, Trenton tweezed items taken from Bernadette's room.

He unwrapped the ends of the tissues to expose two of his finds, the bag of pills and a picture of an unknown man standing in front of a cottage.

The other picture he returned to his pocket as it concerned him the most. If she saw it, there'd be no way to stop her from digging so deep she'd end up like her father.

"Drugs, a picture, and money. Jackpot." Hailey bent to examine the picture. "Why'd you take money?" Genuine concern and confusion lit her gaze.

"I didn't take anything of value. Look closer."

"*Oh.*" Hailey whistled low.

"Tilt it back and forth—"

"I know how to do this. Didn't see it coming, though." Specific examination ended with a confused look. "They got the right paper but used the wrong ink? If you're going to all that trouble—"

"Exactly. Not completely professional, but damn close."

"Maybe Armond is the older man Bernadette was seeing on the side. Could be the pills were just shared among friends." Hailey's uncertainty confirmed she'd dig until reaching rock bottom.

"My sister said the kids she interviewed at school were very tight-lipped. The teachers were worse."

Hailey rubbed her jaw, her tell for withholding information.

The trick to getting it came in avoiding direct questions, hence, he waited.

"I remember this guy." Hailey tapped the picture. "Name's Armond Boyér. He taught graphic design at Beaumont High years ago. Girls fell all over themselves for a second of one-on-one time with him."

Trenton frowned then arched a brow in question. "Yet the terrible duo didn't fall into that trap? What made you and Leigh immune? And for the record, I don't remember him."

"We had more sense. He came the year after you graduated, I think." Hailey tapped the photo while pondering. "He quit to go teach at the Gifted Elite. Broke a lot of hearts in leaving. You gonna share all this with Lieutenant Colson?"

Trenton considered the picture he withheld and confirmed the need for a deeper dive into the man's past *and* present record and activities before replying, "Eventually, yes, but not until I prove none of this links to your father. The question on my mind is this. Pills wouldn't be difficult for her to find, but how'd Bernadette get hold of rag paper?"

"Rag paper? Oh, the stuff made from cotton and linen fibers used to make money." Hailey tapped the bag against her hand as if trying to shake loose answers to vital questions.

"When money is made, paper is squeezed with thousands of pounds of pressure during the printing process. It makes the bills thinner and crisper. And since casual counterfeiting bills are made with cellulose paper, a counterfeit pen makes it change color." Trenton gestured to the bills. "That feels like the real deal, one-quarter linen and three-quarters cotton."

"Armond was an art history and graphic design teacher. He never worked with metal, needed if you want to print from plates and not a scanned image. And I wouldn't think he'd be involved with drugs, would you?" Hailey continued to study the items after setting them on the console.

"Nowadays, casual counterfeiters scan and print at home. The problem with normal scanners is they can't replicate the fine lines. Hexagons become blobs that are lighter and messier. Even the best printers lose detail if viewed with a magnifying glass."

"Which Bernadette would research and know," Hailey murmured, deep in thought.

"Another problem. Even high-end printers aren't aligned properly for money, front to back. Negating all that, they won't have the color-shift ink. The bills would look muddy in spots."

"I'm surprised counterfeiters don't bleach real money then reprint it into larger bills."

"Been there, done that." Trenton snorted. "Research Ricky Scott Nelson. He took one and five-dollar bills, masked some of the genuine images, soaked to remove them and denomination numbers, then created a template to photocopy new images from fifty and hundred-dollar bills onto the original currency."

"What about the imprinted watermarks?"

"Didn't have them pre 1996." Trenton eased back onto the deserted road and accelerated.

"I can check the basics of Armond's financial situation, but I don't have FBI resources. If he's hidden valuables and assets within shell companies offshore, they'll be difficult for me to find. That'd be more in your domain," Hailey grumbled.

"Which means you want to snoop inside his house." Hailey had developed workarounds to lack of resources, much to his frustration.

"You're thinking Armond is just her sugar daddy. You didn't find any other link to him in her room?" she asked.

"No. Seems he might be the older lover, but we won't know until we dig deeper. Why don't you take that aspect, and I'll look into the drugs and bills? It'll take time to have both evaluated."

That way you'll stay away from the worst of the danger.

"You're still hiding something. What?"

Trenton cut his gaze back at Hailey, knowing she wouldn't quit or back down. "Leave it, Hailey. You've got enough to keep you busy for now."

"Not a chance. This is all or nothing, and I'm all in. If you don't talk, I'll take what I have to Laurent, who'll put his version in the paper."

"No. Absolutely not. I forbid it. You are not equipped to go after counterfeiters or drug dealers."

"You *forbid*? Since when did you become my guardian?"

"Since your impulsive behavior started getting my sister in trouble. You never could resist a mystery." He wasn't as worried about his sister since the killer hadn't set his sights on her.

"I won't quit. You may be down here for a visit, but I live here. Drugs, counterfeit money? That spells trouble. I can't walk away."

"You're risking your neck for something you shouldn't be involved in, Sparkles."

"I live here. I'm already involved."

"Listen, I'm going out on a limb here with keeping you in the loop. Don't cut it off."

"Talk. Or read about it in the paper."

Trenton ground his teeth and squeezed the steering wheel. "Damn it, Hailey."

Chagrined, Hailey shrugged. "I do appreciate your help. Really. Think about it while I call Mom." Snatching up her cell, she avoided his gaze and swiped the screen.

"Fine. We'll discuss it later." He'd lost the argument before it started. He could refuse giving the information, but it would risk her neck in the long run.

Cecile Arquette answered her cell on the first ring.

"Hey, Mom. How're you holding up?"

A long sigh preceded the low noise she made in her throat as Trenton listened to one side of the conversation.

"Okay. Trenton and I are just heading home, now. Yes, I agree, Leigh's lieutenant is like a dog with a bone."

Again, Hailey used her hands in conversation as much as her voice.

"I had an interesting chat with Bernadette's mom today. Babette is a good soul who's experienced too much loss. I don't know how she keeps her head above water." Her gaze drifted out the window, her fingers twisting in the soft curls of her ponytail. Several nods later, she closed her eyes, her voice going soft. "She shares a lot of your life philosophy, Mom. It was like listening to a milder version of you in a lot of ways."

After a minute, she disconnected the line and shook her head.

Trenton dropped her at her office with a promise of a discussion to come later. Having her residence above her business was convenient but offered easier access from those bearing ill intentions.

A reprieve from her tenacity allotted time to package and send evidence to the lab, along with ordering his thoughts and priorities. They'd been best friends for years, and he still hadn't found a way to divert her focus once she'd latched onto a thread.

She'd already had three near misses, one at the bayou, another while driving away from Landry's house, and then in her own office. He'd walked away from her once but vowed never to do it again. She owned too much of his heart, and he'd die protecting her.

When he parked behind her vehicle at the office, it took several minutes to prepare for the inevitable confrontation.

Gunther greeted him at the first floor business entrance with a sniff and wag of his tail.

At least one friendly face.

Subtle scents of vanilla and an unknown spice attested to Hailey's heritage and use of the space. It wasn't until he approached the receptionist's desk that he noted a competing scent of pine from Elizabeth's candle.

"He doesn't usually accept people so quickly. He must really like you." Elizabeth looked up from her computer and offered a coy smile, her head tilting to the side as she nibbled her bottom lip. "Would you like to share my lunch? Hailey said y'all have been busy." The message in her eyes betrayed another meaning. Gesturing toward the building's rear, she added, "There's a break room in the back..."

"Ah, no thanks. I've got work to do."

Bored with her failed conquest, she shrugged and turned her attention back to the computer screen. "Take the beast, too, if you don't mind. I'm not a zookeeper. He's been super antsy today."

Extricating himself from the situation, Trenton pivoted and headed toward the door with Gunther catching up when he patted his thigh. The wolf dog's curiosity had led to a bonding of sorts.

Out in the hall and climbing the stairs to the loft, he considered his options. If he caved and offered all intel, he'd have to keep a closer eye on her. The idea held merit.

She looked up when he opened the door.

Hailey sat on the window seat, her dark hair haloed by the angle of the sun. "Hey, boy. Sorry I didn't bring you up. I wasn't planning on staying long."

"You got absorbed in your research," Trenton supplied.

"Yeah, going over my notes now. You hungry?" she said after tipping up a plastic cup and tapping the side. The muffled crunch detailed her current choice of snack.

"Let me guess, Captain Crunch?"

"Hey, don't knock the classics. Cereal is fast and portable."

"Thanks, I'll pass. What have you found so far?"

"Not much. Armond is married, one kid, lives within his salary, and carries a moderate amount of debt. I don't think he's our counterfeiter. Just a pervert who likes young girls," Hailey offered with a grimace.

"That's not verified. Just because Bernadette was obviously infatuated, doesn't mean he reciprocated."

"True, but if they were having an affair and she wanted more, maybe he decided to silence her demands."

"Or maybe she got in trouble with her supplier using fake bills."

"That does sound more likely. Won't know until I confront Armond."

"Until *we* confront him," Trenton warned.

"No. This is a woman's intuition thing. Let me ask a question and shake his hand, I'll know. Oh, but I'll need a copy of that photo. I can handle the interview while you dive into his finances."

Trenton sighed knowing he wouldn't win the argument. "Fine, but take Gunther with you. Do you know where he is at the moment?"

"Summer conference for those kids wanting a jump on the next school year."

"Text me when you arrive and when you leave."

Hailey gave him a serious side-eye in lieu of an argument.

"Are you still determined to give your last haunted tour tonight?"

"Take a wild guess, Trenton. And before you say a word, Leigh's coming." She snickered before adding, "I think her lieutenant is also coming."

"Sounds like fun. Don't forget the upcoming meet and greet with my folks. You can bend Asher's ear about swamps and kittens, then turn your focus on Jaxon and computer hacking. Maybe he'll give you a few tips."

The last juicy morsel ensured both Leigh and Hailey would accompany him to the planned cookout. A phone call to each of his brothers would ensure neither would have a conversation that led to more trouble.

At least he'd been granted a stay of execution in divulging the last of his finds from Bernadette's bedroom—a picture of Henri by Bernadette's side.

A mishmash of tourists and locals formed in front of the office with bright-eyed participants eager to begin their tour. The pet-friendly jaunt didn't include any four-legged companions other than Gunther tonight. As usual, he elicited much focus with his size and confident nature.

It wasn't until he made a beeline to the person hidden in part by others that Hailey's internal radar went on alert.

What is Casper doing here? The teen's presence spelled trouble.

Despite the late hour, Hailey wanted her last excursion down memory lane sharing her knowledge of history and folklore to inspire others to continue learning about the rich culture of the bayous.

Too many tourists thought of locals as country hillbillies who distilled liquor while hexing enemies with black magic. Quite the opposite was true, considering the land's raw beauty and the richness of the local fare.

There'd be time tomorrow to sort out the mysteries of drugs, death, and counterfeit money. Tonight, she needed a break, even though half her makeshift family joined the tour in a bout of overprotective fervor.

Leigh used to be a regular, even helped on occasion during college years. Now she stood with Laurent and Trenton, discussing who knew what while glaring daggers at her lieutenant. Her boyfriend was absent.

"Good evening, ladies and gentlemen. Thank you for joining me tonight for a stroll through a part of history rife with passion, betrayal, murder, and mystery."

On average, evening excursions drew more tourists. Tonight, friends and family rounded up the numbers, a bone she'd pick with them in the morning.

As they stood in front of the first house, a little humor added to her dialogue lightened the mood inspired by dim illumination and foreboding quiet. Drawing a light chuckle from some helped her "take the crowd's temperature." This wasn't the venue that honed her talent to read people, but the knowledge came in handy.

Between recounting a gruesome scene of death over lost love, she kept an eye on two twenty-something-year-old men near the back. Frequent leers in Casper's direction, lack of coordination, and whispered comments dictated trouble brewing. Alcohol on the later tours wasn't prohibited, but drunkenness wasn't tolerated.

During the stroll to their next destination, a slight nod warned Leigh to keep an eye on the inebriated souls.

Her friend crowded closer as Hailey weaved her next tale and watched their eyes light up as their mouths formed perfect Os. She needed no script since growing up with recounts of eerie events. She'd even added tidbits over the years, learned after touching a wrought iron gate surrounding one of her target houses.

Increasing wind carried leaf litter and bits of gravel to add to the spooky atmosphere, but her audience quieted at every stop to listen. Responses of small gasps, *oohs*," and *ahhs*" demonstrated her success.

Despite exhaustion from the long day, she reveled in her role. In the coming months, she'd miss the sharing and comradery.

Trenton and Colson remained close by while Leigh chatted to Casper during a short break. Hailey took up position directly in front of the group, smiling and engaging tourists' questions.

Her next stop, the highlight of the tour, began in the historic graveyard filled with pirates, war heroes, and famed Vodou priests.

It was there, in front of a gravestone, when sudden commotion in the back disrupted the tour. The incident happened so fast, Hailey only saw the legs of a man arcing through the air before a thud and grunt of pain denoted his landing.

The crowd parted enough to see Casper break the hold of the second man and put him down with a leg sweep.

As if understanding the men's intent, Gunther bolted to Casper's side and growled at the moron laying on his back. The inebriated idiot didn't make a move to get up.

"When a girl says no, numbnuts like you should listen." The teen bent to stroke Gunther's chest, the wolf dog taking note of Casper's shoulder and whining. "It's all right, boy. He's a good one too."

What does she mean by that? Who's good?

Casper waved off Leigh and Colson's help, declaring the situation handled. "No, I don't want to press charges against these idiots. I'd say they've learned their lesson." Holding her hands up and out to engage the stunned audience before taking a bow, she added, "Wouldn't you all agree?"

A resounding chorus of agreement and applause filled the air.

Both men asked permission before standing. The two stumbled away amid curses about witches and bitches.

Casper downplayed the exchange as the result of liquor and men having no sense, her cracks drawing guffaws from the men and approving nods from the women. Trenton looked like he could chew nails and spit rust. Leigh grinned and shrugged.

How did Casper know I'd lead the tour tonight?

That question and more tangled Hailey's emotions and made it difficult to concentrate as she drew the group's attention once more.

No haunted tour would be complete without a graveyard haunted tale. In front of a towering mausoleum, Hailey imparted the finer points of a man accused of killing his family while they slept.

She elaborated on details of her story but caught Leigh's cocked brow in Casper's direction in her peripheral vision.

The youth fisted her amulet and appeared to be having a quiet verbal altercation... with no one. "*I don't care if you did or didn't kill them. Now's not the time,*" she hissed. Ambient light caught the youth's chagrin before a noncommittal shrug ended the incident.

The kid's not *crazy. She's talking to spirits.*

Hailey replayed past interactions with the teen. If she had the ability to speak with the dearly departed, it would explain a lot. It also raised more questions.

"Let's continue the last leg of our tour before we visit Pappa Budreaux's for drinks. Shall we?"

The ensuing route took them through a narrow alley where she relayed the story of yesteryear when the pub's side door doubled as an entrance for civil war clandestine meetings. Confederate soldiers had helped stop General Franklin's march through the land route joining West Louisiana and Texas.

Clearing her throat, Hailey continued her course. "Folks, at the end of this alley and to the left, you'll find the perfect café brûlot, Mint Julep, or anything else you can dream up. Thank you for making my last tour memorable."

Another round of applause filled Hailey with satisfaction as she watched the group toddle off murmuring about their favorite part of the evening or planning their next trip.

Casper hesitated, glancing first at Trenton, then Colson, before turning to follow the other tourists, hopefully not to the bar.

Leigh stomped over and huffed her disgruntlement. "Through the damn graveyard, Hailey, really? You had to take *that* route tonight?"

"Oh, knock it off, the way you've been stuffing your face lately, I did you a favor."

"I see we have two of the seven dwarfs present tonight." Colson handed Leigh his handkerchief and pointed to the perspiration on her forehead. "Bitchy and Sweaty present and accounted for." Exaggerating a glance around, he added, "Should we be on the lookout for more?" Amusement glinted in his eyes.

Hailey poked the smug and arrogant bastard in the chest. "Listen, she may be under your command, but I'm not. Leave her alone, asshole."

Gunther growled a warning, too, which caused zero change in Colson's demeanor, except a widening of his grin.

"Aw, being an ass is part of my manly charm." The statement, issued via a straight face, broke slightly with his shoulders shaking.

Hailey's first direct social encounter didn't set well, unable to reconcile his ballbuster reputation with the smartass present. She did, however, grant him kudos for having a sense of humor. Maybe there'd be hope for him down the line if Leigh's boyfriend dropped the ball.

Trenton scrubbed a hand over his chin, partly hiding his smile. "You've done it now, man. No return policy in effect, and believe me, it lasts. You've been marked, fair warning."

"That's okay. I was beginning to wonder if Leigh had emotions or not. At least now I know." Colson snorted before meeting Leigh's glare and adding, "Bring it on."

"Why don't we take this to Pappa Budreaux's and discuss it over a drink?" Trenton, the peacekeeper, stepped between his sister and Colson, nudging her away with an arm around her shoulders.

"I'm not bitchy." Despite Colson's brash and ill-timed attempt at humor, Hailey still appreciated his presence on his night off.

She and Trenton led her protection detail through the alley toward the street. They'd parked near the tour's destination and wouldn't have far to walk.

"Do you have frequent problems with drunks?" Trenton paused at the mouth of the alley to let Hailey take the lead.

Tourists enjoying a weekend night of revelry and music clogged the sidewalk wearing brightly colored dresses and skirts. Live jazz music poured from bars that promised a distraction from the day's worries.

"No, but Casper handled tonight pretty well. Did you find anything about her that's... strange?"

Trenton snorted. "As soon as I started digging, I got a call from the local SAC telling me to knock it off. Her adopted father has one heck of a reach. His absence does not equate to neglect."

"Really?"

"Yeah, and in no uncertain terms. I think my boss was a bit spooked."

"Hailey, move! Falling gargoyle!" Casper's shout echoed from the end of the narrow alley.

The words registered in time to see a statue bearing down on her. Spread concrete wings, beaked nose, and taloned fingers revealed the approaching horror in graphic detail.

Trenton yanked her back against the block wall, grunting as a mortared claw skimmed his arm to leave a bloody trail through torn cloth.

Hailey felt as much as heard the massive stone piece smash against the walkway. Large chunks bounced off the walls of the alley and out onto the sidewalk.

Gunther yelped, caught by a chunk ricocheting of the wall.

Hell.

She didn't need more trouble.

Her wolf-shepherd mix then directed his ire toward the rooftop in boisterous regard. If he could've climbed walls, the culprit would've breathed his last.

"Damn. Are you two all right?" All pretense and familiarity evaporated from Colson's tone in instant favor of formality and business.

Casper's appearance took Colson by surprise, but not Hailey, even though she'd watched her leave with the group earlier.

"Thanks, kid. What were you doing *behind* us?"

"Um, I circled back to the graveyard to do some stone etchings. You'd be surprised how many stories are buried under those stones. Unfortunately, my pencil broke." She held up a pencil then stuck it in her backpack. "Lucky for you that it did."

"Meet any friendly ghosts?" Trenton's narrowed gaze belied the flippant tone.

Neither phased the teenager, obviously cut from sturdy cloth. "Yeah. You'd be surprised what they could tell you." A side glance at Hailey and she added, "You of all people should know that. Don't you educate your friends?"

Trenton moved closer to the teen, his way of throwing interviewees off balance, especially smartass kids.

Casper adopted a Cheshire grin. "Not much intimidates me, dude. Nice try, though. I assume you've been told to leave me alone unless you have formal questions?"

"Which, in fact, I do. How is it you were looking at the roof the exact moment someone decided to flatten Hailey?"

"I'm a kid, not some decrepit, creaky old person. Kids tend to keep their eyes open." Casper's taunt was a challenge.

She doesn't like authority. Okay.

"Either way. Thank you." Hailey moved between them without touching either. There was more to the situation, but now wasn't the time.

Leigh scanned the building's southwest corner, stating, "I know this town, and this corner is not where that thing is normally perched."

"Had to be someone who knew I'd give a tour tonight. Of course, marketing brochures do list me as the tour guide."

"That thing must weigh a ton." Leigh grabbed Hailey by her light jacket and nudged her toward Trenton. "Trenton, keep her safe. Colson and I will catch up with you later."

"These buildings connect all the way down the block, Leigh. Plus, there're any number of fire escapes and entrances into these stores." Hailey indicated the street where the assailant could escape via many exit points. Not that anyone had seen a face. "You're wasting your time, guys."

"Forget it, Hailey. Let's go back to the loft. I'll tell you what else I found in Bernadette's room and about the body in Melford's pond." Trenton nodded to Casper then tugged Hailey toward his SUV.

Chapter Twenty-Two
Hailey

Morning dawned with dark clouds and a strong breeze marking the gulf storm's swift approach. During the next two days, shop owners would board windows, line storefronts with sandbags, and check generators.

Hailey stretched, yawned, and extended her arm to rub Gunther's back.

He wasn't there.

It amazed her how he'd adopted Trenton. Her furry companion tolerated most people but had never taken such a liking to another male. The times she'd run into Victor, Gunther preferred a warning growl over an offered paw.

It wasn't a territorial issue.

Trenton wasted a perfectly good breakfast ranting over her need to push boundaries amid his announcement of canceling the family barbecue due to bad weather.

Insistence on accompanying her to the Gifted Elite Academy didn't fly. Gunther was all the backup needed to interview Armond Boyér.

Grumbles followed her out the door during her attempt to escape his tirade and Leigh's gargoyle jokes.

Cecile Arquette's familiar Cajun swing ringtone cued Hailey into Hamchet's grapevine efficiency as she braked for two deer flitting across the road.

Tapping the Bluetooth button on her steering wheel, she answered the first questions prior to prompting. "I'm fine, Mom. Leigh's fine. So are Trenton and everybody else."

"Why didn't Trenton and that new lieutenant catch the culprit?"

"Mom, it was night. All those buildings connect, and the assailant could've hopped down any number of places or even hidden in one of the adjacent trees. There's only so much manpower."

"They should have security cameras—"

"*They,* meaning most of the store owners, don't do enough business to justify the purchase. Listen, I gotta go, but I'll talk to you later. Love you, Mom." Hailey clicked off to make her turn.

The school grounds presented more like an upscale private college. Manicured lawns with a riot of summer blooms in structured flowerbeds lined the winding road leading to the two-story main building. White columns upheld balconies on either side.

Welcome to the rich and famous.

A call in advance informed her of the teacher's whereabouts and proved a necessity to get past security at the gated entrance. Her ace in the hole to breaking Armond was the picture in Bernadette's possession, a copy of which Trenton texted to her earlier.

Having an affair doesn't make him a pusher, killer, or counterfeiter, she reminded herself as she parked beside a black Chevy. With the students gone, only a few staff members remained.

"Okay, boy. Ambassador time." Yanking Gunther's dual-purpose vest from the floor of the back seat, Hailey settled it over her companion's head and snapped the buckle on the side. "This'll keep you cool and let others know you're well-mannered. Play nice and make friends the way we've practiced, okay?"

An eager *woof* signaled his readiness to meet and greet. He bounded from the open door when called, a big doggy grin on his face. Gunther excelled at his job.

Marble steps led to a grand double-door entrance where ornate handles in the shapes of GE welcomed visitors. Inside, marble flooring defined an elegant reception area with tiled walls. The cost of the one room could buy a cottage.

A fake smile graced the receptionist's face sitting at her desk to one side. "Hi, can I help you?" She gasped when looking up to see the canine sitting patiently by the door. "Um, dogs aren't allowed in here."

"She's a certified service dog," Hailey lied on two counts.

He wasn't certified, nor was he a girl, but had never been challenged. With his longish hair, gender wasn't obvious to those not looking. The official vest obtained from a friend, plus Gunther's charm, worked wonders.

"Really?" Curiosity overcame hesitancy as the young woman circled her desk.

"Meet and greet, Princess."

Hailey hated dumbing down her fierce protector. For reasons unknown, she'd found most people were less afraid of a female Princess than a male Gunther. Of course, the deception only lasted until someone noticed the physical discrepancy. With his long coat, most never did.

"Hey, girl. You sure are big. So beautiful, too." The petite brunette knelt to accept the paw, accompanied by a slight whine and drooping ears. "Aw, I wish I had a treat to give you. What a pretty girl. There's no need to be shy." Rubbing the dog's chest, she continued to coo and make eyes over her newest friend.

Works every time.

Gunther could open more doors than any master key.

"I'm here to visit Armond." Using his first name lent the pretense of familiarity.

"Down the hall, take the first left, third door on the right." Her gaze never left the fur ball she fawned over until he stood and offered his signature bow before striding to Hailey's side. "If you ever need a dog sitter, look me up."

Empty hallways echoed the slight squeak of her tennis shoes. When she knocked on the teacher's door, she half expected to see at least one teen inside with mussed hair and buttons mismatched during a hurried attempt to appear presentable.

"Come in." The voice was low, soft, and sexy.

Figures.

"Hi, Armond. Mind if I call you Armond?" Instead of waiting for an answer, she moved into the small, windowed office and held out her hand over his desk. "I'm Hailey Arquette."

Armond ignored the gesture and returned his gaze to the papers before him, the pen in his hand tapping out his impatience. "I've already answered tons of questions. What can I do for you?"

In his favor, the man didn't balk at Gunther's entrance and sitting by her side.

"Answer some more."

"You're not a police officer."

"Were you expecting one? It can be arranged."

The man was good, kept his expression neutral, likely practiced in front of a mirror. On a wild hunch, Hailey leaned forward and briefly placed both hands on the sleek oak desktop.

Brief being the operative word after a sordid vision flashed in her mind. Heat crept up her cheeks as she snatched her hands away.

On the desk... really?

"What else can I possibly add to what I've previously said?"

"Well, let's find out. In case you're interested, I'm already aware of a few things, but let's start with this." Hailey went for the direct approach. Retrieving her phone, she pulled up the photo of Armond found in Bernadette's room.

Had to give the man credit. He never flinched, nor did his gaze snap away from her screen. Rather, he looked up and confronted her stare with one of his own.

"Miss Bordelon was a student here. She had an exceptional mind and was destined for great things. Such a shame."

Cutting through the crap, Hailey closed her eyes to recall sordid details of what she'd just *seen*.

"Okay. Let's try it this way. "Green eyes, blonde hair, ponytail. You laughed when pulling it. Long scar on her right side from... an appendectomy. And really? On the desk? It was dark outside. I see—" The description made him aware she knew of multiple dalliances. Bernadette had black hair.

"All right. Enough! So the rumors are true..."

Unruffled, Hailey arched a brow, and grinned when ink dripped from the pen over the teacher's fingers.

With a muttered curse, he retrieved a handkerchief and wiped it up. Although he didn't speak, his accusing glare spoke volumes.

Thank you, angel on my shoulder.

"The photo was found hidden in Bernadette's bedroom. Were you aware she kept a journal?" A few lies could go a long way.

Armond leaned back in his chair, his face clouding with uncertainty and a flash of anger. "Just because it's written, doesn't make it true. I have nothing else to say. And you have no proof."

"That's fine. I've gotten enough to write my story and offer it to the AP. I can certainly arrange to talk to the blonde and her parents. A murdered student from this school makes for good copy. Oh, to answer your unasked question, I'm an investigative journalist and licensed private investigator. My current story concerns a student and her illicit affair with a married teacher at an elite boarding school." Hoping the bluff would pay off, Hailey started to stand.

"Wait. I have a family. We've just had our first child."

True or not, the statement was immaterial. Hailey wondered about the percentage of men who cheated on their pregnant wives. Women who'd willingly given up their figure, if temporarily, to bring new life into the world.

"So, you got bored and wanted a younger model with a firmer body?"

"No. It wasn't like that, and I didn't kill Bernadette. We had a brief fling, but when my wife got pregnant, that ended."

An obvious lie.

Increased white around his eyes coincided with the tinge of anger and desperation in his voice.

Those responses were under his control, which begged the question, *how solid is his self-control?* She didn't want to bring up the possibility of counterfeiting or drug running, although the latter seemed unlikely for reasons she couldn't name.

"Please. Sit. I will tell you what you need to know." Once again, he reigned in his emotions and relaxed when Hailey sat and leaned forward.

"I don't have time for games. Did you give her money?"

"What? No. Look at my records. I have very little expendable income." He snorted. "A lot less now with a new baby."

"If you're hiding something offshore, I'll find it."

A steely look of determination flashed over his expression before he glanced out the window. "Okay. You're the pit bull who refuses to relinquish its toy. Like I said, Bernadette and I did have an affair. Yes. But I broke it off when I discovered she was involved with… other things."

"Like?"

"I saw drugs in her purse. When I questioned her about them, she said she wanted the extra money. She had plans that didn't involve Texas, or even the US, for that matter."

"What type of plans?"

"The kid had an incredible mind. She could've done anything, and her parents shielded her from outside sources who'd want to use her for their own benefit. Bernadette knew what kind of money she could make. She was impatient."

"Who supplied her with drugs?"

"I don't know. One of her friends, I guess."

"Did she talk more about anyone in particular?"

"Well, come to think of it, yes. A student, Casper, real name Olivia Decuir, and all-around pain in the ass. I don't know what type of relationship they had, but it was strained. Casper's a new student."

"Where were you the night Bernadette disappeared?"

"Taking care of Hannah. My wife was beyond exhausted due to our daughter's ear infection."

"Yeah? Who's her doctor?"

"Pearlman. I'll text you the picture of the prescription bottle, complete with the date it was filled."

There was nothing humble about his confession and defense. The questions remained, did the cocky man cover a set of core values more sinister than illicit sex? What was Casper's involvement, if any?

Leaving the deeper financial research to Trenton made sense. Armond was a slick bastard with years of hiding his fetish. Trenton had faced those types in his line of work and better understood how to play the game.

Of more interest was the drug angle. If Bernadette's killer had tired of dealing with self-entitled brats, maybe he or she decided the income from the school wasn't worth the trouble. Or maybe the supplier found another, more amenable dealer.

A second interview with Casper needed to happen without a guardian present. A dicey situation at best.

Chapter Twenty-Three
Hailey

This time when Hailey knocked on Casper's door, the girl opened it with a quirk of her lips. "Well, don't you look stone-faced this morning?"

"Hi, Casper. We need to talk." It was difficult not to show irritation at the gargoyle joke. They would follow her for weeks.

"I don't invite strangers in when adults aren't home." Crinkles around her eyes and lips nipped between her teeth declared the lie.

This young woman did whatever she pleased, and they both knew it.

"No problem. Why not step out on the porch with Gunther and me? There's a nice breeze blowing, and I could really use your help."

"I've saved your life twice. Isn't that enough?"

"About that. First, thank you. Second, how is it you were at Henri's store the same time as me? And why'd you go back toward the graveyard last night?"

"I thought I heard something weird from that direction. As for the other, Henri has to know someone was snooping in his shop because of the broken glass. I'm sure you're aware of his reputation. I'd be a terrible investigator if I didn't follow my instincts."

Hailey recognized the avoidance and the lie but let it go. "How'd you get me out of the antique store?"

Instead of slamming the screen door in her face, Casper rolled her eyes but ambled out to sit in a rocker. The constant fiddling of the amulet she wore was a habit, but not a nervous one.

"You'd be surprised what we can do. But let's not get sidetracked. How about being grateful we did get out of there, unseen, and that I saw the gargoyle before it flattened you?"

"What *we* can do? Who's *we*?"

"I have friends. Special friends. Not quite like you, but special nonetheless. Have you asked you mom about your sister?"

"I don't have any siblings." If the purpose of her sidebar equaled a distraction, it worked. "Not sure what you meant by 'not like me,' but I think we've gotten off on the wrong foot." Hailey put out her hand hoping for the brief contact of a handshake.

Casper leaned back in her chair and crossed her arms over her chest, commenting, "I'd love to learn through touch. Nice talent."

That hit too close to home, so Hailey deflected with, "We don't know who moved the gargoyle from its original position."

"Maybe the fiddler on the roof?"

Gargoyle jokes and musical references from a kid... of course.

"Armond says you might've been Bernadette's supplier. I know you're working undercover—so, are you investigating Bernadette, Boyér, or the school in general? Who do you work for?"

"Armond is a pervert. I don't work for anyone, and I've never sold or dealt with drugs. I believe in natural healing."

"But you *are* in a unique position to discover things."

"You have no idea." A small smile played about her mouth.

"People are dying, have died. I need to get to the bottom of it."

"Your father's death? He wasn't connected to Bernadette or the school, directly."

"How do you know?"

"I have my own way of investigating."

Hailey stared at the teen's shoulder, aware of her hair moving, but not from a breeze, lacking on this side of the home.

"See something interesting?" Casper asked. "I understand you're a late bloomer. Some are." A casual shrug replaced further explanation.

"More like, feeling something."

"Training will teach you that distractions get you killed," said by the teen as if from years of experience.

"Why don't we work together? I promise nothing will be repeated to the police or Trenton."

"I'll tell you what I know, but if one word goes to print, or if it comes back to bite me in the ass, well, my dad's connected. Trenton's already found that out." A vague hand gesture accentuated her point. "Ask your questions."

"Who put the totem in my truck?"

"Didn't know about that, but I can look into it."

"What do you know about my dad's death? How was he involved with Henri?"

"Still working on that. I believe he was taken by surprise and didn't know who exactly killed him. How about you answer a question of mine?"

"Shoot."

"How much crap do you get about your eyes? I think they're really cool. Sarah said you're like, descended from some kind of Vodou queen. What was it like growing up in your house?"

Hailey breathed in deep, not willing to go off on a tangent but not wanting to shut down her source. "Trust me. Rumors are vastly overrated. I grew up in a normal house with normal parents."

"Well, damn. That's disappointing. You won't be normal for long, though."

"Why? What makes you say that?"

"Rumors. You're going to develop some kind of special talent, other than the touch thing. Are you aware there are others like you?"

"Where?"

"Around, here and there. Well, not exactly like you. Everybody has their own talent. You'll see."

"Why do I get the feeling you're an old soul?" Hailey tightened her shoulders to prevent the shudder from becoming visible.

"Because I'm advised by those who are."

Hailey looked around. "Yet your father leaves you alone, what, most of the time?"

"I'm the independent type. Back to the issue at hand."

"Okay, about the root cellar. You knew exactly where to go."

"I had a hunch and an anonymous tip. The same person killed both your father and Bernadette, then used the root cellar as a dumping ground."

Hailey watched Casper's frown dissolve into a vacant stare as she gripped her medallion, appearing to see something far off. She'd seen her grandmother do the same many times. "You sound sure of that. How'd you confirm it?"

"Again, my source wishes to remain unidentified, at least for now." Casper cocked her head to the side, her gaze nowhere near touching Hailey.

"Both my father and Bernadette were killed with a poison, an herb, common enough if you know what to look for."

"How do you know?"

"Trenton just told me. I'd like to talk with your sources." Hailey watched the teen tilt her head to the side. At the same time, a lock of hair was tucked behind her ear by unseen hands.

"No. Not at this time."

Hailey must be insane for considering joining forces with a reclusive kid, but then again, Casper wasn't just *any* kid. She had incredible instincts, and something else.

"What else is going on at that school?"

"Not sure yet, but the whole place is creepy wrong. I'll let you know when you can help."

Casper's confidence wasn't out of proportion considering the situation at the antique store and how she manhandled two men during the ghost tour. There existed an old-world knowledge about her that defied her stated age. She'd proven smart, adaptable, and able to take care of herself.

Plus, having eyes and ears inside the school could prove useful.

More than one investigative road led in Henri's direction, Hailey's new focal point. She thanked the young woman but thought about her long after getting back in her truck.

With each mile driven, several things became certain. Once in her mother's driveway, she stopped and retrieved her phone to make notes before details slipped away.

Current evidence suggested non-connected aspects linked the murders. Finding the bridge would lead her to the killer.

At first blush, the drug trade didn't appear to involve Armond. She'd found no excessive expenditures.

Her father's death didn't connect to anything, yet it clearly entwined with Bernadette in some way. Her dad wouldn't have known, much less been involved with a young girl. His moral compass didn't point to illicit sex, drugs, or counterfeiting according to her mother.

No one knew him better. She and her mom were due for a painful conversation.

A lie by omission was still a lie. Whatever monsters her mother held chained to her conscience must hold a key to unraveling the twisted events leading to solving the mysteries. Pain would magnify its grip if Cecile Arquette now feared for her daughter's life.

She let the screen door slam behind her to announce her entrance along with, "Mom."

Unnerving quiet created more alarm than recent events. She couldn't remember a time the house didn't have soft strains of music creating a peaceful atmosphere.

"Mom?" Hailey called again and veered through the living room and down the hallway.

Light filled the small gap between the bedroom door's bottom edge and the floor. Soft sniffling sounds emanated from inside.

Pushing the door open several inches, she scanned the room. Her mother sat on the bed with a box of tissues by her side and a wastebasket at her feet. It was almost full of crumpled sheets. Her gaze lifted when Hailey pushed the door wide.

"All these years, I've been so confused. I thought he just left without saying goodbye, which didn't make sense because I knew he loved us."

"Your judgment is always spot on."

Her mother's watery smile disintegrated into a sob before she blew her nose. "I almost wish I was wrong. At least then he'd be alive."

Gunther padded forward on a whine then rubbed his shoulder against Cecile's lower legs.

"Oh, sweet boy. You are such a comfort. I'm so glad you found your way into Hailey's life." She buried her face in the dog's fur, her shoulder-length hair draping over Gunther's shoulders.

"Is Lieutenant Colson harassing you?"

"No, but I'm well-known as an expert in indigenous plant life, which makes me a prime suspect."

"As if you're alone there. Half the county is, too, Mom. Including Bernadette's boyfriend and his family."

"And that other girl the lieutenant asked me about—"

"You mean Casper, Bernadette's supposed friend?" Damn if Colson and Trenton didn't have their ways.

"Yes. I couldn't remember her name."

"They won't get anything from her, but I did."

Hope graced her mother's expression. "And?"

"And I need to know more about Dad's gambling buddies. First, I have to know, Mom. Did I have a sister?" Hailey sat and covered her mother's hand with her own. Overwhelming grief prevented experiencing her mother's flashbacks.

Cecile gasped and held her free hand over her chest. "How—"

"Let's just say I'm coming into my own. Please. Did I?"

Cecile's gaze drifted to the floor, her eyelids closing as if on a painful memory. "Yes. A miscarriage."

Another lie by omission.

"Mom, let's talk on the back porch over some boiled peanuts." She needed to stand, to run until she had no breath, anything to release the grief welling up inside. Neither would help.

Cecile nuzzled Gunther's head before standing. "I told the lieutenant—"

"And now you can tell me. I need names, dates, and locations as best you can remember. C'mon. You get the drinks. I'll get the nuts."

On the porch, Cecile's gaze took on a thousand-mile stare with current events seemingly forgotten as she toed the rocker back and forth.

Countless memories of sitting on the step with a bowl of snacks and sweet tea while Trenton, his siblings, and her parents laughed over life's vagaries brought a knot to her chest. At that stage in their lives, Trenton's parents were workaholics. Her home had become the place to hang out.

Nudging Gunther's nose away from her bowl of goobers, Hailey smiled when her mom offered him a piece of boiled liver instead.

"You were saying they'd rotate houses for each game night."

"Yes, the locations changed, at least initially. Your dad would say he was going to so-and-so's house for a night of cards. A different member hosted the group each week. Odd that we never did."

"When did that stop?"

"I'm not entirely certain. He became vague with details, and I didn't exactly keep track. It'd gotten to the point where he'd just say, 'Goin' out. See you later.' I never met any of the new crowd, and don't have a name to give you."

Cecile explained group dynamics as they pondered the vast woods beyond her home. Her mom seemed to relive the past, picking out details in order of time, like reciting a sequence of numbers to get to the end.

"Jimmy Nicholman, the gentleman who used to own the hardware store outside White Castle. Jacob Guerin, who worked for Schiffer's Realty. Then, of course, Father Ryan."

"What? Father Ryan gambled?"

"He entered friendly games of poker, dear. Nothing immoral. They'd ante up with popcorn, cookies, and hard candy."

"Okay, wait. What about Jacob? He worked for the same realty company that's handling the sale of the farm where they found Dad?"

"Well, yes. But you have to realize, hon, Hamchet is a small town. They're the only realtors here."

"Seems odd that small town gossip can't cough up something, a description, whatever." Hailey blew out a frustrated breath. "Think back, Mom. Did Dad develop any new friendships around then?"

"Not that I'm aware of. He did go see Father Ryan the night he disappeared. Said he needed a clear path but wouldn't explain further."

"Father Ryan?"

"Yes, but his lips are sealed tight, according to Trenton."

"I hate being left out of the loop," Hailey muttered.

"Whoever killed your father is still out there, Hailey. Asking questions will stir them up and put you in danger. Both Trenton and Father Ryan know it. Leave this to the police."

"If I do that, they'll arrest you and call it quits. I'm not gonna let that happen."

"Neither will Trenton or Leigh. Dear, do I need to remind you they both carry guns?"

"On some days, so do I, Mom. So do I."

Chapter Twenty-Four
Hailey

Thorough research required specific items—laptop, note pad, coffee, and chocolate. If the latter comprised dinner and existed in the form of sugary sweet cereal, well, everyone made sacrifices. Her supply of chocolate bars had dwindled, and Hailey hadn't made time to restock.

From her window, she watched shadows encroach along the empty street below. Trenton's text declaring he was en route meant he'd bring pizza.

In her current state, she wanted nothing more than to cuddle on the sofa with him and soak up his strength.

He hadn't yet shared information about his delve into the funny money, too pissed off after discovering she'd interviewed her dad's known gambling buddies during the afternoon. Not that it mattered. She'd turned up zilch.

Three of the original six still lived, each willing to have a conversation with her. Nicholman, a widower in his late sixties, had even invited her in for coffee.

He'd retained the strength of a younger man with a calculating gaze under thick heavy brows. A call he received during her visit came from Trenton, hot on the same trail.

He hasn't lost his touch.

Trenton knew how to network and managed to stay abreast of current events despite being away for so long.

Figures.

Jacob Guerin had spoken well of her father, and with genuine regret over his death. Well into his sixties, he lived a modest life within the means of his suspected income.

Her thoughts circled back to Henri. Common sense required more research before snooping through his life. He was a venomous snake and required the wariness due any dangerous reptile. If knee-deep into the drug trade, it stood to reason he'd be busy at night, which made her timing perfect.

An incoming text message contained a picture of a pill bottle with the name and fill date highlighted, along with a receipt, stamped with date and time of pickup. She did a double take at the cost. No wonder records revealed Armond's vehicle as one of the older models on the lot.

"Well, Gunther. Looks like Armond's kid really was sick. And damn, those were expensive prescriptions. Though, nowadays, I guess that's to be expected."

A familiar SUV pulled to a stop in front of her building. Trenton hopped out and slipped the strap of his computer bag over his shoulder before fetching a large square box. His heavy scowl and stiff stride foretold of the rant to come.

"He brought pizza, Gunther. See? Men can be trained too. You just have to keep at it and be consistent," she said then met her old friend at the door.

After depositing his bag on the table and not breaking stride, he slid two slices of pepperoni and cheese wedges onto paper plates and brought them over to the window seat.

"I had an interesting conversation with Lieutenant Colson today." Trenton handed her a plate, then sat beside her.

"Did he manage to find a laxative? I know of at least four who have tried to direct him."

"Despite his brief stint here, he knows of your reputation, which, in part, extends to Leigh. I find that interesting as well as disturbing."

"I find that stalkerish, but on to better things. What did you learn about the counterfeiting ring?"

Trenton flattened the line of his mouth before shaking his head. "There's been reports of it surfacing, but not in this immediate area. Northeast Louisiana, Mississippi, Alabama, and Florida. All along the coast and gradually creeping west."

"You think someone's bringing it in via the coast, hitting key points?" Hailey used her finger to swipe a long string of dangling gooey cheese into her mouth.

"Possibly, but I don't see how it ties to Bernadette."

"Too bad we can't get answers from a corpse," Hailey snarked."

He eyed her empty cereal bowl with disdain. "You've got to start eating better. I'm gonna hit the grocery store tomorrow since your stock is low and you'd rather eat crap than shop. Whatcha working on?"

Hailey slammed the lid down on her laptop, not wanting Trenton to pry. "Just doing some research."

"As long as you're not planning to sneak into anyone's house or business, okay?"

Exactly what I'm planning.

"Movie?" She eyed stacks of DVDs in a rack under her flat screen.

"Sure." His tentative answer attached unseen strings. "Is it an action film?"

"*Beauty and the Beast*? It's my favorite." Hailey tossed out the title to gauge Trenton's level of preoccupation.

"Sure you want to watch another animated fairy tale?"

He hadn't recoiled in disgust the way she'd expected. Something about his demeanor screamed subterfuge.

"Okay. You find something to stream then, while I take Gunther out."

He started to protest, until she fisted hands on hips and tapped her foot, waiting.

"Okay, okay. Go ahead, but watch your back."

"Always do." She didn't tell him of the continued itch between her shoulder blades. The feeling had simmered under the surface and made her edgy all day.

Possibilities of what Trenton might be planning plagued her steps down and out the door. As soon as her canine cleared the doorway, he bolted for the woods.

"Gunther, no!"

His growing curiosity with the forest had to stop before it became a problem he wouldn't survive. Part wolf or not, other nighttime predators were as fast as they were deadly and could take him down. He'd once faced off with a black bear who concluded it not worth the time or effort to confront her canine's persistent and agile moves.

Instead of entering the shadows, he circled the trunk of a large oak on the forest's edge.

On approach, she used her phone's light and studied the ground where he sniffed. "Cigarette butts. Damn. Don't suppose local wildlife has a preference for filtered versus unfiltered." Stooping down, she picked up several and put them in her pocket. "Shit, it's still warm. Guess I'm not paranoid, and you're more vigilant than I thought, boy."

Touching the brown stripe she'd painted previously, she saw nothing but gloves, dark clothes, stocky build, and boots. A black mask covering the face denied a visual of anything but dark eyes.

The coming conversation with Trenton wouldn't be pleasant, but his resources were both superior and faster.

She found him sprawled on one end of the couch but knew it was for show. Nothing about him was relaxed.

"I found something I need analyzed. Can you send it off?"

Trenton was on his feet in the next instant. "What?"

"Well, Gunther found them. These were at the edge of the yard."

"Son of a bitch!" Trenton snatched a plastic baggie from his satchel on the counter and held it open for her deposit. "I'll take care of it."

Lack of additional discussion confused Hailey. He knew something she didn't.

"Okay. Spill it. What's up?"

He should know better than to bluff. There were times he held onto information, but he wouldn't lie. She waited. The silence growing.

"I ordered security cameras the day I arrived. They'll be installed tomorrow."

"What? You can't do that."

"Already done. I told your landlord they'd stay if you left."

"Damn it, Trent." It was time to draw a line in the sand, but that's what the overprotective, smug Agent Insufferable expected. Instead, she'd toss him a bone, one she'd already gnawed on.

"I've got some information on my father's gambling buddies."

"Yeah, I talked to the lieutenant."

"More. Stuff Mom remembered after talking to him."

That snapped his attention away from the flat screen. "What?"

"Dad went to see Father Ryan the night he disappeared—to clear his head."

"And you suspect our priest?" A flash of irritation crossed his face.

"No, but we both know he's more likely to bend for you than me in giving information."

Continued probing with questions would end in stalemate for her, not because Father Ryan didn't want the case solved. He'd always held firm about not wanting her in the middle of any investigation.

Not to mention, sending Trenton on that dead-end path would leave her able to search Henri's home.

"You're up to something, Sparkles. What are you planning?"

"What do you mean?"

"You wouldn't help like this without a reason. Give me your phone."

The non sequitur boded ill. "Why?"

"I'm going to install an emergency app. If you get into trouble, all you have to do is push a button, confirm it, and it'll automatically alert your emergency contacts."

"As long as you don't install malware." Hailey handed over her device to avoid suspicion. "Who are you putting as emergency contacts?"

"You're gonna snoop. I know it. I just don't know how or in which direction."

"You didn't answer my question."

"I'll list Leigh and myself. Sad your dog has more sense but lacks the required dexterity to make a call."

"He's even better, sharp teeth. Are you gonna hang around after the dust settles?" A vague hand gesture indicated her back yard. She'd grown used to his presence. Even more, she needed him.

"Don't know yet. Thinking about it." Dropping back onto his end of the sofa, he stretched out and picked up the remote.

"Us swamp people aren't so bad, you know?"

Trenton eyed her with confusion. "You and my sister drove me nuts. It was either leave or crawl into a bottle."

"That's not why you left."

He ignored her in favor of switching channels. The firming of his jaw declared he had something to say, yet he held his tongue.

When she'd gotten serious with Victor, he'd left. Losing her best friend and longtime confidant had been a serious blow. They'd gotten comfortable enough again that she didn't want a repeat lesson and would avoid it at all costs.

Red-orange wisps lit the morning sky, supporting her mother's warning of an approaching storm. Local forecasts insisted everyone seek shelter by late afternoon.

Leigh and Trenton were in the kitchen when Hailey shuffled out wearing boy shorts and a tank top. Trenton paused his cup halfway to his mouth. His audible gulp drew Gunther's attention.

"Put on some clothes, Hailey. It's too early in the morning to stomach that kind of view."

"Oh, damn. I forgot I'm sharing a flat with a virgin. Sorry, guys."

Leigh snickered, taking down a bowl for cereal. "I'm doing laundry here this morning before the storm hits, Hailey. My washer's still on the fritz. Sort your stuff and leave it in the hall bath so I can do it too."

"Wait." Trenton held up a hand. "Please, let me get my shower first. I don't want to trip over tampons and Band-Aid-sized pieces of cloth."

Hailey snorted. "Been that long, huh?" It wasn't often she could make Trenton blush and enjoyed the view.

After eating and assuring Trenton she'd spend the next two days helping her mother can green beans and make jelly, she loaded Gunther into the back seat of her truck and pulled away from the curb, insisting Leigh had more experience in dealing with security companies and camera installation.

Before she and Gunther started out of town, she dialed Laurent, her walking social encyclopedia. He answered on the first ring.

"Hello?"

"Hey, brother from another mother. How's research into the Gifted Elite progressing?"

"Tightest lipped people I've ever met. A tough crowd indeed. I did, however, luck out at their year-end fundraiser."

"Of course, you did. What cute teen could resist your perfect hair, sexy eyes, and Adonis-like body?"

"Ha. Their gaydar isn't formed well enough to know they don't stand a chance."

"You're a tease."

"Yeah, but you love me anyway."

"I do. What'd you find out?"

"Heard about a confrontation between Casper and a man matching Henri's description."

"How bad? Where?"

"In front of Á La Mode—a group of students came in town for treats. She was warning him to stay away from the students."

"And now you have a verified source, hence printable. Good work. Funny you should mention Henri."

The more she learned, the greater the probability existed that someone dangled carrots to manipulate the Gifted Elite students into nefarious pursuits. She had no proof, but the thought wouldn't dissipate.

"Oh, no, no. No you don't. I heard about your escapade at the antique shop. You don't go to his house. Not without me."

"I'll be careful tonight."

"Oh, no. Promise to text me before you go, or else I'll rat you out to Leigh and Trenton."

"I'll take Gunther with me."

"Which is great but not enough. Give me the address and I'll meet you there. You got gloves, baggies, and your lock pick set?"

"Yes to the first and last, no to the middle."

"I'll meet you there with baggies in hand, but if he's got snakes in there, you're on your own."

Chapter Twenty-Five
Hailey

To sneak into a suspected killer's home took brass ones the size of a Leviathan. Hailey felt as prickly and would become just as extinct if caught.

She preferred her chances with the current high winds rather than the man.

A *For Sale* sign wavered in the breeze on the corner lot where she parked. Facing her truck out, she waited for tonight's partner in crime.

Cloudy skies had played hide-and-seek to filter the moonlight with the cross breeze whipping her bangs and ponytail through the open window.

Spending the day helping her mother can beans might have fooled Trenton, but Leigh had given her the stink eye when stopping by to check on their progress.

Earlier, she'd considered her options. Bringing a gun might offer a hint of safety, but the thought of Henri using it to splatter her brains against the kitchen wall made her leave it in the truck. Gunther and Laurent were great backups, as long as she didn't get caught *inside* the house.

This home, listed on Henri's DMV records, didn't fit if he made money through drug running, but she still wanted to check it out.

She and Gunther hadn't taken two steps from the truck when her sidekick looked back toward the intersection and whined low. His alert for a friend gave away Laurent's position seconds before he strode around the corner and down the grass shoulder, lacking his usual jaunty step.

"Hey, thanks for the help. How about you stay in the truck with my boy here?" Gunther rubbed against her leg.

"That might not be the best—"

"If you see our target turn down this street, get Gunther to start a barking chain. It'll send any neighborhood dogs batshit crazy. There's a treat bag of jerky in the console."

"How about you change your mind and not go in at all? Leigh told me about your adventure at the antique store. She—"

"Damn, she has got to stop ratting me out."

"He could've killed you in his store. So, no, I'm not sitting in the truck. I'll take Gunther for a walk. We'll look like a neighbor and dog taking a stroll."

"Okay. His whistle's in the glove box. Use it if you see Henri." Hailey didn't wait for the inevitable argument before turning to go.

Most of the homes looked older but well-kept from what she could see. A few had lights shining through the window.

Henri's house was dark, eerie, and radiated menace despite lacking a car in the driveway. There was no garage, but a wall of wax myrtle separating the structure from his closest neighbor would provide cover.

Small grayish-white berries forming amid the fragrant wispy olive-green leaves offered both color and fragrance. Her mother would love it and not mind the occasional light pruning needed.

Halfway down the side, she looked back to see Laurent waiting while Gunther cocked his leg against a maple tree. Dew glistened on neatly trimmed grass with the drop in temperature. She hoped Henri had a floor mat since damp shoes were a factor she hadn't anticipated.

The side of the home sported two windows, both locked. Around the rear, a large yard dotted with specimen trees fronted a green living barrier to the abutting yard beyond. A small deck offered seating and a stainless-steel grill.

Mullioned French doors were locked tight and revealed no sign of a security alarm, which meant she didn't need her magnets. Locks secured each rear window.

If her hunch proved correct, Henri wouldn't use this place as his base of operations. It was too public, had too many neighbors, and used just for show. She'd found no evidence of drug dealing in the antique store, but the painting there still rankled. Considering its value to her mother, it might have been part of a blackmail plot.

Four windows and a door with glass insets spanned the home's rear. Retrieving her lock pick set from her jacket pocket, she pulled on her gloves and set to work.

It didn't take long to open the simple lock.

A small kitchen with dark stone laminate countertops opened to an eating area and great room behind. Ambient light filtered through the large living room windows and another one over the kitchen sink.

Separated by a bar, the open dining/living area was spacious with an area rug anchoring the dining table and a fireplace on the side wall. A flat screen television occupied most of the space above a thick wood mantle.

Although she didn't need it yet, she retrieved a flashlight from her jacket's side pocket.

Two doors opened off a short hallway with scuffed hardwood floors. Sparing no time to search the open space, she opened the first door to a master suite. Again, windows provided weak ambient light, enough to see the spartan space was masculine with earthy colors.

A bedside table held a wrought iron lamp with a deer in flight among short reeds. The dresser on the far wall was bare except for a matching lamp.

No need to search the master bath yet, she'd save it for later. White tile matched that in the kitchen and aligned with the minimalistic style seen so far. Henri hadn't wasted time on niceties, favoring comfort instead.

Door number two hit the jackpot, a home office. Unlike her mother's favorite space, no bookshelves lined the walls. There were, however, several pictures of interest.

Between the windows on the end wall hung a glossy eight-by-ten of Henri standing beside three other men, each wearing black tactical pants and polo shirts. It reeked of military influence.

Hailey pulled the blind down over the window before clicking on her mini flashlight. If she'd guessed right, the pictures she'd take using her phone would lead to another thread they could trace.

In the back of her mind, she wondered if Casper had already been here.

An L-shaped desk situated for a yard view allowed the user to relax without putting his back to either the door or window. Maybe Henri was paranoid.

Does he have reason to be?

Two lamps, one on each corner, would highlight the separate workspaces. One side held a laptop, the other was bare except for a framed picture of Henri and an unknown woman dressed in slacks and billowy shirt. An upswept hairstyle seemed out of place for one of Henri's friends. Maybe they were something else.

Business partners?

Three drawers on the right held their secrets behind locks easily picked. The top held a thin notebook. Nonsense syllables, dates, and amounts occupied three columns, the fourth held special notations. Immediately, she started taking pics with her phone.

Bingo.

Flipping the pages ahead, she estimated about fifty sheets of documentation, too many to photograph. Inability to decipher the hurried scribble didn't thwart her excitement. She decided to take the whole thing.

Sudden screeching dropped her heart to her stomach when a strong gust outside scrabbled branches against the home's exterior. With a hand to her chest, she took several deep breaths to slow her heart's rampage. At least it hadn't started raining yet.

The second drawer held an unexpected find. Whether the money was real or not didn't matter as far as pointing a dirty finger at the sleazeball. Three stacks contained bundled twenty-dollar bills. Another three stacks behind them featured hundred-dollar bills. Her mind whirled too fast to do the math.

Odd to keep it here.

That part didn't add up either. Taking a picture wouldn't prove it counterfeit. Instead, she slipped a crisp twenty-dollar bill from the bottom of the closest bundle into an evidence baggie.

The last drawer was almost empty, except for a stack of older photos. A picture of each would help identify Henri's contacts. She turned each photo face down after snapping a pic to keep them in their original order.

Again, her heart all but stopped and the heavy phone dropped to the desk upon seeing the last picture. Tears burned her eyes as she studied the two men standing in front of a high dollar Go Fast Vehicle, a sleek and expensive-looking boat.

She'd learned about GFVs when Leigh attended the police academy. Both law enforcement and drug runners used them. The latter generally retrofitted their vehicles.

In the photo, fiberglass covered the boat's upper deck with the entirety painted to blend with the sea. Twin outboard engines provided speed, while the open cockpit revealed access to the cargo hold.

Bald cypress towered over a maze of bayous, sloughs, and ponds behind them and could've been any spot within hundreds of miles.

Anywhere along the coast of at least five states.

Her father stood beside Henri, his expression the polar opposite of the dirtbag's grin. Disparity between their outlooks marked another riddle to solve.

To the side, a small shack offered many ideas for possible usage, none of them welcome.

Dad was involved with drugs and counterfeiting?

Maybe Henri was a dirty ex-cop who'd transplanted to greener pastures in southeast Texas. His short stint in the military could've provided the opportunity to make necessary contacts.

No feasible explanation of the figures standing together by the speedboat made sense. Everything she thought she'd known about her dad went out the window with a snapshot bearing irrefutable truth.

Sudden barking in the distance trumpeted Gunther's alarm. From her position, she couldn't see headlights crossing the living room or hear the grind of an engine coming to halt. The fact she heard the dog so clearly meant he and Laurent had moved closer.

If Henri saw Gunther, he might recognize her distinctive four-footed partner on sight and look for trouble.

In shoving the stack of photos back in the drawer, her fingers touched something smooth, with buttons. A cell phone. Who would lock a cell phone inside their desk?

In a flash of desperation, Hailey tucked the last picture, notebook, and cell phone in her pocket before closing the drawers.

There wasn't time to make it out the back entrance. Instead, she hopped on the desk for easy access to the window. Of course, the blind didn't retract with the first downward yank. On the second try, it slipped from her hand and spiraled up with a loud snap.

The window wouldn't open because the latch was stuck. Panic intensified with each attempt.

The thud of a door closing signaled the homeowner entered the house.

Scrambling off the desk, she ducked into the closet and eased the sliding door closed. Her fingers shook while sweat coated her palms.

She recognized his grumbling threats as Gunther continued his tirade outside. Other neighborhood dogs had picked up his alert.

Trapped solid, she saw no escape. If he entered the office and saw the shade up all the way, he might check his desk, perpetuating her living nightmare.

Footsteps thudded in the other room followed by curses. More threats.

They all boded ill.

When a loud crash sounded from the other room, she almost passed out. Tinkling sounds indicated broken glass hitting the floor.

Henri's roar filled the house.

Hailey clasped her hands together and sent a silent prayer to Èrzulie Dantòr, protector of women and children.

Did Laurent just chuck a rock through Henri's window?

The unexpected intervention steadied her fingers enough to crack the door open an inch. In her mind, she pictured her friend running.

Thank you, buddy.

On the heels of the commotion the front door clicked opened. Henri's sudden silence created its own foreboding, like a predator preparing an ambush.

That was her cue to run. She was out and through the back door to the prickly hedge in record time. It was a miracle she remembered to lock up behind her.

Swaths of moonlight guided her across neighboring backyards. Wobbly legs refused to enable her to climb over the fenced third yard, so she circumvented it and skimmed the tree line to keep running.

Neighborhood dog ruckus quieted with Gunther's silence, apart from the occasional bark elicited during her not-so-stealthy escape.

When she reached the end of the block, she saw Laurent in the truck, ducked down with the windows open.

Spiny leaves picked up by the wind stung her cheek before reaching a now-quiet Gunther.

Henri was nowhere in sight.

Stolen money, notebook, and cell phone, not to mention a few snapshots, all testified to Henri's guilt. The question uppermost in her mind revolved around how much *he* knew about *her*. Next thought— how long until Henri was hot on *her* trail?

Apex predators often reacted with reflex, without caution or logic. If he'd taken the shot at her in the bayou, left the totem in her truck, or tossed a gargoyle over the roof, then his next attempt would be a direct attack, not a subtle warning.

"Damn, *chére.* You cut that too close. Don't ever do that to me again."

"Move it, Laurent. He'll know someone's been inside and recognize your broken window as a distraction. We gotta get out of here."

Gunther sensed her urgency and grumbled his complaint.

"That man is *très mauvais.* I don't care to meet him under any circumstance. After I threw the rock, we hid behind some yew bushes across the street. Thank God your dog is well-trained."

"Yeah, he is a smart one. Let's get you to your car." In her mind's eye, she saw as much as felt Henri's ballistic need for violence upon finding precious evidence missing.

She'd been prepared to uncover items of nefarious business dealings. That came as no surprise. To find a photo of her dad in front of a drug runner's boat would haunt her forever.

"Well?" Laurent pivoted in the passenger seat to face her directly.

"I can't. Not yet. Give me a few minutes." Her fingers still shook.

"Ah, *chère*, whatever it is, we'll deal with it. We're family."

"Call Leigh. Tell her to meet us at the loft first thing in the morning." It would take her that long to get her heart rate under control. Tonight, she needed to sort facts and develop a working theory. Several, in fact.

She didn't want her mother to find out through police channels about the drugs and money she'd found, but involving Leigh and Trenton would prevent Lieutenant Colson from opting for a quick closure. Her father was not going to be a notch on his record.

Tears streamed down her cheeks with the shock of realizing a truth yet to be uncovered, the specifics of how her dad was involved.

Chapter Twenty-Six
Trenton

Gunther preceded his bipedal partner through the door and chuffed eagerly when seeing Trenton. Soft footfalls behind signaled Hailey's hesitation and wariness.

Which meant there existed a reason for said reservation.

Trenton stood from his spot at the table where he'd occupied his time with research, his chair squeaking on tile in sliding back. He should've known something was wrong when she wasn't home. A note saying she'd be at her mom's house till late had made sense, but he should've called Mrs. A sooner.

"Where have you been? I was just getting ready to ping your phone. You—" Taking in her expression, the lid to his laptop slammed shut with the force of his concern. "What happened? What's wrong?"

He stalked to her side then gripped her shoulders and held her at arm's length. Cursory inspection included a sweep from head to toe, then spinning her around to check her back. Curses erupted while plucking leaves from her hair.

Gunther whined.

"What the heck, Hailey?"

Before the answer arrived, a draft of warm air rushed in with the door opening again. Leigh stepped between Hailey and Trenton, shoving him back and facing off with her friend. *"Deio gitlac melacle."*

"No. Nuh-uh. You don't call her an idiot and fool in your twin-speak. Talk human."

The torrent of his sister's angry rant continued with intermittent expletives thrown in, including hand gestures. Gunther whimpered as he inserted himself between the two women.

"Knock off the twin speak, guys. You know I can't understand it when you talk that fast," Trenton admonished again and gripped the closest upper arm of each woman.

"This is between us. Back off or become a permanent falsetto, Trent." Leigh jerked from his grasp and led Hailey to the window seat where she spoke in fits and starts. "How'd you get out? Did Laurent go *inside* with you?"

Hailey's haunted gaze was answer enough.

"Did you touch anything, like, without gloves?" Leigh asked, raising her hands in supplication.

Hailey shook her head, continuing the outpouring of details with intermittent hiccups emphasizing specific points.

Dawning came with Trenton's next circuit of the room. "Laurent calls Leigh instead of me?"

"Take a breath, brother. He knows me better," Leigh advised.

Leigh's arrival had offered Trenton someone who'd communicate in simple English when ready, but he didn't like secondhand or filtered information. He towered over the two, alternately raking his hand through his hair and pacing the open space. Sporadic growls erupted from his throat.

With shoulders slumped and exhaustion lining her face, Hailey met his stare then uttered words that chilled his blood.

"I was doing my job, investigating."

Gravity forced him onto the seat beside her, his mind whirling with images of her dismembered body left for gator bait.

When she began detailing her finds in English, she pulled a plastic bag from her backpack.

Trenton snatched it from her hand and whirled to hold it against the light of the end table lamp. "Son of a bitch."

In the next instant, he'd yanked her to her feet and hauled her close. Holding her against him equaled the affirmation of life he needed.

Gunther growled but didn't react as fast as Hailey, who shoved him back and tried to drop him with a leg sweep.

In response, his reflexive move spun her around. Before she could counter, he'd cuffed her hands. "Stay. I've had enough of this."

This time when he got in Hailey's face, Gunther stalked forward.

Trenton held his hand out and reinforced the nonverbal command with a firm, "Down."

The wolf dog obeyed.

"Trenton, listen—" Hailey began, only to be cut off.

"No. I ask, you answer. That's how this is going to work." Nudging her to sit, he took a seat beside her.

"Where *exactly* did you find this bill?" Holding the baggie in front of her face pissed her off. Good.

"In a house."

"So, not the antique store. Were you invited into said house?" Trenton arched a brow, waiting.

"Sort of." Hailey glanced to Leigh for support, who merely shrugged.

"Were you invited into said house, specifically tonight?" Trenton emphasized the last word.

"No, but I assumed it was an open-ended invitation to wherever, whenever."

"Jesus." He shook his head. "Next question. Who owns the deed to this house?"

"Can't say exactly."

Fury boiled in his chest, threatening to explode. "Who do you know that goes into the house?"

"Um, Henri. You heard him at Joseph's shop. Said to come see him anytime."

Leigh stood transfixed, listening then blurting more intermittent twin speak. Her chest rumbled a warning with each of Hailey's answers.

Trenton closed his eyes and dropped chin to chest. "Hailey. The man is dangerous. His record... no, never mind. I'm not going into that now. What else did you find? I know there's more."

Hailey's vehemence interrupted his tirade.

"We have a situation, here, and I'm not talking about you, Trent, who's about to get your ass kicked. Take these damn cuffs off me, now."

"With all the times he threatened to get Dad's cuffs and use them on us both, I'm surprised you don't carry a key in your back pocket." Some concern, but mostly amusement flashed across Leigh's face.

"Actually, I do, just can't get to it easily."

Leigh retrieved the key and unlocked the restraints. "You could've gotten your ass killed tonight."

"Going alone? Are you nuts?" Trenton choked on his words.

"Not alone. Laurent went with me. Gunther too," Hailey reminded them.

"Neither of which knows how to use a gun."

Leigh snatched the bill from Trenton and examined it under brighter light. "Damn. You are resourceful. You really should think about joining the force."

"No. That's not where this is going!" Trenton turned his eyes to the ceiling in a silent prayer for patience. "She broke into Henri's house, snooped, *and* stole. Can you at least attempt to back me up here, Leigh? I'm trying to save her life."

Leigh looked from Trenton to Hailey. "What else did you find?"

Trenton growled and stalked away. "You two are impossible."

Hailey retrieved the phone and photo from her pocket. A small sob escaped her throat.

Trenton returned and accepted the photo then murmured, "Oh, no, Hailey. I'm sorry."

"It doesn't mean he was dirty." Hailey's voiced escalation encouraged Gunther to rub against her. Angry tears over her father trailed her cheeks until swept away with hurried swipes.

"This phone," Leigh snatched the cell from Hailey's grasp, "...exactly where did you find it?"

"Locked in a drawer with photos and money. Lots and lots of money."

"The problem stands. We have no idea where this cabin and boat are located." Leigh gestured to the photograph. "That's what we need to find. There are miles of marshes, bogs, and swamps amid the forested wetlands. I don't know how to narrow it down."

Hailey glanced between her friends.

"*She* won't. Don't you get it, Leigh? Hailey doesn't carry a badge." Trenton's rage gave them all pause.

For a second.

"That's not just an ordinary phone, it's a satellite phone. We can see where the calls originated," Leigh continued as if Trenton hadn't spoken.

Trenton should've taken control of the investigation from the beginning. In doing so, he could've shut both women out of it, for the most part.

"Yes. That'll give us a general area," Hailey confirmed with a nod.

"All this was obtained through less-than-legal methods," Trenton reminded them. "We can't use it."

"*You* can't. *I* can." Hailey pointed to her chest. "We just can't use it in a way you'd prefer."

Trenton gripped Hailey's upper arms, not relenting when she winced. "I. Can't. Loose. You. Again! Understand?" His face was inches from her, willing her to acknowledge the words he couldn't speak.

When she closed her eyes, he took a step back.

"Did you find any other fingerprints on the bills from Bernadette's room other than her own?" Leigh directed her question to Trenton.

"Yes, but there's no match."

"How about from the corpse in the submerged truck?" Hailey asked, her tone tentative.

"Again, nada."

Leigh unfolded Henri's cell phone then twisted her lips in a grimace. "Good luck unlocking this. Damn thing is fingerprint coded."

"I have the card he gave me when I stopped to pick up my new lens at the hobby shop. If we can pull a print from it, we're in."

Trenton groaned. If he didn't let this play out, he'd be forever wondering where they were and what they were doing.

Leigh settled at the kitchen table after grabbing several paper towels. "Hailey, there's fingerprint powder in the office. Grab the talcum-based tin and your laptop."

"No. I'll do that. Hell, if I didn't know better, I'd swear you two were kin to the ragtag group in Pennsylvania."

"*Hmm*, be nice to meet them someday." Hailey smiled, arching a brow.

"No! And that's final. I couldn't handle it." Trenton held his hand out. "Give me the card. I want a proper trail on this. That much *is* legal."

"You're gonna claim jurisdiction? Why? The phone was stolen." Hailey gestured with her middle finger as she stalked off toward the office.

"I'm temporarily sidestepping your supervisor, Leigh. I don't know him well enough, and I don't want this botched."

None had addressed the elephant in the room.

"Dad…" Hailey began when she returned but couldn't find the words to continue.

"Don't go there, Hailey. We don't know the whole story yet." Trenton held his hand out for the card. "C'mon, park it. At least this is something I can teach you without it pricking my conscience."

"That picture could've been photoshopped for all we know. My father wouldn't have gotten mixed up with drugs."

The weak defense didn't change Leigh's expression of pity.

"C'mon, Trent. Sending this cell off will create too much of a delay." Leigh sat beside him and sighed. "At least let us get into the phone. Then you can have it back."

Hailey palmed her forehead. "No way. I forgot the ledger. I'll be right back."

"What ledger?" Leigh asked.

Before she could shove her chair aside, Trenton grabbed her arm with a firm, "No."

"I'm not going to look for trouble."

"Where *are* you going?" He asked.

"To my truck. I left something on the console. Information and adrenaline overload has muddled my brain." She held her hands up to show she hid nothing.

"Fine. Let's go." No way would he let her out of his sight just yet.

"You don't trust me to walk to my truck and back?"

"I don't trust whatever asshole who's been after you not to take a more direct approach."

Hailey didn't look back after patting her thigh for Gunther to follow. The trio descended the stairs all but silent, minus the thud of sneakers and paws.

Trenton's anger hadn't diminished. His inability to identify a specific threat complicated life. It turned out that Hailey had greater need of a babysitter than his sister.

When they reached the exit, he simply hauled her behind him with an uttered, "Stop." He opened the back door to the small parking lot and froze. "Hailey. Go back upstairs and lock the door."

* * * *

Hailey

She stumbled into the solid wall of Trenton Briner and almost bounced. "What's wrong?"

It took a minute before the lack of light registered the problem. Peering at each corner of the building, she noted the moonlight's reflection on broken glass scattered in the dirt. Someone had disabled the new video cameras and security lights. No doubt, they'd find a bullet or two lodged in each device.

Must've been small caliber to not be heard over the wind.

Strong gusts stung her eyes with dirt and leafy debris in a warning of damage to come. A small dust devil picked up bits of detritus and tiny sticks to define the funnel.

From what she could see, all three of their vehicles remained intact, with her old pickup slotted between Trenton's SUV and Leigh's F150. She shot off a quick text to her friend.

"Go. Now. Upstairs." With a not-so-gentle shove, Trenton sent her stumbling back deeper inside the building.

"Gunther, protect him." Not one to follow directions, she moved to watch from the cover of the block wall. If she'd grabbed her gun, she could've been more use than fodder.

Trenton had drawn his weapon, held in neutral position with muzzle down, before darting forward.

Alerting to an unknown scent or presence, the wolf dog bolted forward past the vehicles and headed toward the woods.

"Gunther, come!" Hailey repeated her command twice before the canine broke off and returned as Leigh joined her by the door.

The dog acknowledged Leigh's presence with a chuff.

"Someone was here." Hailey pointed to the broken glass.

"Kinda gathered that by the lack of light," Leigh said then padded toward Hailey's truck, ready to enforce a lethal response.

Gunther paced Leigh into the night as Hailey followed.

Trenton opened her truck's door and glanced inside. "It's gone. Wouldn't have mattered if you'd locked up."

Each of the three stared at the woods beyond.

"Damn it." Trenton holstered his weapon.

Hailey slid her fingers along the truck's door release, then the seat and console. "Bugger wore gloves. Give me a minute to check my trees."

"What? I'd make a rude comment if I didn't think you were serious." Trenton again took the lead to the edge of the woods. "I don't want to know, just check."

"Somebody's in a mood. And for your information, I just painted stripes around the tree to give it a small clean slate. If our uninvited visitor touched without gloves, I might get something."

Consistent with her luck, she got no clear readings. "He'd already pulled on his gloves, which muffled his aura."

"What was in the ledger, Hailey?"

"Strings of numbers, names of animals, dates and times... oh no. I may have just lost the information needed to solve this mess."

"Let's get someone out here to dust for prints. We'll call it a break-in for now." Trenton scanned their surroundings. "Son of a bitch got the notebook."

"Sure. The tech guys love being called out in the middle of the night ahead of a storm." Leigh snagged her phone and made the call. "This isn't like the city, big brother."

"Damn it. If I'd had my head on straight..." Hailey had no one to blame but herself. After showing the notebook to Laurent, she'd left it in plain sight. Maybe if she'd let him follow her home like he'd wanted, the damn thing would be in her hands.

"Had you been caught an hour ago, you could've been killed." Leigh urged them both back to the loft. "C'mon. There's nothing to do here now."

"Henri's a sly bastard, but at least we have his number," Hailey advised in leading her up the steps, followed by Gunther. "We'll get him."

"Before he gets one of us," Leigh agreed.

Chapter Twenty-Seven
Hailey

Morning dawned with the fringes of severe weather bearing down on the coast. Stronger winds would soon sever small saplings, tear loose shutters and shingles from rooftops, and send furry and feathered creatures scurrying for cover. Small consolation that the National Hurricane Center downgraded the system to a Tropical storm.

A long night of studying her notes left Hailey exhausted and frustrated. The link central to her father, Bernadette, and Henri still eluded them all. Gambling could link Henri and her father, but excluded Bernadette due to time's passage. Drugs could link Henri and Bernadette yet would exclude her father for the same reason.

Recent confrontation, arguments overheard between her parents years prior, and intuition confirmed Henri was neither welcomed nor a tolerated topic of discussion in the Arquette household.

How could her father have been so deficient in character or assessment to form that association? The only conclusion she could draw included blackmail stemming from his gambling. *To do what?*

She knew nothing of gambling addiction, hence at two in the morning when she couldn't sleep, opened her laptop and started research that would outline the following day's plan.

After a fitful three hours, she'd woken to Gunther's two-ton wake-up call. Sitting on her chest was his version of *"C'mon, damn it. I'm sitting cross-legged here."*

"Okay, fur ball. I'm up. I'm up." The rich aroma of Creole bread pudding urged her to move faster.

If Trenton continued to cook, she'd have to convince him to stay, maybe even find him a girlfriend.

God knows he needs to get laid.

The problem was, she didn't know of anyone who was good enough for him *and* could put up with his crazy schedule. A sly rejoinder in the back of her mind declared, *it'd break your heart.*

Outside, wind whistled under the eaves and blew an old plastic trashcan down the street. It certainly wasn't a day to be out and about, but the longer she waited to find Henri's cabin outpost, the higher the probability he'd have cleared out and vanished after knowing someone hunted him.

Even Leigh wouldn't approve of today's plan, hence the layer of subterfuge and deceit.

Leigh pulled the spicy casserole from the oven. "Trent cooked. I'll serve. Hailey, you can clean."

"C'mon, sleepyhead. You're late," Trenton declared as he took a plate from the stack on the table and passed the others down.

"Be back as soon as I take Gunther out." The fact no one challenged her came as a surprise.

Something's up with the badged duo. If only Gunther could talk.

In counter thought, if the intruder got what he wanted last night, there was no need to hang around.

An eerie apprehension settled on her shoulders in stepping into the blustering wind. Her canine partner, however, appeared to love experiencing nature unhinged. He took his time sniffing where investigators had parked the prior night, then relieved himself against one of Trenton's tires.

Two gazes settled on her the minute she stepped back into the loft. "What?"

"We're trying to sort this mess while figuring out what you're up to." Trenton narrowed his gaze as he scooped two large spoonfuls of bread pudding onto her plate.

"Me? Nothing. Can you not see we'll be in the teeth of a storm later today? Let me guess, you both still plan on working. You should sit tight too." Hailey pointed to the one considered her non-blooded twin. "Don't tell me that odious lieutenant is making you go in—"

"It's all hands on deck, or at least in the office. Trenton wants to go too. However, leaving you alone is asking for the worst kind of trouble," Leigh hedged.

"You both need bells around your necks," Trenton muttered. "I thought of sneaking a microchip into your food, so at least I'd be able to track you for a digestive cycle."

"Yeah, but then you'd have to recover the chip." Hailey snickered and offered Leigh a high-five.

Trenton set his fork down and sighed. "Listen, the least you can do is give us twenty-four hours, Hailey. Can you do that much?"

"What makes you think I'd be dumb enough to go out in all of that?" Hailey gestured out the window toward the woods where leaves turned their underbellies to the wind.

"You were on your computer last night. I saw the light under your door," Trenton countered. "I checked your notepad, but you didn't write anything. That equals strategy and deception."

"You should have come in and kept me company. We could've found some way to occupy our time." Sexual innuendos always forced Trenton to back off.

Something in his eyes—the way his jaw clamped shut and his mouth firmed into a straight line pointed to thoughts she couldn't entertain until later.

It was Leigh's turn to snicker.

"Thanks, but prepubescent pimples and gangly colt legs don't do it for me." A slight twitch of his left eye betrayed tension.

Hailey turned her attention to her friend. "*Kigvod rocalwi tuamadi...*" Continued twin speak conveyed her message if not her intent.

Snapping her hand out to the side, Hailey caught the gooey glob of cheese and egg tossed by Trenton along with the comment, "I remember how."

"With no practice, like, for years? Guess it is like riding a bike." Hailey giggled.

"Keep it up and I'll feed your dog this casserole," Trenton flicked his gaze from Hailey to his sister. "Can I get a little support, here, Leigh? Not because of the Y-chromosome, but shared blood?"

His sister rolled her eyes.

"You wouldn't feed him that. It has onions in it." Hailey loaded a forkful of casserole, waiting.

"Stop. Both of you. We'll search as soon as the worst of the storm passes." Leigh slapped the table, staring between the two facing off.

Trenton grumbled and held up his hand in preparation for a possible incoming casserole missile.

Leigh pointed across the table. "You, stay here today. Trenton and I will be back as soon as possible. We'll discuss the next step."

After cleanup, the two possessing badges left with doubtful glares tossed over their shoulders.

The problem now existed—how to find Henri. Again, Hailey cursed herself for wearing gloves during her little B&E.

At least I took pictures of the ledger's first pages. She'd kept that nugget of information to herself.

Hailey tweezed her phone from her back pocket and swiped the screen.

The first entry differed from those that followed. It had no columns or dates, just names of animals and coordinates, likely her best bet.

Because of the storm, it's too late for Henri to leave by boat, but he wouldn't leave money or drugs behind.

She located three sets of coordinates using her phone's app. Each set corresponded to an animal in Henri's records.

The first entry, "Roadrunner," could be the name of his boat.

Sounds 'bout right.

High-speed, low-profile vehicle plus nighttime. Even Henri wouldn't have fled via water in the dark. Not for a long haul.

Trenton had confiscated her pistols and keys, thinking to stop her from snooping, but Victor had taught her to hotwire a vehicle while making modifications years prior.

"I don't believe Trenton sees you as a true threat, Gunther. Doesn't matter. If we find Henri, we'll call Leigh for backup."

It'd serve Trenton and Lieutenant Colson right.

Chapter Twenty-Eight
Hailey

Strong bursts of wind blasted Hailey in the face as she snaked her way over the grassy, uneven path locals would call a road. Muddy tracks detailed passage from the prior night since they held water from the early morning rain.

The air was heavy with the threat of the main deluge still to come. Clouds boiled overhead, building to a crescendo that would soon wash the earth clean.

Hiking through gator country during nesting season miles from civilization wasn't her smartest move, yet time was paramount, and she wanted to get back before the worst of the storm.

Slipping her phone from her back pocket, she huddled over and checked its reception. One bar. Two more steps and she had none.

At least she'd pinned the destinations on her map. That coupled with her knowledge of the area, she'd sweep her targets and be home before Leigh or Trenton.

The first destination equaled an empty lot in the middle of nowhere but its proximity to the river made it a likely rendezvous spot. Tracks there appeared old.

Her second location was just as secluded and also lacked evidence of recent travel. With her bang stick held ready, she proceeded.

Low land and inclement weather forced her to park a half mile from her third destination. Her furry partner hopped out behind her.

The path showed evidence of recent travel in smashed rutted tracks. No sight or sound of a vehicle alerted her to others present.

Gunther perked his ears when rounding the road's next curve, dense with tall grasses and straddled by cedar and gumbo-limbo trees characterized by resinous, peeling coppery-colored bark.

Deeper in the shadowed woods, the harsh *Kee-ahh* of a red-shouldered hawk raised the alarm of an invader in its territory. Increasing winds muted other swamp songs from crickets, cicadas, and various unseen inhabitants.

Hailey paused to study the ramshackle cabin coming into view. Like its suspected owner, it'd seen better days.

Two of the four boarded windows contained holes large enough to invite any number of vermin looking for shelter.

Odd.

One opening was big enough to admit a child, assuming he or she could jump three feet to reach the sill. Part of the sagging roofline appeared ready to cave with the next strong gust.

Buttonbrush and baccharis interspersed with spikerushes and sedges around the structure blocked sight of its foundation but were low enough to view a vehicle if present.

Farther out, narrow glimpses of white caps between cattails, bulrushes, and marsh grass attested to nature's growing force. Henri would be a fool to take a boat out in this weather.

"Gunther, you stay outside. I don't want you getting into it with a raccoon or any other critter I find in there."

Five yards from the broken wooden steps, she signaled her companion to *down*. He did so on an indignant chuff but had a view of the front and side wall.

The first two stair treads tested strong enough before acquiring her full weight. She eyed the posts failing to hold the sagging porch in wind screeching through the roof's many holes.

Two broken upper floorboards warped at the ends provided gaps large enough to create a cozy den underneath. An unidentified hiss as she stepped above them warned the inhabitants didn't fancy visitors.

Even if the front door was bolted from inside, it looked old enough to cave with a well-placed kick. A strong gust shoved her forward, stopped with her palms against the jamb.

Her mind was immediately assaulted with too many visions to assimilate. She snatched her hands back before the images dropped her to her knees. One face did stand out in her mind.

Henri.

Nothing could've heard her approach, which didn't negate an unseen security camera.

Using the hem of her shirt, she grabbed the rusted knob, which turned under her fingers.

A long squeak announced her entry. Inside, she blinked at the amount of floating dust highlighted by filthy windows along the back.

To her right, a cot against the north wall instigated thoughts of who, or what, might have slept there last—or, if small enough and slithered, might still be under the green wool blanket.

Seeing the inside was empty, she leaned her bang stick against the wall.

On the opposite side, a rectangular table butted against wood-plank walls with an oil lamp in its center. The latter lacked any sign of dust or long usage. Scarred floorboards continued to the kitchen area where a pump centered in rotten boards offered water to the steel sink beside it.

The disparity of old and new instigated more uneasiness than the filth under her feet. Warped two-by-six lumber substituted countertop space with empty open shelves above. To her relief, no snakes coiled in the visible areas.

Stranger still was the fact someone covered the front windows with plywood, yet the side and rear-facing ones were left without solid barriers to the interior. Glass panes had long since been broken. Long scratches on the interior of the back door could've come from any number of creatures.

Territorial marks?

Near the front, a round jagged pool of light highlighted dirt on the floor through the side's window frame. The worn and battered desk appeared out of place.

Taking a deep breath, she lightly slid her fingers along the surface to see if she could pick out another face.

Various flashes of Henri counting money or pills flitted through her mind. Another man stood facing the river out back. He looked familiar, but she couldn't identify him from her perspective. Another image entailed a woman, dressed in black slacks and a long-sleeved white shirt, the same who'd posed for a picture.

Lack of dust on the desk surface indicated its recent addition. Dirt and rodent droppings dotted the front, but not there.

There was no space big enough to conceal a person, except under the bed, a section she declined to check. Henri didn't strike her as the type to hide.

Like the desk in Henri's home, the user kept these drawers locked. Declining to test the strength and cleanliness of the wood-slatted chair, Hailey pushed it aside and crouched. Her backpack held a lock pick set, but when she gripped the drawer and pulled, it opened without protest.

Several pens and an open bag of hard candy lay amid paper clips and a ruler in the top drawer. Before inserting her hand and checking the bottom surface of the desk, she made a visual inspection and used the ruler to sweep the underside.

Nothing marred the smooth expanse.

Yay, no spider bites today.

The bottom drawer's depth allowed for legal-sized hanging folders. A dozen dirt-smeared red, green, and blue files rested haphazardly on their rails, showing signs of rifling at some point. Resting two fingers on the side rail, she nudged each file open to see if anything remained. The visions assaulting her now were all of Henri.

Damn. He's cleaned everything out.

In frustration, she'd shoved each folder back then lifted her foot to kick the drawer shut when a slip of something white caught her eye. It'd snagged on the inside corner of the drawer between the last file and rail.

The shudder rolling over her shoulders had nothing to do with the slap of winds testing the building's structural integrity.

A light tug released the tri-folded paper. If it concerned her father, once read, there'd be no shield, no hiding behind what she'd always believed.

Her father was a good and honest man. It came down to faith.

It was a simple white unlined sheet, like what she used in her printer, yet had the potential to change her life.

Do I want to know?

A sudden inrush of wind coincided with the back door slamming wide and bouncing off the wall.

Always the predator, Henri stood in the doorway and smiled. It was the type of cold grin shared by serial killers preparing for playtime.

"Hey, puss. Long time, no have. Time to rectify that and find out if reality matches fantasy."

Hailey took in the baggy jeans and stained t-shirt overlapping his belt. Arrogant as he was repulsive, Henri carried no visible weapon.

Which doesn't mean he doesn't have one tucked in his back waist.

Her stomach clenched. Acid scored her throat.

"I wouldn't brag about something you either don't have or don't know how to use." Hailey made to stand, aware her only weapon lay too far away to use.

Henri took a step inside and shut the door. "Well, now, why don't we find out?" His gaze took in the single-shooter bang stick before his chuckle filled the air. "I don't think so."

She stood no chance of escaping through the front door before he'd be on her, so, she faced him. He had a solid hundred pounds and six inches compared to her slight frame.

"You killed Bernadette." She made it a statement.

"This your idea of foreplay? Certainly turns me on, so, yes, I'll oblige. I did."

"Why carve up her body?"

"To match the others. I have friends with particular tastes."

Another step forward and his grin widened. He hadn't directly admitted to killing the others.

"Why?"

"She wanted too much, was too pushy. She'd learned far too much to live. I followed orders and put her out of my misery."

"Who's your boss?"

"Nobody you'll get to meet, sweetie. In fact, a few minutes from now, you won't even care. Where's your meddlesome partner, by the way?"

"Calling for backup."

"I doubt that." Henri held both hands up, one holding a cell phone. "No reception. Anyway, once they do get here, all they'll find is your body. So, why don't you ask what's really on your mind?"

Hailey fisted her hands, willing her heart rate to slow. "You killed my father. Why?"

"Now, there's the million-dollar question. Your dad was talented in many ways. If not for him, I wouldn't have that fancy boat tied up out back, nor the hefty bank account waiting for me after leaving this hellhole."

"He wouldn't sell drugs. And you're not smart enough to counterfeit bills."

"Ah, there it is. You're right about the first. He was clever enough to figure out how to spin gold out of twine, but not how to hide a note pointing a finger at me."

"Make twenties and hundreds out of one-dollar bills? He wouldn't." Shock punched her in the chest, knocking the breath from her lungs.

Henri took another step closer. Four feet separated them. His gaze landed on the white tri-folded letter on the floor. "*Hmm,* looks like I missed that when clearing out."

"Would it happen to be your confession?"

"Naw, it's something I confiscated from your dad." Henri grunted. "He figured if things went south, cops would know where to look. I certainly couldn't be having that, now could I?"

"You're a pig."

"He'd have done anything to save his precious family. The painting I took as a warning tipped the scales after the visit I paid your mom."

"What?"

Henri answered with a question of his own. "Did you know your mother was pregnant when he died?"

Hailey recoiled from his words.

"Yep. Paid her a little visit myself. Told her to get her husband in line or something real bad would happen. Sorry about your lost sibling. I hear *stress* can cause a miscarriage."

Hailey's mind stuttered to a halt.

Henri shrugged. "I told your dad it'd be one less mouth to feed. That's when he lost his shit. Came at me with murder in his eyes, so enraged he couldn't think. Had himself under animal instincts, but that didn't save him."

"You're the animal, you bastard, and you'll pay, both for Bernadette and my father." Hailey grimaced when Henri pulled a gun from his waistband and set it on the counter.

"The only thing I'm gonna *pay* is attention to your luscious body as I plunder it. Hell, I can take hours and still have plenty of time to escape the worst of this crap. I'll go someplace where I don't have to battle the elements."

"You can't outrun this weather in a boat."

"Don't intend to. I been waiting all morning for you to show. Knew it was you in my house. Why I've got a brand-new pickup waiting at Jonston's Bridge. From there, I'll toddle up the highway and head north."

The bastard would expect her to turn and run toward the front door. When he took another step toward her, she dashed forward and ducked to the side, trying to dart around him and to the back. Once outside, she stood a better chance with Gunther's help.

The wide arc of his swing caught her upper arm and spun her around. She used the momentum and stepped into the punch and aimed at his face.

His pivot prevented the direct strike. Faster than he appeared, he grabbed her foot when she tried a leg sweep.

A hard yank sent her crashing down on her butt.

Crouching, he blocked her next kick with one hand and shoved her back with a punch to her chest. His greater strength sent her head bouncing on the floor with a solid thud.

She'd never imagined he could move so fast.

In anticipatory glee, he chortled and reached for his belt. "Any last words?"

Fingers of his left hand wrapped around her throat as he sat on her thighs, the intent clear. In the next instant, his arms flew up, his eyes wild as he cried out, "What's happening?" Both arms flailed wide, windmilling to keep from toppling backward.

"Get off me."

"Witch! I'll kill you."

"Not today, asshole." The bulk of his weight made it impossible to move.

A sudden presence filled her mind. She felt *something* other than Henri's weight. Swinging her gaze left and right, she saw no one else.

Suddenly, Henri's head snapped back as if punched in the jaw. No blood streaked his flesh. His teeth remained intact; his mouth open in shock while his gaze darted around for the threat.

His weight still pinned her to the floor.

Unable to move, Hailey tilted her head back and let out a long soulful howl declaring, *"Pack meeting, Gunther."*

"Bitch. You think you're a wolf now? Let's see if you screw like one." Despite his bravado, fear tinged his words.

His weight shifted again when an unseen force knocked him sideways. Still, he adjusted position to fasten her hands held over her head in a punishing grip. "Nothing's gonna stop this. Been thinking about it for a long, long time."

The smile on his face burned in her thoughts until a flash of black fur blocked out the stream of light. A low growl was the sole warning of Gunther's attack.

Self-preservation threw Henri's arm up to protect his neck. His scream echoed in the small confines when strong canine teeth pierced soft flesh. His shifting weight freed one leg.

With his other hand, he snatched a knife from his boot.

Hailey intercepted the weapon's arc, able to send it skittering away with her concurrent punch to his crotch.

His weaker position and facing two threats gave her a temporary advantage.

Or is it somehow three threats?

Henri fell to the side but continued to grapple with Gunther, each growling their rage.

She scooted back and crab-walked to her bang stick, watching as Henri dragged her dog back toward the counter and his gun.

Her timing was better, aiming the power head at his shoulder at the same time he reached his weapon. With all the force she could muster, she thrust forward as he twisted his body to avoid contact.

The loud boom echoed in the small confines, followed by Henri's scream of pain.

Surprise etched his features but didn't negate his determination. With one arm in Gunther's jaws, he palmed the gun and swung outward just as the force of her shoving with her stick rocked him backward. He swept his free arm wide for balance but maintained hold of his weapon.

Blood seeped from his shoulder.

Unmitigated fury radiated from him in waves. Like a trapped animal, he gave no notice to his injury. The first shot he fired hit the front wall.

Her only weapon spent, she dropped it in favor of latching onto his wrist and gun, twisting to avoid his wrath.

Gunther redoubled his efforts as Henri pulled his bloody arm free. Undaunted, her canine captured the softer parts between Henri's thighs in his powerful jaws.

The gun clattered to the floor.

Henri's snarl lost volume as breath *whooshed* from his lungs in an ear-piercing scream. A satisfying falsetto resulted from her dog's powerful grip.

Better access adjusted Gunther's target, now clamping his jaws on his opponent's shoulder. Hailey gave Henri the benefit of her booted foot to his crotch as she reached for the pistol.

Shaking fingers sent it skittering out of reach.

"Burn in hell, you bastard."

Blood soaked the front of his shirt as he fell, his body twisting under the power of Gunther's force.

Adrenaline washout sapped her strength, yet she held the upper hand. "Gunther, break."

It took two more commands for her protector to release his prey and stand by her side. She didn't need the gun, now under the cot, and wouldn't let Gunther kill unless Henri attacked again.

The bastard's gaze ricocheted around the room until settling on the cot. Eyes narrowed and shoulders hunched, he looked at Gunther.

"You'll never make it. The next order I give will be a kill command," she promised.

Keeping his gaze locked onto the animal, he scooted back using one arm. It wasn't until he reached the door that he stood, turned, and bolted outside.

"Gunther, no. Let the cops track him down. He's wearing lead in his shoulder that's gonna have to come out. He won't get away, and I won't be a killer." It wasn't like the thug would file a complaint about a dog bite, but if he was found dead with one, it might have a very different outcome for Gunther.

It was then she noticed the slip of paper, the folded letter. Blood spattering the top reminded her of the cost of obtaining it.

Sitting on the floor, she sighed. What could be worse than that already learned?

Cecile,

Please forgive me. I've brought the house down around our ears with my weakness.

Whatever you hear in the coming months, I'm doing what I have to do to keep you and our children safe. Henri's boss is sending someone to pick me up, says if I do this one thing, my debt is clear. I swear I'll never gamble again.

If he stays true to his word, I'll be home and you'll never have to read this.

You know me,

I'll love you forever.

Jon

Tears bled the first line of words together before she could wipe them away. All this time she and her mother thought he'd abandoned them. Her dad's heart was in the right place even if he couldn't see his way clear of the hornets' nest. He died not knowing his wife lost their second child.

Perhaps Henri kept the note to blackmail his boss if their scheme ever came to light.

For long minutes, she merely sat with tears flowing and Gunther nuzzling her face. The growing tempest outside had nothing on what she'd held within for so many years.

The trek back to cellular reception allowed time to digest what she'd learned. She'd discovered the specific link between her father and the counterfeit money, but not the head of the snake. Henri wasn't smart enough and had admitted to receiving orders.

At least her mother might have a little peace in reading the letter.

Chapter Twenty-Nine
Hailey

Nothing topped a long hot shower to soothe away aches, pains, and exhaustion from answering questions. Nothing, that is, except for the promise of a choco-waffle shell packed with Chunky Monkey, hardened dark chocolate, and covered with sprinkles. The thought made Hailey dress faster and head downstairs to her truck.

The storm's downgraded status inspired small groups, either fearless or stupid, to gather and celebrate whatever triumph or victory they claimed. Leigh, Trenton, and her mother waited at Á La Mode to both celebrate and commiserate.

"C'mon, boy. They'll have something for you too."

Gunther was excited to hop up and go for a ride. They each deserved a break, after which, she had a long journal entry for her diary. Maybe she could turn it into a book someday. Once the pain subsided.

There'd be a period of groveling in her future. Her ears still rang from Trenton's lambasting her character and lack of sense. Her mom and Leigh would parrot the prior day's events interspersed with Trenton's expletives to round out the conversation.

Her truck was old but handled the winds with little trouble. Gunther swiped his tail back and forth, a big doggy grin on his face.

Rounding the last bend in the deserted industrial park, Hailey reached over to rub his ears. He sat in the passenger seat, alert and watching the shadows coalesce and blend in the thick woods outside his window. By morning, the storm would blow through, and cleanup would begin.

From the corner of her eye, she saw a truck approach the intersection, speeding up instead of slowing down.

Myriad thoughts revolved through her mind a split second before impact. Collision occurred just behind her door with sharp pain in her shoulder and an ear-splitting crash.

Conflicting forces threw her against the side window with the addition of Gunther's weight for an added wallop. She'd had no time to stop and no place to swerve as it T-boned her vehicle and sent her skidding sideways onto the shoulder.

Something wet flowed over her temple and cheek with a copper odor. Her vision tunneled and darkened even as her vehicle came to a tortuous stop.

Shaking her head didn't clear her sight or the image of Gunther, his lower half lying on the seat with his head and shoulders draped down onto the rubber-matted floorboard.

Time became a gauze-like entity she couldn't track. Her thoughts refused to focus.

From far off, she heard the squeal of screeching metal and knew someone opened her door. Her eyes wouldn't clarify the sight, nor could she identify the humming sound. Darkness pulled her deep within its grasp.

Return to consciousness came in layers with unfamiliar odors and sounds compounding a headache the likes of which she'd never experienced.

Something bounced under her shoulder and jolted her head against a cold, hard, waffled surface. Her first coherent thought revolved around Gunther.

Hazy vision refused to define more than colors and ridges. Her nose told a story of sweaty feet, soured milk, and an undefined rottenness not worth contemplating.

Soft jazz music played from somewhere beyond her field of vision. The sound was tinny, like that which issued from a small speaker.

A radio. Am I in a van?

Slight flexion of her legs delineated the flat surface against the soles of her feet, perhaps a rear door. She couldn't define the exterior view, but two squares of dim light increased the probability of barn-style doors. Driving rain battered the van's thin side panels.

Mental stock of her injuries included pain in her left shoulder and left side of her head. Several blinks helped clear her vision, enough to detail part of the vehicle. Rope bound her hands in front, but her ankles were free.

If she could get out, running was an option.

The problem remained, she didn't know her location, where she was headed, or who was driving.

Her last impression of Henri included a man on the run. Coming back for her now wouldn't negate the pile of evidence stacked against him. He might not be the sharpest tool, but any rat knew when to abandon ship.

The next hard bounce elicited a groan despite her efforts to keep quiet.

"Ah, awake are we? Good. We'll be arriving at your final destination shortly."

The male voice struck a familiar chord in her memory but wouldn't slide into place. Cranking her head back, she saw short dark hair and a sharp-angled jaw.

Armond Boyér?

"Why? What did your affair have to do with Bernadette's drug dealing?"

"Nothing if she hadn't snooped. Curiosity is your downfall. What a shame. Tell me, did Henri enjoy you before you shot him?"

"Not hardly. I sent him packing, with an extra ounce of lead. Why didn't you kill me while I was unconscious?"

"Two reasons. First and primarily, Henri is going to take the blame. Considering his temper issues, he would want a slow and drawn-out revenge. Shooting isn't his style."

"But it is yours? It was you who shot at me in the bayou."

"Yes. I tried to warn you, but you're just too damn stubborn. Had to go snooping in my business."

"You're the counterfeiter. Did Bernadette find your stash and demand a cut?"

"Greedy bitch wanted half." Armond laughed as he slowed to make a turn. "She thought I was the mastermind of it all, didn't realize I've connected with a bigger fish for wider circulation. Paid off, too, till you stuck your nose in it all."

"Sorry. No, wait. Not sorry."

"Five years of work you've screwed up. Five years." Armond snorted in derision. "Pansy-assed bitches on the school board don't even know who's pulling their strings. Someone new is taking over now, and I can't find the source. Guess they'll find out soon enough, though. Wish I could stick around to see it, but that little bitch Bernadette stirred up some of the other girls I've sampled. They'll have a fucking lynch mob after me."

"You wanted Kenny to take the blame for his girlfriend's death."

"That would've worked, too, if not for that lazy ass Henri. Always wanting to take shortcuts and have an insurance policy."

"My father?"

"That, too. Henri wouldn't tell me where he'd buried the bodies. Said he left evidence leading back to me."

"What evidence?"

"The necklace I gave Bernadette. When you found the bodies and it wasn't there, well, it made the threats moot. I don't know where the damn thing is now, not that it matters."

"Did you put the totem in my truck and try to squash me with a concrete gargoyle?"

"Not hardly. I don't play with dolls, and yes, I heard about that. I wouldn't expend the energy to shove a statue off a rooftop."

"How do you know all this?"

"My contacts have spies in every department."

"Yet Henri got away with a bunch of your cash."

"Did he now?"

That gave her pause for thought.

Is Henri dead now?

"Trenton came back to Texas because of a threat to his sister. Why draw him here?"

"That was another of Henri's mistakes, wanting to play instead of setting a definitive example. Said he'd met someone on the dark net from the east coast, a psycho who collected women. He had visions of doing the same."

Hailey felt the force of a sharp turn tug her sideways. "Henri wanted to kidnap and hold women?"

"He had visions of setting up his own harem, the fool."

The threat Trenton conveyed from Pennsylvania had been real but was now extinct.

"Was it him who ran me off the road near the Landry house?" Hailey needed to make sense of all the death and tragedy filling her life.

"I suppose so. Sounds like something he'd do." Armond slowed to a crawl on the pitted trail and angled the van right. Strong wind slid them to the side.

"So, who was the corpse in the truck?"

"Homeless guy Henri brought back from Houston. Few more miles in here and the only way you're leavin' is in the belly of a gator. 'Fraid you're at the bottom of the food chain tonight."

"When Henri's caught, he'll turn on you to save his own skin."

"I may only be a lowly art history teacher, but last I heard, corpses don't talk."

"Only to medical examiners."

"Not if they can't find the pieces. I do believe in feeding gators smaller portions. It helps their digestion. At least that's what I've found in my experience."

"Sick. How many have you killed and left for carrion predators?"

"Only the three who challenged my right to rule this section."

"Section of what?"

"Doesn't matter. Tell you what, you be *real* nice, and I'll make it quick. Might even get yourself some endorphins for the end. You won't feel a thing. In deference to your aversion of Henri, I won't even drop your body parts in the same place. How's that sound?"

Hailey shook her head. She'd need a different mindset to survive. Armond wasn't just a predator. He was intelligent, resourceful, and vicious. She'd also witnessed his arrogant side that begged for exploitation.

Rolling her shoulders, closing her eyes, and taking a deep breath, she forced her body to relax. Every captive situation offered the possibility of escape, however small. It only appeared to those alert enough to see it.

His obvious plan to take advantage equaled a window to turn the tables. If assured of success, the predator would lower his guard.

Convincing him she believed in her ability to change his mind about killing her equaled a pivotal key. All she needed was his uncertainty, a slight preoccupation, a split second in time.

"If I cooperate, will you let me live?"

Armond startled and snapped his gaze around to stare. Internal debate indicated by a fierce frown revealed he pondered her attitude, if not the outcome.

"You don't strike me as the type to capitulate that easily." A slight hike in the corner of his mouth morphed into a grin.

"I'm not as young as the girls you like, but my experience makes me better."

"Had lots of practice with that federal agent, have you?"

That took her by surprise. "Um, no. And for the record, *ew.*"

"Huh, that's the thing about you youngsters. You never see what's in front of you. That, and you have no appreciation for history."

"Are you a native of Texas?"

"Not hardly. I moved here from up north. My, ah, extracurricular activities have gained me a base foundation, a life here in the bayou."

Whether the storm cut off access to his destination or anticipation of her offer shortened the trip deeper into the bayou, Armond pulled to a stop and pivoted in his seat.

"I suppose here's good. There's nothing for miles except swamp, tidal salt marshes, and interconnecting waterways."

"You know enough to avoid flooded areas, especially during a storm?"

In their previous conversation, she'd strived to obtain information related to Bernadette, not his knowledge of Texas bayous. The majority of Texans had no clue how to navigate and survive the swamp.

"I should. It pays to be a history buff. These systems of trails joined by early settlers became known as the Old Spanish Trail Highway. We're on Indian paths that circumvented the heavier forested and swampy areas and followed higher ground with natural ridges."

Striking up a conversation was the fastest path to stroking his ego. "You're a survivalist, then? That takes guts in these parts."

"Would that I had the time, but no. I happen to know people who *are* acquainted with navigating this area. I learned enough to get to my meeting points."

Again, he narrowed his gaze in judging her sincerity then shrugged as if it didn't matter.

A flash of silver glinted off the blade he retrieved from under his seat before he opened his door and slipped out.

A minute later, the barn-style doors opened to flood the van with midday driving rain. Armond hunched his shoulders and grabbed for his hat that flew off on a strong gust of wind.

"Still feel like cooperating?" His knife reflected ambient shafts of light as he slid inside. Though not latching the doors, he closed them to within inches.

Hailey nodded with a simultaneous raising of her shoulders and ducking her head. While she didn't have a submissive bone in her body, she could fake it to save her life.

"Roll onto your back."

Instant compliance earned a nod of approval.

"Unbuckle your belt and open your jeans."

With her wrists tied and rope wet, the maneuver would be difficult at best. After fumbling a minute with her belt, she let out a whimper.

"I can't. My fingers are numb and won't work right. A little help please?"

"Open your legs."

His kneeling and tentative crawl suggested suspicion. He kept the knife tight in his right hand.

When he reached forward with the blade, she understood his intent to deal a mortal wound. She had no viable defense. Her breath hitched on a sharp gasp as the knife closed the distance.

A strange howl filled the van and buffeted her ears. At the same time, Armond flew backward as if kicked in the gut.

Hailey hadn't moved.

The motion sent him careening into the doors and falling out, his arms flailing to help break his fall.

He landed on the soaking ground with a loud *"oof."*

Nylon rope burned her skin as she scooted out into the driving rain.

Armond regained his feet but hadn't retained his knife, which nestled in the grass mere feet to her left. Both froze with indecision.

"That's a mistake, asshole." Snapping a front kick sent him back to land amid leaf detritus even as pain rifled through her knee and up her thigh. "Face me like the spineless wimp you are." Without hesitation, she scooped up the knife.

"Why bother? I brought a gun." Rain plastered his shirt to his body in his dash for the driver's door. A swipe at his face cleared small leaves sealed to his cheek by the driving wind.

It was senseless to engage him with an injured knee and bound hands, nor could she stop his retreat toward the driver's door. She wasn't a killer.

Running proved her only option.

Bolting through the aged forest offered cover, but she had no idea of her location. Thinner brush to her left offered the best temporary direction.

A glance over her shoulder saw him taking aim. As he fired the shot, his gun arm flew up and out, sending the bullet meant for her off to her right.

She didn't stop to contemplate the strange occurrences or unseen benefactor, instead choosing to flee.

Armond had driven them to a forest full of black willow, ash, swamp oak, and aspen. Soft ground sucked at her sneakers as the next round struck the tree she passed.

It provided incentive to increase speed while gauging her distance and direction. Slipping on the thick carpet of detritus underneath saved her from the next shot.

"You'll never make it out of here alive. A bullet is less painful than a gator attack or a snake's bite."

He had a point, but she preferred neither. No sound of pursuit could override howling wind in her mad thrashing through guinea grass and around thickets of orange thorny bush.

The crack of another round made Hailey duck despite not feeling the kiss of metal tearing through flesh. Thoughts of Leigh finding the truck with Gunther inside brought tears to her eyes, blending with raindrops slashing at her cheeks.

Verbal threats became more distant, indicating her kidnapper was not brave enough to chance the swamps with her.

Her lungs burned for air. Sharp pain knifed through her injured knee. She kept going despite the increasing hobble in her step until blazing fire in her left side forced her to take cover for a break.

Ducking behind the wide, buttressed base of a cypress, she listened for footsteps while reversing the recovered blade and working to slice her bonds.

The only sound heard above the wind's roar was the pounding of her heart. Bile was bitter and scorched her throat.

Armond was a predator, but one most comfortable in a concrete and glass jungle. This was her territory, her turf. She understood bayou life, its cycles, dangers, and warnings.

The distinct sound of an engine's roar signaled he'd opted to leave, likely thinking the storm and swamp would take care of her remains. She couldn't wait to see the look on his face when she next confronted him.

A mental catalog of resources included her appropriated blade and the knowledge imparted during childhood story time.

The strongest weapon is my brain. Thanks, Mom.

Discovering he hadn't taken the time to toss her cell equaled a minor victory, not that there'd be service even if it survived the storm.

She needed to find an appropriate staff for use as a longer-range weapon. A broken limb would do nicely.

Her unknown location made it unwise to follow the road. The bastard might lay in wait, at least for a while. She needed to think ahead.

The night would be pitch black with heavy cloud cover, both a blessing and curse in her current circumstances. Unsure of how long she'd been unconscious in the van and injured, she needed a safe place to rest.

If there was a river nearby, she'd have a direction, as it would likely lead to civilization sooner rather than later. First, she needed a longer defensive weapon.

As children, she and Leigh had called four-foot walking sticks "wizard staffs." The one she found allowed her to make enough noise to warn and not startle carnivorous inhabitants. Surprising alligators, especially when nesting, increased their penchant to attack.

Despite many claims that Texas gators were less aggressive than those found in Florida's Everglades, she didn't care to test the theory. She'd never been to the sunshine state but rationalized the plentiful food supply in her area might keep the local reptiles more timid concerning humans.

She used her knife to sharpen one end of the limb she'd found, leaving the opposite to aid in walking and probing grasses too tall to circumvent. Tentative thrusts tested solidity of covered branches and found hidden holes.

Hailey was no prepper, but her mother's teachings instilled the knowledge to survive. She couldn't hear the sounds of rushing water ahead over the howling wind, but before long, thinning brush led her to a river too wide to chance crossing.

By now, Leigh and Trenton would be searching for her, regardless of the driving rain. Unfortunately, they'd have no direction or clue where to search.

In the meantime, a small fire would lend warmth and protection but wouldn't be possible until the weather cleared.

The ground grew soggier at the edge of the wood line.

Thickets of mangrove roots extending from black pudding soil merged into large trunks stretching more than fifty feet in the air.

Ahead, where they extended below the river's water line, many varieties of creature called the underwater habitat home, from one-inch gobies to sharks. Turbulence created another obstacle to crossing even if it weren't deep and wide.

Again, her mother's words came back to roost. *"Birds, fish, reptiles, and amphibians often nest on the west side of a river."* Nailing down a general direction was easier than dealing with what lay ahead.

Survival.

Common sense dictated she stay at least twenty feet from the water's edge, not a problem since she couldn't get to it.

Finding a shorter stick, she shoved it perpendicular into the ground where light would stream unfiltered from branches and mark its shadow when the sun made an appearance. At least she'd know which direction she traveled.

Next on her to-do list—build a small shelter away from the water and find something to eat.

Cattails and frogs it is.

Tomorrow, she'd stay in the open as much as possible while avoiding close proximity to the river.

Mud would protect exposed skin from mosquitos when the rain stopped. The smell she'd have to accept. Pathogens were less of a concern than bites that would invite other predators.

Alligators hunted at night, a time she hoped to pass without becoming a snack. Fallen sticks and limbs piled up would've made a decent shelter if not for wind and lack of binding material. A platform within a tree using branches and palm fronds would have to do.

Either way, she'd get a fire going as soon as the rain let up. Knowing Trenton, he'd have every available eye in the sky searching as soon as possible.

She hadn't noted conspicuous mounds of dirt indicating a gator's nest until nearly stepping on one. Most existed close to the water and consisted of dead vegetation mixed with mud. They typically held up to forty eggs.

A low drawn-out hiss warned of uninvited company regardless.

Without hesitation, she grabbed the nearest overhanging branch and climbed. Snapping jaws underneath warned of the predator's persistence. Had she been a few feet farther from the tree, she'd be in the gator's jaws, beating its snout and attacking its eyes, one of its few vulnerable spots. The knife at her back waist would do little good in her frantic state.

Great. Treed by a gator and stuck here for the duration.

Memory failed to call up much about the reptile's determination except the fact they were patient. How long would it take the beast to wander off, or at least far enough for her to drop down and make a hobbled run for deeper cover?

If stuck overnight, she could wedge herself in the fork of intersecting limbs and wait it out. Come dawn, a nesting female would likely go search of food.

By that time, Hailey would be hungry and tired, too, but alive to brag about it. From there, options included finding her way back to the Old Spanish Trail Highway or following the river.

That decision would come in the morning and depended on how much her injured knee swelled. Either way, Armond wouldn't be looking for her, wouldn't expect her to survive.

Her mind swirled with known facts then postulated about what she didn't know. The teacher claimed he hadn't tried to kill her with the gargoyle or put the totem in her truck. He also claimed to have spies in various departments.

Her thoughts drifted to Casper and her suspicious presence both at the antique store and the haunted ghost tour. Yet the young woman's actions suggested an inclination to save, not kill.

Which left Victor as a possibility.

Has he pulled one over on me?

Chapter Thirty
Trenton

Trenton loosened his grip on the wheel after skidding to a stop behind Leigh's truck. How was he supposed to do his job when Frick and Frack found trouble at every turn? If Leigh's boyfriend felt the same compulsion to watch over them, why wasn't he present?

Colson's message stating Hailey had been in an accident didn't come close to conveying the scene he now surveyed.

Lightning split the sky in jagged spears crashing down in the adjacent field while the crack of thunder overrode the fierce wind's attempts to level the landscape. Rain defied the best attempts to remain partially dry.

Flashing lights from two sheriff's cruisers strobed across the landscape. Behind them, two unmarked SUVs sat haphazardly parked.

Leigh's heated argument with the man towering over her drew his attention. With her friend in trouble, few could turn her from a determined path.

Colson isn't prepared for the tide of Leigh's wrath.

The young man hadn't learned to deal with women, detectives or not.

"Leigh? Where is she?" Wind and driving rain swallowed Trenton's words.

"Don't know, and numbnuts here won't call for a chopper." With hands fisted on her hips, she wasn't going to budge.

"Damn it, Leigh. We're in the midst of a storm. They can't take off now, and you know it. Besides, for all you know she could be cutting across this field to get help. There's very little blood here," Colson pointed to the semi-open field encompassing hundreds of acres.

"She wouldn't leave Gunther behind, first of all. Second, if she had to hoof it alone, she would've gone home. It may not be closer, but it's familiar."

Each shouted to be heard over the wind.

"Lieutenant Colson." Trenton started to pull rank but instead shook the offered hand and decided to listen to the detective's logic.

"Agent Briner." Informality from the prior weekend during Hailey's tour evaporated in the face of his responsibilities. "Perhaps you could talk sense into this one." Gesturing to Leigh, the lieutenant continued, "We'll call in air support when they can respond, when and if it's needed."

Leigh ignored her supervisor and turned to him. "Granted, her cell phone and backpack are missing. *However,* Gunther was draped off the front seat to the floor. I got him situated for now, but you know as well as I do she wouldn't leave him like that. And this was no accident."

Understanding dawned before he scanned the damage to the vehicle. "She's done a lot of crazy things, but she'd die before walking away from Gunther," he agreed, his stomach souring.

Circling Leigh and crouching beside the vehicle to study the damage, he noted the discrepancies between what he saw and what he knew as truth.

"Someone T-boned this vehicle." Turning to view the angles and bushes that would've veiled its approach, Trenton added, "She was ambushed."

Glass shards, likely from the other vehicle's headlights, lay scattered around the driver's door and rear tire well.

"Figured that. Plus," Leigh pointed to the horizontal indentation signifying the worst of the damage, "...I'd say the vehicle used was modified with a push bar of some sort."

Trenton picked up her train of thought. "No sign of skid marks indicating the other driver tried to stop. The intersection is clear from that direction."

His sister pointed down the dirt lane to where the other vehicle would've waited.

Scanning east and west ends of the deserted road Hailey had traveled, Trenton realized he no longer missed hillsides dusted with wildflowers and craggy mountains in the background. Southeast Texas was again his home, hurricanes, family, and all. "Hailey never saw it coming."

"The fact the other vehicle drove off indicates pre-meditation, I'll agree with that. I've already got units looking for her. However, no pilot is going up until this blows out." Colson held his hands up to indicate the wind flattening shrub grass around them.

"I'll call the vet while you start the search. I think Gunther's okay, just shook up. Hailey will have my head if I don't make sure, though." Leigh ignored her lieutenant and gripped Trenton's arm.

"Already on it." Trenton retrieved his cell on his way to his SUV to make some calls. When he returned, the lieutenant had his hands full.

"I've already spoken with Trooper Henley, State Police. This ties in with the counterfeiting and murder, so there won't be a problem with resources," Leigh advised.

"Hey, wait a minute." Colson circled Leigh to face Trenton. "Are you claiming jurisdiction here? I believe we should've had a few conversations before now. What is going on? Counterfeiting? What counterfeiting?"

"I'll explain in a minute. Is your CSI on the way?" Trenton paused, estimating transit and reaction times, then addressed Leigh. "How thorough is your evidence collection team? Whatever they collect, we can send it to the federal lab and get priority."

"Yes. And the team is solid. Colson's anal enough to supervise." No trace of timidity tainted Leigh's tone, despite her supervisor towering over her. "But I don't know how much they'll get. Everything's drenched."

Trenton turned to Colson and declared, "I don't care about the arrest. You can have it." Appealing to what might be the lieutenant's concern proved incorrect. "I just want my family safe."

"I don't give a damn about the collar." Colson trailed Leigh around the hood of the vehicle as she gloved up. "I'll put Gunther in your truck, Leigh."

Leigh stood back as Colson moved to open the door, hesitating before getting closer to the animal who'd gone utterly still.

"I'll take it from here. He knows me." Leigh reached in slowly to rub Gunther's chest. "How's it going, fella? How 'bout we take a ride? We'll find your mom while you're getting checked out."

Trenton studied the driver's door handle. Rain slashed at the outside of the window. Its interior wasn't dry, but it hadn't been soaked. "Underside of this might be the best place to get a print here."

Looking over the seat, Colson huffed a disgusted sigh. "Really? I hadn't thought of that." His attention turned to the white, paneled van pulling to a stop. Swiveling his head back in Leigh's direction, he added, "You'd already called them before you called me."

"I am a detective. I *detected* foul play, hence, CSI's presence."

"We've found no trace of Henri. Could be he's trying to finish what he started at the cabin." Colson addressed Trenton, "We got plenty of prints there, both Henri's along with a few of another, as yet unsub. Hailey's prints were excluded."

"I don't think this is Henri's work. It has to be our unidentified subject." Leigh interjected. "Hailey said he was shot and had a truck waiting at the ridge. We found fresh blood there, too, but no vehicle or Henri. I'm thinking he headed for high ground or across the border."

"Does Hailey still keep a change of clothes in the back?" Trenton had already sheathed his hands and searched under the back seat.

He retrieved a t-shirt and tossed it to Leigh. "Scent cloth when we're ready."

"We've got one dog on the way. Damn rain. Hailey was probably carried to her kidnapper's wheels."

Chapter Thirty-One
Hailey

To elevate one's knee while propped in a tree took skill, patience, and luck. The latter held through a night of intermittent naps.

The morning dawned dry with less wind, the worst of the storm having passed. In the quieter wake, horse flies, mosquitos, and all manner of biting bugs came out to feed.

Gravity assisted Hailey's descent from the lowest branch after determining the immediate vicinity clear of jaws and claws.

She clamped her mouth shut against the pain knifing through her knee. It'd been twenty minutes since her new leather-skinned BFF toddled off in search of easier prey.

A distant splash marked movement at the water line.

Mud applied to exposed skin helped lessen winged predators' penchant for snacking while wishing she had clogged sinuses. The smell rivaled the worst of anything experienced, until remembering the flies in the root cellar.

Her homemade walking staff assisted her hobble-step deeper into the woods and out of immediate reptilian range.

Seams of her denim jeans had stretched from the pressure of her knee's swelling despite its elevation during the night, but she didn't want to split the fabric and lose what little protection it offered. With each step, pain shot up her thigh and down into her calf.

Due to her inability to move quickly if needed, she decided to retrace her steps and search for the Old Spanish Trail Highway leading out.

Prodding each area as she walked, she avoided stepping into a hidden lair, but hustled just the same after hearing a hiss nearby.

Exhaustion clouding her mind relegated her focus to the basics of survival. Thinking of her phone, she retrieved it to check for a signal. Soaked and useless.

Her mind had stayed busy during the darkest hours, putting together final pieces of the puzzle. Three questions remained unanswered. Who placed the totem in her truck, and who attempted to crush her with a concrete gargoyle?

Last and most importantly, what unseen force had intervened on her behalf and saved her life, at the bayou with Trenton, the cabin with Henri, and when Armond intended to kill. Was it a part of her natural gift, yet to unfold?

Armond's reference to an expanded distribution ring got relegated to the backburner. She'd leave that to Trenton and the sheriff's department.

The teacher's claim that someone new was muscling their way into the gifted school detoured her thoughts to Casper, wiser than her years and trained as well as any cop, despite her age.

Her own "gift" drove Trenton to distraction at times. What were the extent and limitations of Casper's talent?

Exhaustion plagued her steps, but dehydration was a bigger threat. If she had basic supplies, a plastic bag and a piece of string, she could collect moisture from transpiring leaves of berry bushes. Filtering and boiling water from the river wasn't an option, as proven by spending the night in a tree. She couldn't maneuver fast enough to stay safe. Juicy cattail roots and a few carefully selected berries started her day.

Yum.

Strong remnants of the storm blew her bangs across her face and cooled her forehead as she thought about Gunther. A fuzzy memory of him beside her after the crash didn't indicate whether or not he'd sustained major injury.

She trusted that Leigh or Trenton would take care of him and start a search. Unfortunately, her friends wouldn't have an accurate starting point. Dead as it was, her phone couldn't be pinged.

By her estimation, it'd taken two hours to reach a trail where tire tracks indicated recent travel via four-wheeler. From there, she didn't know how far it was to a decent road. It could take minutes or days, which she wouldn't have in her injured state.

Midday passed with an occasional ray of sunshine poking holes in heavy cloud cover. Another meal of juicy berries for lunch brought back more of her mom's lectures on indigenous plants.

She knew open ground was near after passing an increasing number and variety of flowering bushes that required extra energy to support fruit.

When she limped to the edge of the wood line and saw the open expanse of ground yet to travel, moisture brimmed her eyes. She didn't have the strength to climb another tree to take a nap, hence decided to push forward.

In the distance, she made out several groupings of trees dotting the perimeter of the grassy landscape.

She trusted the twin ruts followed through marsh grass would eventually guide her to civilization. She had her walking stick, her mind intact, and the determination to see it through.

At least someone left me a trail to follow.

From behind her, she heard rhythmic steps.

Damn. How'd I miss that?

Holding her staff like a cudgel and taking cover behind a wide tree trunk, she waited.

"Looks like someone could use a ride." Amusement rode the edge of the teenager's voice.

"Casper?"

"In the flesh. How badly are you injured?"

"I can't walk all day, that's for sure." Looking around, she saw no fresh tracks, nor had she heard a vehicle. "What are you doing here? And how did you *get* here?"

"First. I came to help you. Second, well, that's a long story that'll have to wait. How about we get you home?"

"Seriously. The 'stories for later' are racking up. You've got to give me something." Hailey watched the younger woman's approach. Her clutch on the medallion around her neck tightened.

"Fine. I'll show you something, but I won't answer questions. Not yet."

"Plausible deniability?"

"Something like that. It's time you embrace your heritage instead of fighting it." Casper held out her hand.

Denial was on the tip of Hailey's tongue, but she couldn't voice the lie.

"Come on, take it. I know you feel things at times, just like I know who saved you from Armond when he dumped you off."

"What? You knew what he was going to do?" No way would she take the offered hand now. Not yet.

"No. I found out after the fact. Then I came to get you." Casper gripped the amulet tighter and again offered her hand.

A gentle breeze brushed the side of Hailey's neck before ruffling her hair. Soothing, soft, encouraging.

Hailey reached for Casper's hand, aware something huge was transpiring.

She wasn't prepared. Not even close.

Nearly translucent, a small sphere of white light expanded, growing taller with indistinct margins. Contours suggested a girl, maybe younger than Casper.

Hailey held her breath as seconds passed with the form taking shape, though she found few distinct features. She got the impression of faded jeans, t-shirt, and an oval shaped face.

That wasn't what knocked the breath from her lungs.

"Hi, Hailey." The voice was faint but held a musical quality. Long hair blew in an otherworldly breeze, or maybe it was just an illusion. "It's good to finally meet you."

"Your eyes."

"Yeah, it's a family trait."

Hailey fell to her knees, dislodging her grip on Casper's hand. The vision disappeared.

"Where—"

Casper crouched and touched Hailey's shoulder.

The girl reappeared and smiled.

"Who...?"

"Our parents named me Adélaïde, but you can call me Addy. The others do."

"Others?"

"Spirits." Addy gestured to the side. "Ghosts, though I don't know many." she added with a giggle.

"But you died before birth. How do you appear as…" She waved her hand in a vague gesture then noticed other translucent figures standing by, watching. Some were dressed in times of old, maybe turn of the century. Colors appeared muted, so did their facial features.

"Doesn't mean I can't appear older if I choose to. I've learned a lot, even if I have a long way to go." A defensive note cinched the speaker's edge of defiance.

"I have so many questions about your," she started to say life, then afterlife, but settled for, "existence. You've saved my life."

"I think now you have more important concerns. We can talk later." As if settling the matter, the spirit faded, the background seen through her becoming more prominent until the light was gone. *"Bye."*

"As much as I love a great reunion, or, first meeting as it is, I think we should walk while we talk." Casper dropped the hand holding the medallion to her side and let go of Hailey.

Once again, it appeared to be just the two of them.

"The medallion? That's how you connect with spirits?"

"Yes."

"That's how you found me. You talk to them." Hailey eyed the teen in a new light, her mind struggling to put together puzzle pieces.

"Yep, and it's how I knew about the gargoyle." Casper held up her hand to forestall more questions. "The incident at the antique store was coincidence."

"How'd you get us out?"

"That's a conversation for another day." Sweeping her hand out, she added, "Shall we?"

"I don't know where we are? Do you have a phone? Not that it'd matter since there'll be no reception." After a night with little sleep, a knee injury, and the appearance of her sister's spirit, her mind felt muzzy, a mix of fuzzy and muddled.

"Your transportation will arrive soon. I have… friends. Again, not a discussion for today."

"My transportation? What about yours?" Hailey put one foot in front of the other, mindful of her step.

"Again, pre-arranged. That's all you need know for now. Let's take this in baby steps."

That's all Hailey could manage. Prairie potholes, or freshwater depressions, edged the trail and presented specific dangers, but paled in light of recent revelations.

"Trenton's receiving an anonymous call about now, and getting this general area as your location. I'd very much appreciate it if you'd keep my presence here today, well, to yourself."

"Meaning I have to earn your trust first, then again with your, um, friends."

"Exactly."

Swelling in her knee made for painful walking, and her left shoulder wouldn't tolerate picking up anything weighing more than a small stick. Still, Casper was mindful of the slower pace.

Another thirty minutes filled with revelations about spirits created more questions than answers. When they reached another wood line, thinner and with less underbrush, she turned at the distant sound of thumping.

"Looks like your ride is almost here." She smiled then added, "We'll talk later."

"I can't leave you alone out here. Good God, you may be special, but you're still a kid," she argued despite instinct dictating Casper could take care of herself.

Casper held up a satellite phone. "Do you honestly think your fed friend is gonna believe stories about spirits helping you?"

"You called in the anonymous tip."

"No, this is for my pickup," Casper replied.

"You're investigating the school."

A shrug and smile were the only answer received as Casper turned to go.

"Wait. How are you gonna get out of here, and why the need for subterfuge when you could just take me with you?"

"I can't take you with me, but I wanted to make sure you made it to safety."

Their discussion ceased as the distant *thump, thump* of a helicopter announced its approach.

"How do you know that's a rescue and not a cleanup crew for Armond?"

"Trust me." The words drifted off as Casper vanished into the woods.

For a brief moment, Hailey could've sworn she saw the glimmer of a large silver ring inside the tree line, another riddle for another day.

Her swollen leg and lack of strength made the decision to stand still easy. As the helicopter grew closer, she studied the craft for insignia. Not that it mattered. She'd made her choice to take a stand. If the occupants weren't friendly, she wouldn't have the strength or stamina to run.

Familiar letters splashed across the side of the approaching craft formed a lump in her throat. According to Leigh, the FBI utilized a fleet of UH-60s, helicopters that resembled black hawks, like in the movies they used to watch.

Standing in the open, she waved her stick as the craft slowed and descended. The strong downwash of air forced her back and almost onto her butt.

The skids had just touched ground when the side door opened and Leigh jumped out. Her wide grin contrasted Trenton's scowl as he removed his headphones and stepped down.

Neither tried to talk until the blades stopped churning, but Leigh's arm around her shoulders said it all.

"Jeez, friend. You stink."

"Thanks, Leigh. Good to see you too."

"Where have you been?" Trenton took her walking stick and threw it aside. Latching onto her upper arms, he held her out to scan for visible injury.

"I thought I'd go for a walkabout. Wanna join me? I've been hanging out with *Les Dents*." Hailey snickered.

"Teeth? Are you delirious? Ah, you've got a head injury." Trenton fingered the scab at her temple.

"No. My new BFF. I named her myself."

Trenton turned to Leigh. "What's she talking about?"

Leigh shrugged. "Maybe you're not asking the right question."

Frustration twisted Trenton's mouth and narrowed his gaze. "Explain. Now."

"Gator. Nesting season." Hailey had little energy to expend on explanations.

"And you named it Teeth?" Trenton asked with a little less heat in his words.

"Woulda been rude and redundant to call her Gator. 'Sides, that name's already taken."

Trenton groaned, pulling her in for a hug while ignoring her ill humor. "Don't ever freaking do this to me again, you hear?"

"Yes, Mom." Nothing had ever felt better than his arms around her, his heat kindling a fire within her chest.

"I mean it. Damn it. Watching over you girls has always been a full-time job."

"Yet, you left us behind," Hailey countered with a little heat of her own.

"Leigh had a steady boyfriend, and you had... Victor. I thought you'd be okay."

"Not only am I okay, I'm fine. How's Gunther?" Hailey looked around them.

"No broken bones, no internal injuries. Just bruises." Trenton cocked his head to the side and frowned, his gaze studying her injured leg.

"I bumped it." Keeping her knee bent, she rested her foot on the ground.

"*Kiguld dawmc chiolf...*" Hailey edged Trenton back and stood toe to toe with his sister, continuing in their native twin speak.

Trenton was having none of it. "No, damn it. I'm not an overbearing ass. And no more gibberish. I want to hear and understand *every* word from now on. You two get away with too much crap, but it ends now. No more twin speak. No more secrets."

Little did he know, she'd hold one very close to the vest.

Casper.

"Can we just go home? I really need a bath."

Careful of her wounded leg, Trenton swept her up in his arms and carried her to the helicopter, mumbling, "Don't want you to bitch about getting hurt on your ride home."

"Hey, look at the bright side. I found my partner."

Beside them, Leigh choked out a, "What?" Her frown deepened when looking from her brother to her friend.

"Not him, silly. I'll explain later." Hailey's thoughts wavered to the coming conversation with her mother. Perhaps that could wait a day, or three.

It wasn't until they settled that Trenton explained what little he knew about an anonymous tipster.

Hailey smiled when he kissed the crown of her head.

Chapter Thirty-Two
Hailey

Soft, baggy sweats felt wonderful after ditching the wet jeans and t-shirt. With nothing worse than bruises and sprains, she'd heal with time.

Hailey nodded for Leigh to open the curtain separating them from the other ER cubicles.

"You look better already, she said."

"I'm hungry. I didn't get my choco cone."

"We'll stop on the way home."

"Any sign of Armond?"

Leigh's gaze dropped to the floor as Trenton came into view, saying, "His name popped up with airport security. He's fled the country."

"Damn. His family?" Hailey asked.

"Left behind."

Hailey shook her head, understanding what his wife would feel. She'd dealt with it for years. Armond's infant would grow up wondering what became of her father. A different version of abandonment and shame would follow the child into adulthood.

"Ready to go?" Trenton jutted his chin toward the orderly bringing a wheelchair. "We'll get your statement once you're settled."

"Damn straight. I want a shower, a hot meal, and a pack meeting."

Leigh chuckled when he groaned. "C'mon, Trent. You know you wanna be a part of it."

"How'd you girls get started on that, anyway?" Trenton stepped aside for the orderly to wheel Hailey out.

"Gunther started it. We just joined." Hailey gave Trenton her bagged clothes as they made their way through the near-empty hallway and outside. The likelihood of obtaining evidence was nil after an overnight in cleansing rains and high winds.

"Speaking of which, we'll pick your fur ball up from your mom's house on the way home. She's been cooking all morning." Leigh preceded them into the storm's remnants of wind and whirling debris.

Once loaded in the SUV, Hailey could wait no more. "Okay, guys. Spit 'em out. I want details."

"Armond's wife said she had no idea what her husband was into or with whom he was involved." Leigh helped Hailey prop her leg on the back seat before moving to the front.

After buckling her own seatbelt, Leigh pivoted to add, "She did say he'd expected to come into some money soon and that due to a change in financial status, they'd be moving from Texas."

"His financials may have changed, all right. But she and the child are not a part of the plan." Trenton pulled off the hospital lot and onto the main road.

"Why would he wait five years?" Hailey spoke to the group at large.

Trenton slowed to maneuver around a large tree limb covering half the road. "My guess he was building his business in the counterfeiting trade and wanted to move up the food chain to assure his financial future. We won't know for sure until we nail down his contacts."

"Colson is networking with other agencies. This thing is getting bigger by the day. We've no idea how deep or how far it goes." Leigh rolled her eyes. "He's gonna be knee-deep in this for months. At least he'll be off my case."

"Want to explain how we got an anonymous tip detailing your coordinates?" Trenton caught her eye in the rearview mirror.

"How would I know? I was in the bayou without a working phone."

Trenton snorted. "We got Armond's print off the interior underside of your driver's door. He'd apparently wiped down other surfaces but forgot the door latch."

Leigh tapped Hailey on the ankle. "Looks like my supervisor isn't such a dork after all."

"Which means Armond's in the system? From what?"

"Background check for all employees of the Gifted Elite," Leigh supplied with a grin.

"There's still a loose end I'd like cut. The drugs, cigarette butts found in the backyard, the totem doll, and the dropped gargoyle that nearly creamed me."

Trenton caught her eye again, his tone serious. "No DNA match on the totem, not for Henri, Armond, or anyone else we can find. It's just not in the system. Henri has a prior for dealing drugs."

"So, we're looking for a ghost. Great," Leigh said with obvious frustration.

"Well, doesn't that narrow it down?" Trenton grumbled. "We're looking for a male who's never been arrested, never been fingerprinted, and has no military or police experience."

"What about the call giving you my position?"

"Made from a computer whose signal is still bouncing all over the world," Trenton replied. "Whoever sent it is likely a prodigy."

Leigh picked up the conversational thread. "They were able to exclude the men in our lives. So at least that's something."

The happy reunion between Hailey and her canine partner extended well into the afternoon with Gunther bounding around her feet in Cecile's living room.

Their pack meeting lasted a little longer, due to Trenton's additional bass. He'd capitulated and embraced the group's insanity.

Once they'd loaded the SUV with enough casserole dishes and desserts to fill her fridge and freezer, Hailey, Trenton, and Leigh headed to the loft.

Hailey anticipated a long hot shower.

Trenton's gentlemanly manners urged him out as soon as he'd parked. He insisted on carrying her in.

Aftereffects of the storm had left cooler prevailing temperatures with a northern breeze and lots of tree limbs along roads and in yards. Tasks for later.

Leigh retrieved her keys to open the back door. When she touched the knob, it turned freely. "Uh, guys? The back door's unlocked." She stepped back and palmed her weapon.

In the next instant, Trenton dropped Hailey's feet and set her between himself and the SUV to take point.

"Elizabeth probably came out and forgot to lock up."

"We'll see. Gunther, *suche.*" Leigh's command sent the K9 rocketing into the building's lengthwise hall, his focus complete.

He sniffed along the entire hallway before returning to sit at Hailey's side.

The ground floor was clear, and Trenton found the door to their office locked. He took the stairs two at a time to the living quarters. It turned under his hand.

Another command sent the dog through her living quarters.

Minutes later, he returned and whined. Instead of sitting, he stood between Hailey and the door.

She didn't need to interpret his behavior for anyone. Understanding etched all their faces, *"The loft is clear, but someone's been inside."*

A quick rub of her K9's chest and a, "Good, boy" would suffice until she could engage in a proper game of tug, his reward.

Trenton made a stay motion with his hand. "Laurent, maybe?" he asked, making his way inside.

"No, I texted him earlier to let him know Hailey was okay. He's gonna stop by tomorrow morning," Leigh replied while palming her Glock.

Lights flooded the kitchen when Trenton flipped the switch. "You two stay put. I'll clear the rooms."

Several minutes later, he returned, having holstered his weapon.

Hailey didn't need to search to discover the source of Gunther's concern.

In the middle of the kitchen island, a black candle with Hailey's name carved in the side sat beside a length of black string and a folded note. *They* weren't responsible for her heart's sudden staccato rhythm. In front of the items, a black stuffed animal stood on all fours, minus its head. It was an exact replica of Gunther.

Hailey reached for it then paused with Trenton's hand on her forearm.

"Prints." Trenton used an ink pen to lift the flap of the folded paper.

This isn't over. You will pay.

"It's handwritten. By Armond?" Hailey wondered, but that didn't feel right. "I know we can all agree this isn't Victor's work."

"Agreed, and since Armond has fled the country, I doubt he left it." Leigh searched her expression as if it held the answers.

"I agree. When he admitted to carving Henri into pieces, Armond denied leaving the other totem or shoving the gargoyle off the roof. Damn it." Hailey briefly closed her eyes. "We wrapped up the local counterfeiting and the murders. When does it stop?"

"We've locked down the immediate problems," Leigh agreed. "We'll figure the rest out."

"A good thing I've been reassigned to the Beaumont office,

temporarily." Trenton ran his fingers through his hair, glancing back toward the hallway and open doors.

"Can't complain. You haven't seen your family yet, and Jaxon's due home any time. They all miss you, brother." Leigh patted him on the shoulder. "Good to have you back."

"You should stay here until you find your own place," Leigh offered with a smirk in Hailey's direction.

Hailey shrugged then grinned. "We'll help you find a pet-friendly place, Trenton. Welcome home."

As Trenton groaned, Gunther thumped his tail on the floor.

* * * *

Thank you for reading *Perfect In Death*.

Join Hailey and Casper in southeast Texas as they unravel the mystery of stolen gun shipments, murder, and chaos with hair-raising suspense, mystery, and everyday shenanigans.

Read farther for an excerpt from *Deceptive Silence*.

If you'd like to know when my next book is ready, take a second and sign up for my NEW RELEASE email alerts at reilygarrett (dot) com. My original release dates always have time padded in for, you know, life events and such. They usually move up by several months. Plus, I don't spend a lot of time on social media.

Deceptive Silence

Before the sun peeked over the horizon's rim to separate the lush greens, golds, and browns that would comprise the best photo Hailey had ever taken, misty gray held the bayou's secrets tight within its obscure and deadly grasp.

The occasional *pew, pew* of a baby gator replicated the sound of a science fiction gun blasting over open water. No doubt the growl heard thereafter came from the mother warning off other ambush predators.

In self-preservation mode, Hailey's fingers tightened on her bang stick. Only one shot, the 44 magnum proved an effective weapon while the long handle ensured she maintained a little distance from creatures intent on catching their next meal.

Dusk and dawn proved the most dangerous times for exploring the bayou, the best hunting times for apex predators. This morning, she was one of them. Natural light would help obtaining her best shot—with a camera.

On a recent excursion, she'd witnessed a black panther—reported to inhabit China, Southern India, and Malaysia, but nowhere in the US—prowling in search of prey. Without her camera, she'd had no way to show proof of its presence.

Her current position deep in the thinly treed forest allowed her to keep a decent 360 visual while viewing the narrow passage where her trail cam had caught her current target.

After checking for snakes and other meat eaters who enjoyed human flesh, she and Gunther settled behind the broad base of a cypress tree, a sentinel of the swamps. If not for the early start to their dry season, she would've had to hunker down in a boat.

Any amount of discomfort was worth the picture that would put her on the front page of *Wildlife Ezine*. Private investigative work earned her paychecks. This photo would establish her place as a photographer.

Beside her, Gunther perked his ears with the grumble of low voices in the distance. She wasn't the only bipedal creature around; though, running into others this far along the inlet was rare.

She couldn't hear the gist of the exchange.

Two men argued as they walked parallel to her position. They stopped and faced the water with one using his hands to emphasize a point. Their exchange heated and rose in volume until both startled as branches snapped to their left.

Using her hooded telephoto lens, she scanned the acreage bordered by three intersecting canals. Estimated distance put them at the edge of the largest waterway, a dangerous place to stand and not pay attention to surroundings.

Because she was generally curious and considered nosy, she snapped a few bursts to capture the moment on digital media. Both men were canted toward the water. Shoulder-length hair pulled back in a ponytail swung to the side when the stockier of the two pivoted to face the woods to her left.

His companion also wore jeans, but his head was covered by a hoodie. Shorter and wiry, his accent pegged him for a local.

Ponytail spoke with a stiff northern accent. He also wore a long-sleeved tee, common for maintaining a barrier between skin and biting insects. An eagle's head on the back of his ball cap proclaimed him a Philadelphia baseball fan.

From his back waist, Hoodie pulled a gun and took a step back, putting distance between himself and his opponent, shaking his head.

Beside her, Gunther growled when a sharp crack filled the morning air, not the type issued from an alligator or the pop from a pistol. It was louder and lingered longer.

Ponytail, so animated a moment prior, fell back on his butt, his hands clutching his chest. He slumped down in the marsh grass and didn't move.

Hoodie was behind him and couldn't nail Ponytail in the chest. A third person shot him.

Gunther's presence during weapon's training assured he wouldn't react without conscious thought. Still, he didn't like guns and voiced his displeasure with zealous appeal.

Her hand on his collar kept him from bolting forward. In the split-second it took to quiet him, he'd given away their position, to both

Hoodie and whomever shot his companion.

Hoodie's gaze swung in Hailey's direction.

"Duck!"

The harsh command in her ear startled her into hunching her shoulders. She dropped down and behind the tree trunk from the sight of the gun in Hoodie's hand.

Someone had snuck on her up from behind. Her gaze swiveled to either side in her half-pivot.

No one was there.

To prevent light from glinting off her lens barrel, she kept it low and tucked it under her tee. The bang stick wouldn't aide her now. In order to fire, it required pressure, as in slamming it against an adversary.

Hoodie's gaze searched for a target. If he thought she'd shot his companion, he wasn't considering the angle of origin.

Reily's Books

Romantic Thrillers
McAllister Justice Series
Tender Echoes
Digital Velocity
Bound By Shadows
Inconclusive Evidence
Carbon Replacements
Shattered Reflections
Remnants of Evil

Moonlight and Murder Series
Shifting Targets
A Critical Tangent
Pivotal Decisions
Seeds of Murder
An Unlikely Grave
Deadly Interception
Love You To Death

Psychic Thrillers
Mind Stalkers Series
Bending Fate
Silent Depths
Shadow Guard
Whispers After Death
Mind Hunters

Guardian Series
Shadowed Horizons
Shadowed Origins
Shadowed Passages
Shadowed Spirits
Shadowed Intent
Shadowed Visions
Shadowed Deliverance

Hailey Arquette Murder Files
Perfect In Death
Deceptive Silence
Unlikely Justice
Phantom Reunion

Paranormal Romance
Immortal Lovers Series
Unholy Alliance
Blood Union

Standalone paranormal romance
Tiago

Copyright

About Reily

Reily Garrett is a writer, mother, and companion to three long coat German shepherds. When not working with her dogs, she's sitting at her desk with her fur kids by her side.

Author of chilling suspense and snarky romance, her stories span the distance of romantic thrillers, paranormal romance, and erotic romance. Regardless of genre, each book delves into a dark and twisted imagination yet is tempered with romance and a touch of humor.

Reviews by Kirkus Reviews, San Francisco Bay Review, and BestThrillers.com best describe her work:

"This could be James Patterson, Lee Child, and Tess Gerritsen rolled into one, but the dark, twisted methods used by the serial killer could surprise even those readers..." - San Francisco Bay Review

"...steamy, seductive police procedural..." - BestThrillers.com
"...well-researched thriller that remains romantically genuine throughout." - Kirkus Review

Prior experience in the Military Police, private investigations, and as an ICU nurse gives her fiction a real-world flavor. Find Reily at reilygarrett (dot) com.

www.ingramcontent.com/pod-product-compliance
Lightning Source LLC
Chambersburg PA
CBHW051143130726
47988CB00005B/1961